T5-CQC-536

touch

touch

Stories of Contact *by South African Writers*
Edited by Karina Magdalena Szczurek

Published by Zebra Press
an imprint of Random House Struik (Pty) Ltd
Reg. No. 1966/003153/07
80 McKenzie Street, Cape Town, 8001
PO Box 1144, Cape Town, 8000 South Africa

www.zebrapress.co.za

First published 2009

1 3 5 7 9 10 8 6 4 2

Publication © Zebra Press 2009
Compilation and preface © Karina Magdalena Szczurek
Individual stories © the authors
The acknowledgements on pages 225–6 constitute an extension of this copyright page

Cover photograph © Getty Images/Gallo Images/Jason Hetherington
Cover design: Monique Oberholzer

The quotation from 'I Remember, I Remember' by Philip Larkin is reprinted from
The Less Deceived by permission of The Marvell Press, England and Australia

All rights reserved. No part of this publication may be reproduced,
stored in a retrieval system or transmitted, in any form or by any means,
electronic, mechanical, photocopying, recording or otherwise,
without the prior written permission of the copyright owners.

Set in 11 pt on 15 pt Bembo

Reproduction by Hirt & Carter (Cape) (Pty) Ltd
Printed and bound by Paarl Print, Oosterland Street, Paarl, South Africa

ISBN 978 1 77022 046 1

Over 50 000 unique African images available to purchase
from our image bank at www.imagesofafrica.co.za

To those who are not afraid to reach out

contents

Preface

The sheer abandon of a mother's embrace, the proud handshake that seals an accomplishment, the afterglow of a first kiss, a chance encounter with an intriguing stranger, the desire awakened by a lover's caress, a sign of life from a long-lost friend, and the void if all such things are absent. Touch or its absence defines all human interaction. The stories in this collection, written by twenty-two of South Africa's most renowned and most exciting emerging voices, give nuances to the theme of touch, with all its complex emotional and physical connotations.

Touch: Stories of Contact was inspired by Richard Zimler and Raša Sekulović's *The Children's Hours: Stories of Childhood* as well as by Nadine Gordimer's *Telling Tales*. Both collections raise money for worthwhile causes, the former for Save the Children, the latter for the Treatment Action Campaign (TAC). Because of the TAC's indispensable work in South Africa, I also conceived of this book as a fundraiser for the organisation and very consciously invited only South African authors to contribute to the project.

Although some of them do not reside in the country, their work is largely influenced by and embedded in the local literary landscape.

It was important to me not to ask for contributions about HIV/AIDS, however necessary such stories are for our understanding of the suffering caused by the pandemic and the triumphs of its survivors. Instead, I invited writers to reflect on the theme of touch – to celebrate and explore what is most precious and intimate about relationships, about the capacity of reaching out to and touching one another – and in the process to create a powerful counter-image to what is most frightening, even fatal, about touch, namely the possibility of an HIV infection as a consequence of human interaction. It is an attempt to reclaim intimacy – a lost space in South Africa at the moment, as Margie Orford suggested to me when we corresponded about the project. In this sense, it is fascinating to see how many of the stories emphasise the significance of touch in our lives by evoking its absence. The theme has been interpreted in diverse, often surprising and inventive ways. Whether fictional or autobiographical, the contributions focus not only on emotional and bodily contact, but also on such concepts as 'staying in touch' and 'easy touch'.

With the exception of two pieces, the stories in *Touch* were written specifically for this collection. All the contributors have agreed to donate their royalties to the TAC in support of the organisation's essential and effective fight against HIV and AIDS in South Africa.

For their engagement and inspiration, I am infinitely grateful to Nadine Gordimer, Richard Zimler and Raša Sekulović. A bow of gratitude and admiration to Zackie Achmat and the people at the TAC. I would also like to thank Stephen Johnson and Marlene Fryer for their faith in this book; Isobel Dixon for her encouragement and support; and Nicola Menné, Nèlleke de Jager, Alida Potgieter, Loftus Marais, Ben Williams and Frederik de Jager for their help in tracing some of the contributors. Special thanks go to Martha Evans, whose editorial touch has made these stories glow; Robert Plummer, who was wonderful to work with; André Brink for his translation; and Monique Oberholzer for her exquisite cover design. I could not have wished for a better team to collaborate with on this project.

I owe my deepest debt of gratitude to all the contributors: thank you for your enthusiasm, talent and generosity. *Touch* has surpassed my wildest dreams because of you.

KARINA MAGDALENA SZCZUREK
MAY 2009

damon galgut

The Crossing

The morning after the argument, she woke early and knew she wouldn't sleep again. Andrew was curled away from her, very much on his side of the bed. She got dressed and stood for a long moment, looking at the bony shape of his shoulders, the dark outline of his head. Then she went out and down the steps to the beach.

It was just after dawn; nobody else was around. High up above, the roofs of the town caught the light, but down at the shore everything was in shadow. The tide was far out, leaving a cryptic calligraphy of swirl-marks and debris on the sand.

She found herself wandering north, to where the beach was closed off by a headland. It was the sort of point beyond which Andrew wouldn't go, because who knew what might happen on the other side, away from order and civilised eyes? But the view past the promontory was inviting: a narrow strip of sand, edged by cliffs, with a complexity of boulders at the far end.

When the water was high, you might not be able to get around, but now, with the tide out, it was easy. She meant only to go a few steps but, partly to defy her sleeping husband, she went further. And then there was no point in standing still, with nothing to obstruct her on the vacant white sand.

She felt freer, lighter, than she had in days, and it was only when she got to the far end of the beach that her thoughts became tangled again. Perhaps it was because the pinkish rocks were so dense and slippery, or the cliffs suddenly so raw and close, but she felt plunged again into the thickets of last night's argument. It hadn't been a big fight – they'd had worse – but it was especially painful because it was the first one since the wedding.

Since they'd set off on their honeymoon a couple of weeks before, she'd been full of doubts about what she'd done. Or maybe it was more accurate to say that her doubts had become visible to herself. It wasn't anything that Andrew did exactly; though she found him cautious and irritatingly conservative. He was fine as long as he was staying in luxurious accommodation – that *riad* in Marrakech, for example – but the moment they left the beaten track his anxiety became more voluble. Everything was suspect, too dirty or untrustworthy or expensive. She found this dif-ficult to cope with, but she could hardly claim that it came as a surprise: they'd been living together for three years already.

It had been her idea to visit Sidi Ifni, the little town at the top of the cliffs. She'd especially wanted to return here because of the memories it held for her from a previous trip, eight years ago. But that was a different journey, with a different man – part of a youth and a past that were sup-posed to be behind her. On that occasion she and Mark, her boyfriend at the time, had continued southward, into the bleached emptiness of the Sahara. She knew already that there would be no visit to the desert on this trip.

Andrew had tried to like the town at first. He was an architect, and the Spanish Art Deco of the streets around the plaza had perked him up a bit. But she could see he was alarmed by their hotel, although it was also, at least in part, in the Art Deco style. The place was run down, she had to admit. But that was what she liked about it, the seedy ghost of old grandeur.

She'd snapped at him when they were getting ready for bed last night and he'd made some comment about the sheets. 'This is as good as it gets,' she told him. 'There isn't a better place in town.'

'I know. I'm not complaining.'

'You *are* complaining, but you're being passive-aggressive about it. You didn't want to come here, I know that. I forced you.'

'It's all right,' he said mildly. 'But it *is* supposed to be our honeymoon. Not some hippie holiday.'

'Is that what's bothering you? That I came here before with some-body else?'

'*You* keep talking about it, not me.'

'I don't keep talking about it,' she said, unaccountably tearful all of a sudden. But she knew that it was true: the memory of that previous journey kept flickering around the edges of this one. It wasn't that she had any unresolved longings for Mark; he'd turned out to be a cheat and a jerk, and he was, in any case, also married by this point, and living in another country. No, it was that there were other ways of travelling, other ways of living, and all of them were closed to her now. She had chosen *this* one, this man. For the rest of her life.

In bed, with the light off, Andrew had shifted towards her. 'We mustn't fight,' he murmured. 'Not yet. We can hate each other later, but let's be sweet for the first year or two.' He was speaking in his mumbly-jokey voice, with which he usually approached her for sex. They'd been making love every night – marriage had recharged that side of things, at least – but suddenly the idea of his touch, even before his hand had actually reached her, was like a shock to her skin.

'No,' she said. 'Not tonight.'

'No?'

'I don't want to. Not tonight.'

His hand, resting on her hip, had quivered for a moment, then with-drawn.

That was it, what terrified her: the finality. This flesh, this touch, for ever and ever – she had pledged herself to it. Never to hold another body, or not in this way. It wasn't Andrew she was unhappy with; it was the vow they'd made. She wasn't sure that she could live up to it. The life ahead of her felt like a foreign terrain, through which she might not be able to find her way.

Now the flesh-coloured rocks opened in front of her, the cliffs retreated, and she was on another stretch of beach. With a human figure at the edge of it, staring at the sea. A young man, she saw as she drew closer, wearing ragged clothes. There was a fishing village at the top of the cliffs nearby, and she supposed he came from there. She felt a jolt, a tightening, in her lower body: was she putting herself in danger, being out here on her own? On the one or two occasions when she'd wandered off by herself she'd had a lot of trouble from random men along the way. But that had been in the cities, where everything felt rougher and more jaded. This place was so clean and empty; surely no harm could come to her?

She was, in any case, committed – too close to beat a retreat. The man didn't look at her, but as she approached he suddenly said, as if continuing an old conversation, 'Tonight I go.'

He pointed out across the water.

'What?'

'Kunree Island. Me, I go. Tonight.'

Now he did look at her, and his stare, against his dark skin, was a brilliant green.

'I don't understand.' She glanced out towards the horizon, as if it might offer up an island.

'Yes, yes.' He became animated, a fervour switching on in his wooden face. 'Me, I try, other side, maybe job, maybe money …'

As he went on, gesticulating, throwing out these broken words, a memory stirred from her previous visit, and finally she did understand.

'Oh. Okay. The Canary Islands. You're going tonight?'

'Yes, me. I try.' He smiled, showing a broken front tooth.

This beach, she remembered, was the starting point for illegal crossings into Spain. They saved up for months or sometimes years, these boys, to pay smugglers to ferry them across. Once they reached the Canary Islands – if they got there, in leaky, overcrowded boats – they were dumped and left to take their chances.

'But isn't that very dangerous?'

He shrugged.

'Don't you have a family here? A mother, father ...?'

Again, the shrug. She was chastened, that he could throw off so lightly what felt so heavy to her. 'Morocco no good,' he told her. 'No money, no work. I want new life.' And he looked at her with interest. 'You Spanish?'

'No, I'm from South Africa.'

'South Africa good place?'

'Um, yes, it is, I suppose.' What she meant was that it was good for her, and people like her.

'You take me South Africa?'

'That isn't possible. I'm sorry.' Her difference from him became suddenly apparent, and she felt herself flush. For the first time she looked properly and actually *saw* him. It was a peculiar moment. The ravages of hard living aside, he wasn't bad-looking, with a hard, trim body that he fully inhabited. And what came to her then, seemingly out of nowhere, was a desire to reach out and touch him. It wasn't exactly sexual; nor was it specific. In some general, formless way, she wanted to press up against him – or press her life against his. She wanted to close the distance between them.

She didn't do it, of course. The impulse was shameful and absurd, and when she thought about it later, it became purely sexual in her mind. She'd had a moment of inappropriate attraction; that was all – something to be buried, or remembered with embarrassment.

He didn't seem to notice. 'You first time Morocco?'

'No, I was here before. But this is different. I'm here with my husband,' she told him. 'On my honeymoon.'

'Marriage you?'

'Two weeks ago.' She flashed the ring on her finger.

'Ah, good, good.'

'Well, maybe not.'

'No?'

She hesitated, while the moment between them opened out: the sun had cleared the cliffs and the first light spread across the water. Abruptly, to her own amazement, she found herself confessing, 'I might have made a mistake.'

He waited.

'Yes … my husband … I think I might have chosen the wrong man.'

The green eyes seemed to understand, but she was already in retreat. What did she think she was doing, unburdening her deepest qualms to a stranger on the beach? But before she could move away he had reached out and taken hold of her wrist between his fingers.

'What are you doing?' Her voice could hardly break out.

'Very … beautiful.' But although he made a show of examining the diamonds on her finger, he was after something else. He turned her hand one way, then the other, as if she were concealing something from him. It was the lightest, most delicate of contacts; yet she could feel her heartbeat conveyed to him through her skin.

She had sent the wrong signals and something, possibly dangerous, was about to happen. She was saved by the arrival of a boy, wearing a red shirt. He had come down a path from the cliff and was running across the beach towards them, shouting a word, over and over. The word became a name: 'Abdul … Abdul!' Attached to the man, she realised, who was attached to her.

She saw the moment through outside eyes and immediately snatched her hand away. 'Don't touch me,' she told him, 'you mustn't touch me,' and then she was walking in the direction from which she'd come, not looking back.

Andrew was alarmed by her absence, she could see, but determined to smooth things over. He was drinking coffee on the roof terrace when she arrived, his face a little tighter than usual. He said nothing about their disagreement the night before, but he was working overly hard to appreciate her.

She warmed to his affections, because she loved him, after all; but she was also trying to leave behind that unsettling encounter on the beach. They both took refuge in comforting trivialities: swimming, drinking coffee at a pavement café, playing backgammon in the room. And agreed that they would leave in the morning.

If she didn't mention what had happened on her walk, it was because nothing had happened. Though whenever she thought about the young man – Abdul – with the startling green eyes, it set off a guilty flutter of panic. It had come out of nowhere, that peculiar gesture – taking her hand like that. And what did it mean? From time to time she rubbed the place where he'd held her, as if it were sore. But it didn't hurt, of course; it didn't feel like anything.

She decided at a certain point that he'd been after her wedding ring. That was it: she'd flashed it at him, like a fool, and he'd decided to steal it off her finger. If that boy hadn't arrived when he did, the crime would have followed in a moment. Outraged and consoled by this explanation, she folded the incident away in her mind. She didn't need to think about it again.

Except she did. That evening, a storm came up over the sea. From the balcony of their room they watched the black clouds rolling in, the white cracks fragmenting the sky. Wind importuned the water to higher and higher protest, and she found herself wondering aloud whether any boats would go out on a night like this.

Although they were on peaceable terms when they got into bed, Andrew didn't touch her that night. The memory of her rejection was still with them both, a warm but definite distance between their sleeping bodies. But when she woke in the morning she felt that he'd moved closer, his even breath hot on the back of her neck.

She had to extricate herself with stealth, to leave the room without waking him. She'd gone to sleep with no conscious plan in mind, but woken with an intention as clearly defined as a duty. She had to find that young man she'd spoken to and explain to him that what she'd told him yesterday was false. She hadn't made a mistake; her husband was the right man; her marriage was a good choice. Even if he didn't understand what she was saying, it mattered to her that she should say it. She wanted to take back the words.

Down on the beach, the storm wrack was strewn in spectacular patterns, though the sky today was flawless. She started slowly northward, but once she'd passed the promontory she went faster, faster. She felt an increasing sense of urgency, as though she had an assignation for which she might be late. So feverish and certain was her mission that it only occurred to her halfway, when she was sliding around between the rocks, that he might not be there. Even if he hadn't gone on his voyage, why would he be standing in the same place, waiting? Anxiety took hold of her, but when she emerged from the boulders into the lit arena again, the figure was there. In the same pose as yesterday, staring out to sea. As if he hadn't moved since she'd left. Her heart stopped or started; it was hard to know which.

It was only as she drew close that she saw the red shirt. It wasn't him at all; it was that boy, a friend or maybe a relative, who had broken into their scene by running across the beach.

He turned a tear-marked face towards her. And she knew. Instantly, as if she'd been carrying the knowledge inside her – since last night, or perhaps even earlier, since they'd stood in this very spot, talking.

'My brother,' he told her, 'he die.'

'Who? You mean the young man … Abdul … the one who …' Her voice trailed away, into what could never be said.

It was absurd: she didn't know him; he was a stranger. Yet she felt an emptiness all day, like a kind of grief. One particular image kept rising in her mind and she kept shoving it away – it was too terrible.

She performed all the necessary motions involved in packing and departure, even though she herself was elsewhere. As they left the town behind, she kept her head rigidly to the front, staring at the road through her dark glasses. The radio was tuned to some music station, which sub-stituted for conversation, but halfway through the drive, Andrew leant over and put his hand on her knee. 'You're very quiet today,' he said.

'I'm just preoccupied; I'm not sure why. It's nothing important.'

'Is it that argument we had the other night?' The first time he'd mentioned it. 'Because I know I can be difficult and I'm sorry if I …'

'No, it isn't that.' She had to speak, to explain, but she let a little silence pass before she told him. 'You know … yesterday … I had a conversation on the beach with a man. A fisherman, I think he was.'

'Yes?' He sounded wary.

'The thing is … he drowned. He told me he was going to make the crossing last night to the Canary Islands. And he drowned on the voyage. I spoke to his brother this morning, and he told me.'

Andrew made a sound – it could have been sympathy or annoyance. 'That's awful. In that storm?'

'He was very young. He wanted a new life, he said.'

'I'm sure he did. We'd all like a new life.' Then, perhaps hearing the note he'd sounded, he changed tack. 'They're in a horrible situation, these people. No future to speak of. I know you think I don't care, but I do. I'm sorry about your friend. Is there anything I can do?'

'No,' she said, then added after a moment, 'He wasn't my friend. I didn't know him at all.'

'Yes, I realise. It's just a manner of speaking.'

They left it at that – but she finally allowed herself to see the image she'd been keeping at bay. It was of wreckage spread across the surface of the sea. And of the young man adrift under the water, his green eyes staring downward to where the marine light shaded away into the deep. A cloud of fish was feeding on his body.

Would it have been like that? How could she know? She would never be shown a shipwreck, or a dangerous crossing over water in the dark. She only had her own life, with its gifts and choices. In their hotel room in Agadir that night, in a soft bed made up with freshly starched sheets, she felt Andrew move towards her tentatively, unsure of his reception. From down in the street, dimmed by the sound of the air conditioner, came the noise of distant traffic, and the voice of a muezzin calling the faithful to prayer. She turned towards her husband.

henrietta rose-innes

Promenade

I haven't changed much, over the years. When I look in the mirror, the experience is much the same as it was when I was a younger man. My teeth have not yellowed and my eyesight is remarkably good. Even my finger- and toenails, I suspect, do not edge out from my extremities as rapidly as other peoples' do. Everyone assumes that I'm in my early forties, when in fact I'm fifty-four – a long way from retirement, but still significantly older than my colleagues at the ad agency. Of course I'm balding now, but even this has helped to freeze me in time. I used to style my hair differently, part it this way and that, grow it and trim it; but I am stuck now with this look, this length: a conservative short cut around the bald spot at the crown. Anything else looks foolish.

It is partially the adipose layer beneath the skin, I believe, that helps to preserve my looks. Slightly plump people, I've often noticed, seem to age better than the bony ones: the skin stays taut for longer, the skeletons submerged. Yes, I am a little overweight, as I have been since my early thirties. I've tried to lose the excess, but my body remains impervious.

A few years back, I put myself through a stern fitness regime – low-fat foods, the gym. There was no observable impact on my weight or muscle tone. I have a metabolism in perfect equilibrium, it seems. Still, I exercise, frequently if moderately. Because what would happen if I stopped?

So it is that every evening after work, at six sharp, I take my promenade along the sea wall near my flat. I clip along at a steady lope: a little more than a walk, a little less than a jog. My fists are bunched before my chest; I thrust them forward and back, kicking my feet one-two one-two, my elbows winging to the sides. Yes, I am one of those speed-walkers. I know it's undignified, but it's the only way to get up any kind of sweat without actually running. I have the gear: special lightweight sweatpants, athletic socks, sweat-wicking tops in the latest high-tech fabrics. (No vests; I really am too old for that.) Once a year I buy a new pair of Nikes or New Balances, a virtuous treat.

On my outward journey, the sea lies to my left, grey or blue or silver. Fifteen minutes at a swift stride from my flat down the steep street, to the sea wall and along the path to the traffic lights opposite the garage and café. Here I sometimes pause to stretch on the strip of lawn, before continuing another fifteen minutes along the promenade as far as the public telephones. Then I wheel around and go back in the other direction, one-two one-two, with the sea on my right, half an hour, pausing only to cross at the lights to the café for the day's *Argus*. I roll the newspaper tightly and hold it baton-like in one hand for the rest of the route home (only unsatisfactory on the weekends, when the editions are too fat for comfort). I always take with me just enough change in the special zip-up pocket in my top – plus twenty cents, because sometimes they put up the price without warning – and my house key. No wallet or cellphone; although the promenade is busy and safe at that time, you can never be too careful. And I like to stay light.

The thing about walking along a sea wall is that your options are limited: you can only go forward or back. You can't head off to one side without falling into the sea, or ploughing across the lawn through the children's swings and roundabouts and into the traffic. The lack of choice is soothing, and I'm quite content to follow my established route, each time the same. It is a beautiful walk, especially on still evenings when the sea is flat and the sky clear, or lightly flecked with peachy clouds. The water glows and swirls like cognac. Everyone I meet, coming or going, is gilded on either the left or right sides of their faces with pink or saffron, and they all seem serene and calm and somehow meditative in the generous light. I know I do.

People comment on that: my serenity. But often I am not calm inside, not at all, especially not in the boiling light of those late evenings. It is a dramatic coastline, and there are often grand effects: towering clouds, beating waves, gleams on the rocks where Darwin, they tell me, once stood and pondered geological time and the ancient congress of molten stone. But it is not these that affect me so. It is purely the light coming over the sea, a brilliant luminosity not encountered from any other vantage point in the city. It cuts me with a kind of ecstasy. As if I'm on the verge of something: some revelation that I'm powerless to halt. I have been brought almost to tears, some evenings on the promenade.

There is a particular moment, when the sky goes coral pink and the breaking surf is chalk-blue, almost fluorescent in the fading light. And then each incoming swell feels as if it is rolling over my body, just under the skin, from the soles of my feet all the way to my fingernails, rolling out over the quick, making me want to reach out my fingers and touch. Although I am a controlled man, I am not immune to these things.

Controlled, that's another word I've heard people – my workmates – use to describe me. I'm a senior copywriter, moderately good at my job; good at controlling words, certainly. Words for pictures of sunsets, often with cars or couples in front of them. But I grope after language to describe the feelings I experience on my evening walks, the light in the air and on the sea. This pleases me: that some things remain beyond my grasp. That they cannot be rendered down.

Perhaps this is why I have no ambition. I've held the same position at the same agency for fifteen years and have no desire for anything greater, for a managerial position, even as the new hires are promoted up around me. Such things, I know, could never fulfil my more obscure longings. I'm happy to run in place.

There are always a lot of people moving up and down the promenade: smooth-skinned models looping along in Rollerblades too heavy for their frail ankles; the old woman who sits on the same bench every evening to feed the pigeons; cheerful ladies in tracksuits, trying to shift a kilogram or two; resolute athletes with corded thighs. Dog-walkers and drug-dealers and beggars, and lovers in each other's arms as they watch the sun go down. Some of them I have seen every other evening for the past three years, which is how long I have been taking my promenade now; others are new. Recently I've started to feel I recognise individual seagulls along the route, although this is surely my imagination.

One evening, a young man comes past me, sweating and steaming in a small cloud of musk. Although covered up in a tracksuit, his body is obviously muscular; not the smooth inflated-looking muscles that you see on some of the gym boys, not well-fed recreational beef, but the hard, functional build of someone who works with his body for a living. Shorter than me, but strong. He jogs fast and purposefully.

I notice him again a few days later, and from then on he intersects regularly with my evening promenade, three times a week: Mondays, Wednesdays, Saturdays. I see him going only the one way. He must loop back, as I do; but his circuit is clearly far more expansive and demanding than my own. Time-wise, he is rigid. I always pass him on my outbound trip, and always, it seems, at exactly the same place, just opposite the traffic lights where I pause to do my stretches. He waits to cross the road there, bouncing on his toes, swivelling his torso aggressively left and right. Perhaps he's heading for the gym.

Always dressed in bright, deep colours, I notice; he must have half a dozen different tracksuits, in pillar-box red, racing green, midnight blue. (These phrases come to me involuntarily.) He always wears the complete assemblage, matched top and pants, which is quite formal – never casual in a T-shirt. A white towel is looped around his neck and sometimes he grasps its ends as he waits at the traffic lights, pulling it against the back of his dark neck. A strong, almost cuboidal block of a jaw. I think he must be a boxer. Something in the way he moves, in the build. Or maybe it is just the way he holds his fists, loosely clenched, that gives me this idea.

My certainty about his occupation grows. Who else but a professional athlete would need to train so often and so hard, swathed in towel and sweat-dark tracksuit? His arms are bulkier than a long-distance runner's would need to be; he is light on his feet with a dancing stride, and there's a kind of sprightly aggression in his movements. Enormous hands, for his height. They make me self-conscious about my own flushed fists.

Two men, changeless, beating the same if opposite route; it is comforting. I've read about boxers' battles to keep their weight at certain limits, and I imagine that we are caught in the same kind of stasis. Like me, he is fighting to keep his body where it is – although, to be sure, at a different, higher level. After a while we start to nod to each other, cautiously.

To test my boxing theory, one day I put up my fists – not sure, really, what I intend. He balls his and twitches them towards his chin. No smile, though. It feels tenuous, the moment: me with fists raised, unsure if this is a playful act. Up close, I see the imperfections – the damaged skin of his brows, the way the scarring seems to have resulted in the loss of eyebrows. I notice that his nose looks broken, his earlobes thick. (Are those cauliflower ears?) Despite this coarsening of the features, he has an appealing face, set in an expression of youthful resolution, lit on one side by the setting sun.

It becomes a jokey ritual, a greeting every time we pass. The lifted hands in imaginary gloves. At least, I think it's a joke. It grows from there. One evening, when we come face to face, he and I do that little step-step dance that happens when two people are walking straight into each other: both to the same side and then both back again. I smile. His fists come up and this time he pauses to spar with me. I flinch – and then I know I'm right: only a pro could direct such a sparkling combination of quick almost-touches to my ribs, my jaw, my nose. The huge fists lunge at me, snap back; so close, I feel a tickle of warm air on my face, and smell his sweat. I raise my hands to parry.

And after that it happens every time: each evening we do the little two-step dance, and spend a few moments trading phantom blows.

A smile never crosses that face, as if the scars somehow prevent it; but at the end, just before he skips to the side and jogs on, he'll give me a look and tip his chin up in brief and surely humorous acknowledgement.

A month passes, two. The woman who feeds the birds looks increasingly fragile, until I start to worry that she'll be overpowered by the sturdy pigeons bickering around her; and then one day she is gone. Shortly thereafter, I see the pigeons have constructed another old woman in their midst. The couples part and reconfigure. But the boxer and I remain the same, locked in our pattern, running and standing still.

Other people loop in other cycles around us, stitching up the ends of their days with a quick up-and-down along the water's edge. I think of ants, crawling in opposing circles; clockwise ants every now and then touching mouthparts with their anticlockwise comrades, passing cryptic messages. Some promenaders I will doubtless never meet, caught as we are in orbits that never intersect. But the boxer and I are in sync.

My days pass mildly; I have other routines. The promenade is not my only circular occupation. I sit on Sunday afternoons in the flat and read the newspaper. I go out to buy myself coffee and croissants. I go to work, where I produce copy about faster, stronger, younger. When I hear my own words on TV, I don't remember ever writing them.

Sitting in my padded swivel chair before my computer station, hands poised to tap the keys, I am trapped in stillness. There is a strong desire to stand, run and swing my arms, dispel this immobility. But I stay where I am and the spasm passes. My colleagues at the other workstations do not notice this fleeting turmoil, do not see that I have paused in my typing to contemplate for a moment some grand gesture. I flex my hands, let them drop mildly back to the keyboard. My fingers renew their automatic labour.

Mondays, Wednesdays, Saturdays. We never speak, but our greetings are progressively more familiar. In our small, intense interactions I notice things in great detail: the fact that his irises are black, fading from that dark centre to amber rims. A chipped tooth in his slightly open mouth.

Our sparring becomes elaborate. I think he might be teaching me to box. It's all very controlled, but of course there is also a little thrill of fear. Huge fists in your face, what can you do but imagine those hands rubbing out your features, smearing your nose, forcing your teeth into your mouth?

That's never happened to me of course, but I can imagine the very specific sensations: nose-break pain, tooth-shatter pain, taste of blood. I do not know exactly what the mock-blows signify – violence or camaraderie. Each thrust has the potential to explode, is centimetres from rocketing into my face, from crushing my chest. I can imagine receiving such blows far more easily than I can see myself delivering them. I try to picture pushing my hand all the way, sticking it between the big fists to press against that jaw. Impossible.

Sometimes, trotting on after our shadow-play, I am trembling slightly, feeling the sting of invisible gloves on my body, the smack of fists. I think of the phrase *glass jaw*. Compared to his stony features, I am all crystal.

One Wednesday afternoon I stay home from work with a cold. I switch on the TV at some unusual hour, to catch the afternoon news: SABC2 or 3, which I would not normally watch. And I see him, I am sure it is him, under the bright lights of the ring, in shiny red-and-white shorts, his knuckles encased in bulbous mitts like cartoon hands. His lips are distended by a gum guard, and he looks smaller with his top off, but I know him by his movements: the sideways skip and jump, fists flung out in that dancing rhythm. He and his opponent in blue are both little terrier-men – is it featherweight? – but they are pure wire-hard muscle, shiny brown with sweat. I don't catch his name over the dinging bell, the shouts of the crowd; and anyway, the commentary is in another language. I lean forward, face close to the screen.

It only lasts a couple of rounds. The one small, hard man drills the other to the floor with sweat-spraying strokes. I feel each blow as a twitch in my upper arms. And then it is over: Blue lies flat on his back, toes up and out; my boxer's hands are raised above his head in victory. Blood streaming from his brow.

Only after the ads come on do I relax my hands and lean back on the couch.

He is absent from the promenade for a week. When he reappears, I am warier of him, almost ducking away from his shadow-strokes; but he is too skilful to touch me. Often I think about speaking to him, but my mouth is dry, and he is exercising so hard, so earnestly; I don't want to break his concentration.

I am not eloquent here, in this conversation of bodies. Still, I have come to depend on these playful altercations, these little knockabouts in which neither one of us falls to the ground.

Today for the first time in months, my routine is broken. What is it that delays me? A foolish thing. A flutter of wings in my chest as I am putting on my shoes, a kind of rushing. Something to startle a man of my age. I have to sit for a few moments, gathering myself. Only fifty-four. I have had no trouble before now. I eat well; my life does not have unusual stresses. I exercise.

As a result I am ten minutes late in getting away. Maybe twelve. I don't check the exact time of my leaving, nor do I feel the need to hurry especially, to catch up. I am rigid in my habits, but not to that degree. The heart flutter has upset me and I'm not thinking of anything else. I set out cautiously.

I do not think of the boxer, of how I have disrupted the pattern of our meetings. I do not consider that my delay will in turn mean that he is not delayed. His circuit from unknown origin to unknown destination will now not be paused for our customary sparring. He will not lose that five or ten seconds, and thus will cross the road five or ten seconds sooner. I do not think of these things, and if I did I would not see the significance.

I feel old and tired and a little sick; for once I do not feel like the bracing sea air, the spray, the demanding sunset light. I do not feel like meeting the radiant youthful figure of the boxer, holding up his hands.

Ten minutes, maybe twelve. Enough time for it all to be over by the time I reach the stretch beyond the children's swings, coming up to the traffic lights. As I approach, I see the small crowd ahead. A car has stopped in the road, slewed at a shocked angle, windscreen spiderwebbed. People standing with their heads down, rapt, staring at something at their centre. An ambulance pulls up. I lengthen my stride.

As I come alongside I see only people's backs and legs. I push my way through. Cooling flesh slicked with sunscreen and sweat, joggers and walkers. A couple of dogs twisting their leashes around their owners' legs, weaving a mesh between me and what lies on the pavement. I step over crossed leashes, squeeze between shoulders.

The boxer is lying on his back, hands at his sides, legs spread, toes pointed up and tilted away from each other. A dachshund sniffs at his bright white trainers. There is blood. My hands, the backs of my hands, tingle as if they have just been slapped. My knuckles tingle. My face aches. I back away.

I walk on. The ambulance drives past me, but it goes slowly with no siren or lights flashing. I walk and walk; something has reset my clock and I no longer know when to turn around. On beyond the café, on along the sea wall, beyond the phones, on until the path ends at the wall of the marina and I can go no more; otherwise I might walk for ever.

Stepping up to the wall that blocks my path, I punch it with my left hand. Not hard, only enough to hurt my knuckles, not to bloody them; I wouldn't know how to hit that hard. I do it just once, then stand staring at the wall for a moment before turning away.

I don't go back along the promenade. Instead I cross the road to the other side, towards the shops and hotels and away from the sea. The ocean is gentle and tired this evening; the sighs of the incoming and outgoing waves seem to confirm, regretfully, the truth of tides turning, time passing. Such flat phrases for that eternal suffering rhythm; but this is the best I can do.

I walk home a different way, through backstreets. It takes me a long time. I stop halfway at a random bistro and order coffee, decaf for the heart, and pick up the newspaper I failed to buy earlier. I don't know where I am in the day. I read the newspaper front to back, the sports pages and the classifieds and the obituaries. Then at last I continue home along an unfamiliar route. I can't avoid glimpsing, in a broken band down the steep side streets, the soft luminous colour that the sea is generating. I can feel that brightness in the corner of my eye, but here where I am walking the world is darker. I'm cold in my T-shirt.

As I pass the window of the Woolworths on the corner, it is old, vain habit that makes me glance into the silvered glass. And I see clearly that age has come to me at last: decades, it seems, since this morning. The expensive walking clothes hang loose. And I know that from now on the years, which never burdened me before, will gather on my body, heavier and heavier in the life that remains. Time has started up again, speeding me down.

I step away from the glass and close my eyes. I raise up the boxer in my mind. Lifting my hands to my chest, I pick up the pace, one-two, one-two, elbows out. Through the evening streets, heading home, I complete my promenade.

andré
brink

Surprise Visit

There is no one at the reception desk to welcome him. This suits him
perfectly. One can only assess the standard of care-giving in an old-age
home if they aren't alerted to your coming. Even more important is that
he wants to surprise her. He has something to tell her, something he has
spent a lifetime looking for and which he must share with her. It is now
almost two years since his last visit. One doesn't feel good about these
long intervals, but what else can one do? Princeton is not exactly round
the corner from Cape Town. And, anyway, his sister Jolene is living right
here in the city, close by, in Claremont, and since her husband's death she
hasn't had much to occupy her. In any case, it isn't as if Mum is really
aware of what is going on around her. For at least three years now, since
the last stroke, she has just been lying here. Waiting. For − well. Still has
some lucid moments, says Jolene, but fewer and further between. Hardly
ever recognises anybody.

He goes through the reception area to the corridor, where he quickly
makes sure that nobody is approaching from either end. Then, following

Jolene's instructions, he turns right. The last time he visited her was with his family, just before they left the country. Her room was to the left then, three doors down. But the home likes to shift them around. A change of scenery? Hardly. His own feeling is that the old people – Mum, undoubtedly – find these shifts deeply distressing. Every time it becomes a radical displacement. As bad as those moves in his youth, from one town to the next, as the bank authorities in their wisdom transferred them across the map of the country. Every time a new school, new friends, new teachers, new everything. He never really learnt to cope with that. The only constant in those years was Mum. His father was always more of an absence than a presence. But Mum, yes, she made the difference. Which was why he finally had to make the effort to come all this way to see her. For the last time? Before he went to the States he had already paid her a number of visits, of which each could have been the last. But she held on. Not without some perversity, he sometimes thought. Always a contrary old bird.

He walks down the passage, his rubber soles squeaking on the green linoleum. Down to the end, Jolene has said, then sharp left. Into a small, undefined kind of space which may once have been a storeroom, when the old red-brick building was still a girls' school. He had actually come here two or three times during his university years, when the girls put on the plays indefatigably penned and produced by the Welshman who taught English and with whom he'd struck up some kind of easy-going friendship. It was mainly cricket that had brought the two of them together. But for some time, at least a year or so, the prof's daughter had provided an additional attraction. She was still at this school then and acted in a couple of her father's plays. A fiery little thing, provocatively pretty. And the plays, invariably crackling with Gaelic magic, heightened her attraction. What was the last one? Of course: *The Isles of the Blest*, when after the show he and she slipped along some corridor into a secluded lobby at the end, which might have been this very space, and briefly wrought their own magic until they were interrupted, at the critical moment, by the avenging fury of a principal.

Three doors lead from here. The middle one must be the one he is looking for, if Jolene is to be believed. Opening into what resembles the waiting room of a railway station. Even smelling like one. Except that this one, large and lugubrious, has darker undertones. What must undoubtedly be the smell of death. When one ends up here there are no further shifts or moves to be expected. It is the ultimate Waiting Room. From here there are only the few steps to the hearse at the door. *Abandon all hope, ye who enter.* Or something to that effect.

There are eight beds in the ward, two rows of four. In each, a small bundle. Like meagre loaves in a bakery, relying on self-raising flour past its sell-by date. There are sounds too, most of them barely audible: sighs, moans, wheezing. Long, thin tremolos from an insect world.

According to Jolene, Mum should be in the second row, in the first bed. But one cannot be sure. Here, too, the Home may be persisting in its ways, believing in the need for change, for desperate variety, even at the very end.

'So just have a good look,' Jolene had said. 'You're sure to find her.'

'Of course I will,' he snapped back at her. 'Why shouldn't I? It's our mother, isn't it? And it's not quite two years since my last visit, for God's sake.'

He bends over the small loaf on the first bed of the second row to stare at the wizened face, smell the sour breath of death. No, this is assuredly not Mum. He turns back to the first row to start at the beginning. This one lies chattering in a near-whisper to herself. Most definitely not his mother. On to the second, the third. The fourth. Then he starts on the second row, now driven on by something akin to urgency. One, two, three, four. He straightens his back and shifts his grasp on the plastic bag in which he has brought his offerings for the occasion. The book: Georgette Heyer. He remembers how fond Mum used to be of her. How the two of them used to read her books together, before he veered off towards the world of science, physics. She herself may have changed course by now. That was thirty, perhaps forty, years ago. She most probably does not, cannot, read any more. Then there is the small velvet box with the pearl necklace. At the moment, in these circumstances, it seems almost obscene. Meant perhaps for the smooth and slender neck of someone in her twenties, possibly thirties. Not ninety-five. There is also a small tub of strawberry yoghurt that Jolene had persuaded him to buy at the café on his way to the Home. And the bottle of skin lotion for her hands. He would have preferred something more ostentatiously expensive for an occasion like today's, but this was another of Jolene's bright ideas. Apparently Mum has been complaining about her dry skin on several recent visits.

He has now completed the round of all eight beds. Could she have passed away in the night? He feels a sudden gasp in his throat, but suppresses it. Surely they would have let Jolene know. The place is known for its solicitous concern and the staff's Christian devotion to their frail-care duties. Still, he reminds himself, there was no one at reception. And there's no one on duty here. No sign of any nurse or staff member in the passage as he came along. Not that this needs to occasion any alarm. He hasn't really been paying attention, has he? If anything, he has deliberately avoided contact with any person who might stop, or question, or even smile at him, and then insist on explanations and reminiscences, once they learn that he is Professor Naudé.

He convinces himself that his examination of the old patients in the two rows of the ward has been much too cursory. He has simply assumed that he'd recognise Mum immediately. But it has been two years. Even before he went to Princeton she had aged and changed dramatically every time he came to visit. She must be ancient now. No use groping back for memories of past moments. Conversations, little jokes, gentle banter, whatever. Everything has changed. He should have made allowance for that. All he needs to do is get a proper grasp on himself and repeat the round. He's come all this way, crossing seas and continents and time zones to visit her. The least he can do is pay attention. Be here for her.

And he has the message to give her. Unless … For a moment he looks back at the door, in a sudden tinge of panic. This may be a sign. He should have kept the news to himself. What would she understand of it anyway? Yet, how could he be expected to keep it to himself? Even when he was at school, when she helped him with his maths, she'd cherished his dreams with him. In those days they weren't even properly focused yet. He just knew he'd be doing something abundantly, wonderfully special one day. And they would celebrate together. Now the day has come. And yet he may have waited too long. She is so very old. What on earth can it matter to her? But he knows with what unconditional dedication she has always believed in him. Nothing can be rounded off before she has been told.

He returns to the door – the door that leads to that cramped space where he and the prof's daughter had enjoyed their youthful, short-lived celebration – and begins once more at the first row. Much more slowly and attentively than the first time, he stops beside the first of the patients in the Waiting Room. Bends over, stares with ferocious intensity at what is visible of the small humanoid face. Inhales, exhales. Even dares to whisper: 'Mum …?' And after a moment, once again, giving it more voice: 'Mum, is that you?'

No. No, this is impossible. He feels a fool at the mere thought that this shrunken little alien might be his mother. My God, all the years, the years they have lived together. It must count for something. Sorry, Madam. I didn't mean to intrude, to stare at the nakedness, the utter vulnerability of your face.

'Mum …?'

No response, no sign of recognition.

Then on to the second. Suppressing the urge to start moving faster again. Now he has to take his time. There will be, must be, a hint. The merest gesture, a sigh, a fluttering of the eyelids perhaps, a dry scraping of the throat, the twitching of a hand, a fleeting change of expression on the sleeping face.

The third. His view is half-obscured by a fold in the bedspread. He glances at the door, which is still closed, then dares to straighten out the fold and inspect the face more closely, the gnarled hand resting against it, the thickened, yellow nails, the scrawny chicken neck, the wispy hair. Like bumfluff, he remembers Mum describing an acquaintance once, in disgust. She was always so proud of her own hair, and from Jolene he knows that she used to insist that a hairdresser visit her every Friday. Look at it now. But this isn't she. That is obvious.

He moves on to the fourth bed. This time he lingers even longer, to make quite sure. The small head among the sheets is sunken and bony, the mouth half-open, allowing a thread of spittle to dribble across one cheek. The face of a stranger, and yet not altogether, not utterly, unfamiliar. Remove fifty or sixty years: could this not have been the face watching over his homework, prodding him, prodding him? ('But Mu–um! I've already gone through everything twice. I promise you. I know it!' 'One can never be sure enough, Nicholas. Just do it for me. One day you'll thank me for it.' 'Okay, Mum. Just for you then.') He can see why everybody always said she'd been such a good teacher. Her patience. Her encouragement. Her persistence. Her faith in him.

He is still peering intently at her when she opens one eye, the right one. Blue and lucent as it should be. And yet not quite, no, not quite. Her eyes always had an intensity of blue not matched by any others. The blue of aquamarine. Of tanzanite. Whereas this eye staring up at him is like a dull, much-fingered marble, like a summer sky drained of its emphatic colour by too much sun. At this moment she opens her left eye as well. This leaves him with no doubt. This small person is not his mother. He moves on to the first bed in the second row, starting the process all over again. But she is not here. They must have moved her to another ward.

He reaches the door and prepares to leave, back to the wavering assurance of the lobby where he may, or may not, as a student, have picked his way through a moment of furtive magic with the professor's precocious daughter before being stopped in panting mid-passion by the screeching Valkyrie. With no magic to rely on today, he may just be forced to seek help from one of the staff after all. Once again he reminds himself of how, even before leaving for the States, the changes in his withering mother had baffled him. As if the processes of ageing had accelerated every time. The intervals had never been very short – three months, four, sometimes six – but never as long as this. He must remember that. Goddammit, he hadn't come all this way to ask strangers to help him identify his own mother.

One more time then. After that, he promises himself, he will ask for help. He will renounce all fleeting memories of magic and rely on the real, the actual, the scientific. He owes it to his mother, to himself, to try once more. Even if it means forcing memory. In search of those minuscule little signs that ultimately define identity. Not necessarily the obvious, visual traits, but the almost subliminal hints and suggestions that make you what you are, and who you are, different from others.

He has been away for two years. But before that – even considering the absences, the silences, the distances – they had spent more than half a century together. She had given birth to him, had coaxed his first steps, had taken him to school the first time, had helped him to read, to write, to make his first subtractions and additions, had shielded him from the unfairness of teachers, the viciousness of schoolmates, had urged him on to his first wins in the hundred yards, the high jump, the first small triumph in the debating society; she had comforted him after his first disappoint-ment in love, had actually smoothed his way to the heart of a second girl by interceding with an overprotective parent to give him a chance. Seen him through school. Through university – no longer really able to help, but always ready to encourage, to discuss, to make the failures bearable and the successes more memorable. Mum. Always Mum. One of these small but unremittingly human bundles in the two rows of narrow barricaded beds in this sterile ward. For years now there has been so little contact between them. Phone calls coming further and further apart. Letters drying up. Those long, early letters in her large handwriting, growing more and more spindly. Always headed by a text from the Bible. What was her favourite one? He gropes for a while. *Wherewithal shall a young man cleanse his way? By taking heed thereto according to thy word.* He is delighted to find it coming back to him. And so much else besides. Now he knows that he will dis-cover her. She is here. I'm coming, Mum. Be reassured. I'm here.

He starts on a final round. The first bed, and the second. The woman with the bumfluff. The one with the dull blue eyes. This time nothing will escape him. He is not content merely to look, to stare. He dares to pull away a spread, a blanket, a sheet to see more clearly. The hands. These, surely, he should be able to recognise even blindfolded.

And then, three-quarters of the way through the round, he comes to a sudden standstill. Yes. Of course! This is his mother. How could he have missed her on the first two inspections?

Here she is. The face is more wasted than ever before. The eyes are closed. The mouth sunken and reduced to a mere slit, with wiry hairs on the upper lip. The hands like two desiccated old claws. But this is she. These hands have held him, coaxed him, cuddled him, given him confidence and assurance. Mum, Mum. It is not only her presence that is restored to him, but so much of himself, his long past – he himself is verging on sixty, and for most of those years she has been with him. He feels tears stinging behind his eyes, but suppresses them.

He sits down on the straight, hard-backed little chair beside her high bed, inclining his head to look at her more closely. To make her aware of his presence. To make her realise what he cannot tell her in words. The simple fact that he is here.

He forages inside the plastic bag. Takes out the book, looks at the title, frowning and straining his eyes, but then replaces it. She will not be able to read it, and seeing it may only distress her. His hand finds the small velvet box, half-opens it, then puts it back too.

The pearls are no longer appropriate. Even the yoghurt is redundant. He could force the teaspoon between her thin, pale lips, but she might not even react. She is almost literally beyond his reach. Can she sense it? Her hands are twitching; her breath comes with a rasping sound, in brief and barely audible gasps. Her face is screwed up in what seems like anguish.

His fingers resume their search. And suddenly he realises that there is something he can do. He takes the bottle of skin lotion from the bag, opens it, pours some of the cool, thick fluid into the hollow of his left hand and dips the fingers of his right hand into it. Slowly, as he starts applying it to the talon closest to him, she seems to relax. The stern, resentful lines on her face appear to soften. For some time she remains negative, even resisting. But already she is relenting. The shadow of a smile seems to form on her mouth. It is almost like that first time with the prof's eager daughter. The slow, languid yielding, the almost imperceptible growing of acceptance, of trust.

Her body no longer attempts to turn away, to resist, to tense in negativity. The skin of her face becomes more pliant, it actually seems as if years and suffering and anguish and hardness are slowly, very slowly, peeled away as he reaches further, through layers of diffidence and protection and self-preservation, towards a deeper self, a deeper truth of herself, which is revealed, exposed, laid bare, now offered in confidence and frankness and trust. Her hand now rests on the outstretched palm and fingers of his own left hand, as with the right he eases the lotion into her dry skin, not rubbing, not applying any force, but insinuating the moisture into her as he feels a suggestion of new life stirring very deep inside her, and she seems to grow younger, only a few years, but younger, easier, brushing away something like cobwebs of suspicion and fear, of stubbornness, of uncertainty. I am here, say his hands as he very quietly keeps on stroking and barely stroking, taking each of her fingers separately in his, gently palpating them, applying a little pressure at a time and then releasing them again. And through the softening, moistening new litheness of her skin she responds: Yes, you are here. And I am here too. You have never been away. You will always be close to me.

Nothing else matters any longer. Only this.

And as he continues caressing her hand, he keeps his face close to hers to whisper into her ear. 'Mum, I've got to tell you. This is what I've come for. You know how I always spoke to you about what I was working on? That thing that always eluded me. The Unified Theory? Bringing together Relativity and Quantum Physics?'

Her eyes are half-open now. He has willed them open.

'Can you hear me, Mum?'

Her eyes are gazing in his direction. Not at him, but as if she is looking right through him at something beyond him, far away, remote.

'Bringing Einstein and Hawking together, Mum. Do you remember?

'I couldn't get any further with it here in Cape Town. But in the States, at Princeton … There are such amazing people to work with over there. We haven't got everything in place yet, but it's so close now. So incredibly close. And last week I … The professor in charge of the project called me in. He said …' His voice catches. Now he can only stare back at her.

Involuntarily his fingers continue to stroke hers. And she seems to be responding to it with a brief clenching of her hand. Or is it his imagination? Wishful thinking?

'I had to tell you, Mum.'

Another weak pressing of her fingers in his hand. The small smile on her lips does not change.

He resumes his slow, almost imperceptible caressing of her hand as he applies a few more drops of the silky lotion. It lasts and lasts, like music that has to run its course and cannot be interrupted before it has arrived at its inevitable and natural climax. A recognition, an acknowledgement that reaches beyond the possibility of words.

This is you. This is I. Yes. Yes.

Her hand now lies motionless between his. The faint smile remains on her lips even as it seems to sink more deeply into her small face. Her eyes are still open, gazing and unmoving. He clips the cap back on the bottle and leaves it on the small table beside the bed. There is no need to tell her anything more. She knows. At least, she knows everything she needs to know.

She may not be here when he comes again. If he ever comes. It won't be necessary. They both know, now and for ever.

By now, he notices with relief, her eyes are closed. He gets up quietly, taking care that the plastic bag doesn't disturb her peaceful slumber with a rustle. He bends over and presses his lips to her forehead. It is hard and cool.

As he begins to move towards the door, it opens and a middle-aged nurse in white comes in. She stops when she sees him, clearly startled by his presence. But then a broad smile of recognition breaks out on her face.

'Professor Naudé!' she exclaims. 'Is it really you? How wonderful to see you again after such a long time.' She frowns briefly. 'But what are you doing there at Mrs Owen's bed? Do you know her too?'

'I came to surprise my mother …' he mumbles.

'Right over here,' the nurse says, pointing at the first bed in the second row. The one Jolene had mentioned to him. Then clicks with her tongue. 'You should have warned us. She'd have liked to have had her hair done for you and everything. Come and sit here. Shall I wake her up for you?'

'I'll just sit for a while,' he says, glancing involuntarily at the door that leads to the small space of failure and frustration beyond. 'Then I'll be off again.'

'But—'

'No need,' he says, without looking at her. 'No need.'

mary
watson

Trinity

There were three of them, and in the middle was Gretchen with a name like a fairy tale. She was the base of the triangle, the bottom line, bringing them together and keeping them apart. Gretchen had found them, Waldo and Priya, and then decided to keep them.

Waldo was not unlike the picture-book wanderer: the skinny, bespectacled man hidden in large crowds of people; the locations (carnivals, haunted castles, markets) detailed to camouflage his red-striped jersey and scarf. Always in long shot, his lanky frame blended into his surroundings. And always, once you spotted him, the one you were looking for. When Gretchen found this Waldo, who had worked very hard to be lost, she felt a similar sense of quiet satisfaction as a child finding the cane or the dog or the picture-boy Waldo himself. It was the satisfaction of having completed a task, even though there was no apparent purpose or use.

Priya had long ago left the tropics, so long, she explained to Gretchen, that she couldn't remember it at all except for the touch of certain fabrics, the smell of cardamom in sweet milk. And then she could only remember impressions, or feelings that were beyond her vocabulary: sometimes a feeling of safe when curled up tight, other times, a sense of wonder at a half-remembered picture. Priya described to Gretchen a picture of a dulled silver-gold – one of those popular pictures of the early seventies – that showed water and silt. She couldn't mark exactly where the silt ended, or where the water began. So it followed that if you could walk on the silt, then you could surely walk across the water. The question had vexed her at four years old and even now she was obsessed with knowing what would bear her weight and how it would feel to step barefoot there: a canopy of leaves, a vat of porridge, a newly iced lake, a thick carpet of brown pine needles in a sheltered wood.

Gretchen first saw Priya dancing alone in an abandoned old forge. Sunlight filtered through the small slit windows in the roof. The audience was small and indifferent; the event had not been well advertised. Priya's body fitted together like jigsaw, the light fell on her in spooky shafts, and Gretchen, in the near darkness, was enchanted. A trick of light rippled the floor and it looked like Priya danced on water. Gretchen had claimed Priya then, just as she'd claimed Waldo before that. Gretchen found herself beautiful. She had long, dark hair, just beginning to line with grey, which fell to her waist, and her thin elegance gave her a sense of composure. She was a neat woman, who delighted in regularity, in clear lines, in things that added up. As a little girl, she had always liked to put her dolls exactly where they belonged.

They were all good friends now, her little gang. She was pleased with the arrangement: supper at least once a week, always someone to talk to, to drop in unexpectedly, and several times a year they went away together. Usually they went for weekends, somewhere not too far, but there would be one long trip where they ventured further and stayed together for a week or two. This year, they were headed to the wintry sea, armed with workplans and piles of books – thrillers and the Russians.

The coast was idyllic and empty. It was not the right time for tourists, and the locals were sensibly indoors. The clouds hung low, and this oppressed Priya, who clawed at her throat, complaining of claustrophobia. Gretchen found it dreamy. They had hired a cottage where Priya and

Gretchen shared the big bedroom and Waldo took the child's room. Priya and Gretchen slept together in the same big bed and sometimes Gretchen wondered at their platonic love – they lay together in the way that Gretchen imagined she would with sisters, if she hadn't been an only child. Or as lovers, if she liked girls. To see her face from that close, and from that angle … But she was neither sister nor lover, and yet they lay so close.

All three together took long walks on the beach and read out loud to each other. Sometimes poetry, sometimes the erotic bits from the thrillers – Waldo did them in different voices. Waldo was one of the girls, the other two liked to say. They could tell him their boy stories; they could show him their new bras. Their other friends liked to warn them that the situation was unsustainable, that naturally someone would end up in bed with another and the third would be left out and hurt. Their position was unstable, the balance wouldn't hold. But Gretchen disagreed, laughing that if Waldo – or Priya – was going to fall in love with her, it would have happened already.

They were all three of them mad about games. They invented word games, Gretchen especially loved number games. They had all bet their grandmothers several times over; Gretchen had won Waldo's but owed hers to Priya three times. Priya had won several prized items of Gretchen's clothing, and Gretchen owned Waldo's burgundy jeans, which she grudgingly allowed him to wear. They only flapped about her narrow waist. They turned everything into a game, but they were always games with an edge of competition – Gretchen especially worked towards some kind of trophy. They most loved racing against each other: running, walking, swimming. Usually the two girls took each other on, and Waldo raced against time. This was where the big prizes lay. When Waldo took an hour to complete an impossible Sudoku square, he washed dishes for a week; Gretchen of course solved the puzzle in twenty-five minutes. Priya cropped a patch of hair from just above her temple for twenty to thirty of Gretchen's push-ups. Gretchen flashed her tits down at the harbour for not being able to name all of the Spice Girls. Priya and Waldo had laughed as Gretchen's cold fingers unbuttoned her shirt. There was a man in the distance, but luckily he was too far to be sure of what he'd just seen. On that wintry beach, people were always in the distance, small specks on the untamed seascape.

Gretchen liked to cook; she was very good at it because she was so precise. She always learnt from a recipe book, not deviating from the ingredients at all. She measured things exactly and she was particularly good with timing. That evening, she was trying out something new, and the other two kept hiding her measuring spoons and so she sent them out to play.

'Take pictures of Priya dancing,' she said, because Waldo could make magic with a camera and Priya's body could do the most extraordinary things. 'With the waves behind her.' What could be more beautiful?

So the pair headed to the beach, and Priya, conscious of Waldo's camera, walked a straight line along the water's edge.

That was when it shifted, when Gretchen's geometry could go no further. She had thought of a triangle, or of three intersecting circles. But their story was not as regular as she would have liked. That was the point that marked Gretchen on the outside, and the moment when the other two retreated.

When Priya and Waldo returned from the beach, Gretchen had set a table with candles, lit a fire and cooked the supper. She was pleased with herself and unashamedly eager to hear their praise for the meal, much too extravagant for such a quiet beach. But Priya was moody that night – she said she had a headache and went to read in the bedroom after supper. And that was fine for Gretchen, because she liked being alone with Waldo. He was one of those men who, when you first looked, you noticed mostly the spectacles, the floppy hair, the thin frame. But looking again showed you the strength of that frame, the startling green of his eyes against the olive of his skin, and the beautiful symmetry of his face. Gretchen did not allow herself to dwell too much on the ways in which Waldo was not one of the girls. Because there lay the invisible line that maintained the balance of their threesome, and it was like religion: Gretchen just didn't dare.

The next day Gretchen saw Waldo outside in the cold morning air.

She paused coming down the stairs and watched as he looked out to the quiet beach, holding a mug of something steaming in his hands. She walked down towards him, but before she reached the glass doors, Priya came up the wooden deck, stamping her feet in their thick, fleecy boots. She missed a step and wobbled a moment. Gretchen looked on, her hand on the wooden frame of the glass door. It was peeling badly and was slightly rotted. Gretchen held her hand on the wood, feeling the rough edges where the paint had torn away. Waldo reached out an arm and helped Priya up the last step. Even as he reached, Gretchen didn't like it. Something twisted and ached in her when she saw him take Priya's gloved hand. He held on to it as Priya stood on the deck beside him and warmed her other hand on his steaming mug. Gretchen watched them, one hand each on the blue mug, the other hand holding on each other. It was a light touch, friendly, casual and muted by the wool of Priya's gloves, but still Gretchen didn't like it. She was reluctant to move away from the doorframe, reluctant to announce her presence. But they seemed to know she was there, for they dropped hands suddenly and turned away – Waldo turned in towards her, and Priya turned out, towards the sea. There was something to be said, but it stayed inside, like a blocked pipe.

Lunch was distracted, and then Priya burst, 'Oh, this is ridiculous. Gretchen, you've probably guessed by now: Waldo and I are in love.'

Gretchen could never have said 'in love' like that, like it was one word. Priya said it easily, without any shame in saying something quite so grand. 'In love' was for Anna Karenina, or else something out of a soap opera or worse, Gretchen thought. Someone else's melodrama, not hers. And then the way Priya told her, as if she were a child whose reaction would have to be tolerated.

Waldo didn't say anything, he just seemed embarrassed.

'But that's wonderful, Priya.' Gretchen would not give herself away. 'I'm so happy for you both.'

After the dishes were cleared, she excused herself, saying that she needed to do some work that afternoon. She was not an artist like the two of them, she laughed in an unfunny way, and her work was so much less inspired. She urged them to head out to the lighthouse, as they'd suggested that morning. And after they'd left, she sat determinedly with her papers and read the heading many times, but got no further. She stayed reading that line, hunched and wretched. After a tear fell onto the judgment, she leapt up in horror at herself and began cooking – measuring and chopping for another too elaborate supper, when her friends might have preferred farm-baked white bread and cheese. By the time they'd returned, something delicious was cooking, and Gretchen had regained her calm.

'Why didn't you tell me before?' she asked, more kindly than she felt. They didn't answer; they didn't know how to say it.

They were guilty, the two of them, and Gretchen didn't want to know. She felt foolish for thinking them even and fair, perhaps with her just a little bit more fair, when it had been lopsided for a while now. Even slowly sinking. Until one day when Gretchen would no longer be able to fit herself in with them, when she wouldn't belong. Already she felt on the outside of a secret, or a joke. Worse, she felt humoured. She had been made into (she felt the anger rising in her throat) the third wheel. Unaligned and off-balance. A dog with three legs.

'Why don't I take the baby room and the two of you can share? That makes much more sense.'

And then, night after night, lying in the little bed next door, hoping that she wouldn't hear anything. Or rather hoping that she would, because then she would somehow be part of it. Then she wouldn't be so left out. And she could reduce it to something sordid: grunts on the other side of the holiday-house wall.

They were shy lovers initially, when the three went out walking together. They were reluctant to hold hands or show their affection, but they grew bolder and by the end of the week they were kissing or holding each other, his arms around her thickly coated tummy as they stared out to sea. A standard image of romance that Gretchen had previously wondered about – why that pose? Why, in the movies, did the woman never stand behind the man? Was it warm and protected like that, or did they not want to see each other? He could look down at her head and search for nits, she suppressed a giggle. But then, she supposed, even if they faced each other, it was hard to see someone from up close. You need a bit of distance in order to read the features.

Later that day, Gretchen realised that it was worse than she thought. There was something else. Something further, something deeper. The jealousy that nagged her wasn't simply about her best friends edging away from her. She realised it when they stood on the causeway, a thin promenade that was a bit like walking a knife-edge, or a tightrope. The tide was low and the water had receded, leaving the smooth sea floor open, like a secret just told. The realisation came when Waldo raised his camera to take a picture of Priya staring intently at the exposed seabed. Just at that moment, Gretchen decided that she wanted Waldo.

The next day – the last of the holiday – Gretchen found herself watching the lovers covertly as they set out to hire bicycles. She was fed up with this new arrangement where Waldo and Priya were the main story, and Gretchen the addendum. It didn't suit her at all.

By the time Waldo came pushing his bicycle from the shop storeroom, the two women were standing together in a prickly silence. Gretchen wondered how she should declare herself to Waldo. It seemed something shameful; she imagined it as opening her jacket and flashing at him, like she had at the harbour. Which didn't seem funny any more. He might look at her appalled, embarrassed. She decided quickly.

'Let's race,' she said. 'To the lighthouse.'

'What's the prize?'

Gretchen hesitated a small second: 'Waldo.'

Priya did not seem surprised. 'Sure.' It was a casual reply.

'And for Waldo?'

'He races against time. If he gets there in twenty minutes, he's not bound to the winner. And he can decide what it is he wants. More than twenty minutes, and the winner takes all.'

It was a neat equation. The race between the two women equalled Waldo's race against time. For Gretchen it helped iron out all the untidy emotions that had disturbed her equilibrium this last week. They shook on the deal and set out.

Waldo shot ahead, with Priya behind him. He did not turn around to see how they followed. He pedalled with strength and tried to leave the two women behind. It had become awkward. He felt an overwhelming urge to pedal away, to be somewhere else. He did not care too much for being offered up like some kind of trophy. Like flashed tits, or chopped hair, or a week's worth of dishes. And to be Gretchen's prize – it reminded him of the boy in a cage in a gingerbread house holding out his finger to see if he was nicely fattened. That wasn't Gretchen but Gretel, and it wasn't even her, but the witch. He felt sorry for Gretchen; she was too eager, too uptight about how things worked, how people should be, and her position in all of it. She had caged herself with her careful ideas. Waldo turned around and saw Gretchen take a corner. Priya must be at the back. All those nights in the master bedroom lying stiffly next to Priya. Not yet, he told her, I'm not ready, and she was impatient, which just made him long to leave all of this behind. It didn't matter to him who won, he wasn't playing any more. He would, after this island, take up his camera and go somewhere out of reach, where he wouldn't feel them snaking towards him. He would go and lose himself in his pictures.

Gretchen heard the sound of the bike falling about a minute after she noticed how bad the road was getting. Waldo was ahead, a faraway dot, and then disappeared. It was a sheltered spot, the road shaded by the cliff face. Crusty patches of frost blotched the surface, and in places there was a thin, almost imperceptible film of ice. It was an unmistakable sound and, without stopping, Gretchen turned and saw that Priya had fallen. She regarded the image for a fraction of a second. Should she go back? Gretchen sneaked a second look. Priya was sitting next to the bike. She looked okay. Gretchen pedalled harder. She left her friend awkward on the downward slope of the verge, her bike turned over beside her, the wheels spinning. She did not dwell on that small glee she felt; she focused instead on the road ahead. The lighthouse came into view as she turned a corner. She judged that she had about four kilometres to go. Gretchen's little demon quietly gnawed at her heart and kept her pedalling viciously. Waldo appeared on the uphill not too far ahead of her. She watched him grow bigger; he was pedalling at a comfortable pace. It had been seventeen minutes since they had begun the race, but Waldo made no attempt to beat the clock. Gretchen felt a taut line pull between her two friends. She thought suddenly of another beach, one far from there, where she had once come across hermit crabs playing musical chairs. Musical shells. She had watched the funny, naked crabs scuttle across the rocks looking for new shells, trying them out, looking to see what would fit. Scraggly and insect-like, they ran lightly across the perfectly spiralled periwinkle shells. She'd wondered what made the crabs come out of their old shells: did it become uncomfortable, did the burden of fitting yourself into someone else's things eventually become too much, forcing you out so that you could find another, hoping that this time it wouldn't pinch? That this new shell would feel like yours, and finally you could stay? But they never stopped moving shells; they couldn't be comfortable. The quick, cold scurry, that zigzag from shell to shell – did they look to find a shell that fitted the pattern of their own distorted bodies; did the whorls encode a message? If Gretchen were honest, would she admit that she had known of something that burned between Priya and Waldo, and that she'd placed herself in the middle? That's where she was comfortable, in the undeclared passion of others. Like the hermit crabs, she had never had her own perfect spirals, but rested deep within others, scavenging off dead matter. Because if you had your own, you were stuck with it, and if you fed off others, you would never get bored. But now she was bored. This game, with Waldo as its prize, suddenly didn't appeal any more. She had won: twenty minutes had passed; Priya was far behind. She was well aware of the costs: Waldo's dignity, the small betrayal of Priya. But that didn't weigh her down too much. What did bear down was that now the game was over. The music had stopped and she was the one on the chair. And all that was left to do was sit on it, alone.

Priya always liked things best just before. She liked it more just before she went on holiday, just before a kiss, just before hearing news, just before eating something nice. The promise always felt better than the realisation of it; she was always just a little bit disappointed. She had liked it much more before Gretchen had forced her and Waldo to share a bed. Waldo was lovely to consider from across a room, but too cold, too stiff when you came close. When Priya heard the sound of Gretchen's wheels steadily approaching, she knew that she had lost, but she didn't mind because Waldo wasn't hers to lose. Gretchen passed, the sound of her bicycle wheels a low hum – she kept a strong, steady pace, unlike Priya's uneven spurts of energy. They had all three of them taken strain from holding an impossible balance these last two years. Like her best arabesque held for too long. The road was slippery, so Priya slowed down, she was careful with her precious dancer's body. She was concentrating hard on the thin film of ice on the new black tar. Like some kind of frosting on treacle that her bicycle wheel was cutting through. That's when she felt the bike falling and, for a second, she floated. Neither the ice nor the treacle had borne her weight. Her hand was raw, her hip bit, and her knee was mildly banged. She was badly shaken, and kept saying to herself, 'I've fallen off my bike.' It was a comforting refrain. Lucky that she had slowed down. She would sell both Gretchen and Waldo to the Devil rather than have a knee injury. As she struggled to get up, she looked far down the road and saw Gretchen's face – small, but unmistakably turning away.

In the minutes that passed as Waldo and Gretchen waited for Priya, they did not talk of prizes or winning. They leant against a low wall, their bicycles parked on the tar. Priya, when she joined them, did not speak of her fall, and she kept her raw, swollen hand closed in its glove. They wheeled their bikes back to the house and were silent as they stepped across the uneven stones. They looked for the last time on the reeds growing on the dunes, the sun almost to bed at three thirty, the knife-edge promenade where a heavily coated man pushed a blue baby in the pram against the wind. The tide was just coming in, filling the pools, closing over the sea floor, claiming it back to itself.

alex
smith

Change

The light didn't work, there were no windows, and the lack of cool air in the darkness was enough to trigger a migraine. Bags of groceries were cutting into Martha's hand, pressing her wedding and engagement rings into her flesh hurtfully – she had transferred all the bags to her left hand so that she could unlock the door between the garage and the kitchen. She had the post, two letters, between her lips, and a pocket of oranges under her arm. The tumble dryer was on and the garage was filled with hot air. She was struggling to find the correct key on her bunch; the first and second keys she tried were wrong. The garage was unbearably stuffy and she was starting to perspire. The shopping bags had stopped the flow of blood to her fingers and her lips were going into a spasm from holding the post.

Ah, thank God, she thought, as the third key slipped into the lock and turned. She opened the door and entered at about the same time as her husband Peter, who had come in through the yard door, holding a bucket and a mop. They would have collided, but Peter pulled himself out of the way and stood flush against the fridge – well, as flush as his belly would allow.

There's no space in this unit, Martha thought. She looked at her husband as she had that thought, and was further irked by the poor combination of shirt and sweater he had on. Out of courtesy, her lips seemed to want to form a greeting, so they curled up, almost, but not quite, into a smile, which was quickly erased by a loud sigh, followed by her bustling into the kitchen and the thump of heavy shopping bags on the counter.

Pssshhh. The iron steamed. Mavis, from Executive Domestics, was ironing in the cramped corner between the stove, the prep sink and the crockery cupboards.

Martha spoke, in fact exclaimed, a greeting, with almost manic friendliness: 'I've bought you a pie for lunch, Mavis, and there's a new loaf of bread for you and I got more sugar too and two jam doughnuts – one for you and one for Mr Gardener. Oh yes, and I bought some Silvo, so when you've finished the ironing you can polish the silver, please, and I got window cleaner too, so after lunch you can do the windows, upstairs and downstairs.' All this Martha revealed as she unpacked.

Peter, with his bucket and mop, not wanting to get in his wife's way, was still in the doorway area between the fridge and the yard, hoping that she had bought more disinfectant. His dog, Muffin, had misbehaved and Peter had discovered the dried wee at the front door after Martha had left for Pick 'n Pay. It was a relief she hadn't seen it first. He'd managed to clean most of it away, but the grouting between the tiles was stained and they were out of household … ah, excellent, he thought, seeing Martha unpack lemon-scented household cleaning liquid, that's exactly what I need. Did she buy dog food? She knows the dog food has run out.

As soon as Martha had put the household cleaner into the cupboard under the sink with the infuriating drain prone to blockage, Peter took it out.

This did not go unnoticed; Martha, struggling to tear open the pocket of oranges, knew that his wretched dog must have weed somewhere. 'It smells like a toilet in here,' she said to Mavis. 'You better open that window.'

Pssshhh. The iron steamed as Mavis set it on the counter and leant across the toaster to open the window. As she twisted the window latch, her chest rested against an expensive Baccarat vase from the Gardeners' previous house and another lifetime.

'Muffin!' shouted Martha. 'Muffin!' The guilty Maltese poodle emerged from a bed under the dining table. 'It smells like a doggery in this *unit*.' She said 'unit' with particular disdain. 'Go on, outside, Muffin! You should be outside.' Gathering up the dog's bed, she commandeered the poodle through the open-plan lounge-diningroom-kitchen and into the garden. Mavis and Peter watched as Martha installed Muffin and his bed on the dilapidated wooden bench strapped up with ropes.

Pssshhh. Mavis paused from her ironing to put away the other groceries. The pie bought for her lunch was steak and kidney. It wasn't her preferred flavour. Chicken and mushroom was what she really liked. Kidneys, she sighed; she had never liked the idea of eating kidneys. She would pick them out as she always did when Martha bought that flavour, which was often.

Peter was filling his bucket with water. Mavis was putting the two jam doughnuts into the bread bin next to the sink beneath the window with the view of Steenberg Mountain. Peter had the tap on full and water was splashing; some drops landed on Mavis's hand. 'Jam doughnuts!' He was jovial at the prospect. 'Excellent, we'll have those for tea, Mavis, you and I. Mrs Gardener doesn't know what she's missing; I don't know why she won't eat doughnuts.'

Mavis wished Mrs Gardener hadn't bought the jam doughnuts. Just that week she had decided to start a diet; now she wasn't going to be able to resist eating the doughnut.

'Did Mrs Gardener remember to buy the dog food?' Peter asked, seeing Martha marching back across the grass.

'No, there is no food for Muffin,' Mavis said. She wasn't surprised Martha had forgotten the dog food.

Peter got out of the kitchen area before his wife reached the glass sliding doors. She closed the door behind her and left Muffin looking in forlornly. 'You're in disgrace, Muffin,' she said. 'You can stay outside now.

It's a perfectly nice day; there's no reason you have to be inside making the place smell.'

In the tiny entrance area, Peter squirted Handy Andy onto the cream mock-granite tiles and set about mopping. His sports coat was lying on the dining table and Martha eyed it with irritation as she passed the table on the way back to the kitchen part of what she called 'the unit'. 'Mavis,' she called, 'I wonder if you could grate a little carrot for lunch. I'll do the salad.' To a new bunch of roses out of water, still in cellophane with a pouch of flower food attached, she said: 'Juliette is coming. I want this unit to look at least half-decent.'

Pssshhh. The iron hissed as Mavis paused to ask, 'Do you want me to grate the carrot now?'

The salad Martha had planned for Juliette had grapefruit, blue cheese and walnuts – expensive ingredients, so as Martha prepared the salad she halved the quantity of blue cheese and walnuts. The saved ingredients would be good for a second salad, another day.

In time, Peter managed to get the yellowness out of the tile grouting. With bucket and mop and Handy Andy in hand, he walked the few paces from the nook that was the entrance, along the length of the kitchen counter opposite the dining table. As he rounded the counter, Martha was in an advanced stage of opening the dishwasher beneath the sink, and again they came close to colliding, but both, after twenty years of marriage, had become very adept at avoiding things. They withdrew their advances and so escaped any unpleasant interaction. Peter edged around his wife and into the yard.

'Mavis, you must please unpack the dishwasher when it finishes,' said Martha, in as friendly a tone as she could, although annoyed that she now had to unpack the dishes.

Pssshhh, said the iron as Mavis lifted it from the collar of Mr Gardener's last remaining Thomas Pink of London shirt. 'It only just finished washing now, Mrs Gardener.'

Martha nodded understanding. She gathered up three French porcelain side plates, three matching dinner plates and three sets of silver knives and forks. 'But are you going to grate that carrot?'

Pssshhh. Opening the drawer of pots and sundry equipment such as graters, Mavis was reminded that grating carrot was something she particularly disliked doing, because Mrs Gardener insisted on the carrot being grated on the finest-sized hole, which took longer and was messy. Bits of carrot always flew everywhere. Why did it have to be the small hole, wondered Mavis, when the large hole was much more effective, quicker and cleaner?

'Remember to grate it as finely as possible,' said Martha, setting up the table for lunch.

'Yes, Mrs Gardener.' Mavis was used to the fact that both Martha and Peter Gardener repeated themselves often.

The ironing board was moved aside and Mavis took carrots in a Woolworths bag out of the fridge. They were medium-sized, a terrible size for grating, too thin and wiry, and inclined to snap during the force of grating. She had once told Martha that the carrots in the bag marked 'large' were the best for grating and, since the Gardeners only ate their carrot grated, it made sense to buy the ones most suited to grating: *large* carrots.

'All clean!' announced Peter, coming in from the yard, leaving sludgy footprints on Mavis's newly washed floor. 'The house smells like an orchard now, doesn't it, Mavis?'

Mavis had to laugh at that, even though she was dealing with the wiry carrots. Martha scowled.

'Just like a beautiful spring garden filled with lemon trees!' Peter said loudly. 'Not so, Mavis?'

Mavis laughed again and shook her head. 'Yes, Mr Gardener.'

Muffin was whining and scratching at the glass door, and Peter wanted to go to his dog, but the most direct route from the kitchen area to the door was via the gap between the side wall and Peter's chair at the head of the dining table – a gap that was small and occupied by Martha, who was at that moment positioning a linen napkin under a side plate. Peter opted for the longer route around the far end of the dining table. Almost at the glass door, he spoke to his dog as if the poodle could hear through glass: 'Poor Muffin! Nobody has given you any breakfast and there's not even any food for you, my boy. Locked out in the cold and hungry.' Peter was about to open the glass door, but he turned back and saw Martha glaring at him. He knew that if he let the dog in, Martha would simply banish him back to the garden a few moments later. With his master so near, Muffin was scratching madly now, yelping, hoping. 'I'm sorry, boy,' Peter said. 'You have to stay out for a while, but later I'll go and get your food and a lovely big ostrich bone. How about that? You'll like that, won't you, my boy?'

Content that her decree had not been breached, Martha was arranging flowers.

A carrot snapped mid-grate and as a result Mavis ended up with a grated knuckle. She sucked the blood from her grazed index and middle fingers.

Peter looked at the mountain through the rattling door; Muffin was throwing himself at the glass. 'I think I'll watch the news,' he said to the mountain. 'I want to see what the markets are doing.'

Martha shook her head and thought how banal it was that Peter always watched the news; all day long he watched the news, the same news, over and over again. A large sofa was positioned between the glass door and the dining table. Opposite it was a television, which, with a click of the remote, began to spew loud commentary on the global financial meltdown. It seemed the American Senate had rejected the seven-hundred-billion-dollar bailout plan.

'This is a catastrophe,' Peter said with glee to Becky Anderson, the news anchor reporting. Becky Anderson responded in her firm-voiced affirmative by quoting figures about losses.

Snip, snip, snip, Martha cut the ends off the new bunch of white roses. The flowers had been a dreadful price, but the unit had to look at least half-decent when Juliette arrived. What difference does it make, she thought, if the stock market halves in value? It's not like we have any stocks or even any money of any substantial sort left.

Mavis, still grating, her knuckle still bleeding, was thinking a similar thing: she had no money saved, no pension fund, no stocks or bonds or any of the other things the Americans on Peter's favourite DStv news station spoke about all day long.

Wall Street traders on the television were shaking their heads in utter disbelief at the news that Congress had rejected the bailout package. Peter was cheered by the mayhem in the markets, although he didn't realise it and would definitely deny his joy, thought Martha.

'This is an absolute disaster,' he said. Becky Anderson replied that there would be a second vote later in the week, so all was not lost.

The phone rang. Quickly, Martha placed her roses into a vase, which she had strategically positioned on the kitchen counter to block the view of the ironing board, and answered. A female guard at the security-village gate asked if she was expecting a Juliette, and Martha said she was, so the Juliette was permitted to enter the grounds.

At the far end of the security complex in which Martha and Peter lived, Juliette followed the road up one hill flanked with fountains and down another hill. Although she loved them dearly, she was dreading the lunch with Martha and Peter. It amazed her, or, more accurately, it made her insufferably tense, to be around them. She took a great breath before she rang their doorbell.

This was an opportunity to let Muffin in, and Peter took it. For Muffin, the sight of the open front door, a glimmer of dog-scented grass beyond the unit, and a guest was a joy as great as joy. As Martha was kissing Juliette on her cheek and saying hello, Muffin dive-bombed the greeting. Peter sauntered over to join the welcome party. 'Down, Muffin!' commanded Martha, but to no avail, so she caught him and picked him up to prevent the dog from clawing Juliette's silk skirt.

Stretching his arms wide open and then folding them around Juliette and drawing her close, Peter relished the softness of their guest's ivory shirt, the warmth of her body beneath and the enthralling notes of a perfume – composed of coriander, coffee, peony and white musk, and spritzed on in the car – now seeped into Juliette's skin at her earlobe and along her neck. 'Can I get you a glass of wine?' Peter asked her, noting once again that she really needn't have had that facelift. Her skin looked stretched, and though she had previously been an extremely attractive woman, she now looked peculiarly taut. Peter was against all forms of cosmetic surgery, primarily because it was very expensive, and because

Martha was always hankering after a facelift or an eye-lift or some kind of skin-smoothing, youth-giving peel. But he wouldn't allow it; age was natural and Martha must accept it. That was his policy.

Juliette knew she'd definitely need wine to get through the lunch. After so many years, Peter didn't ask Martha what she would be drinking – they always shared a bottle of white wine with lunch. Their circumstances may have changed, their living quarters diminished, but their habits were still the same. He poured three glasses of a fine Cape white.

Martha had that low-grade migraine still coming on, so although there was the usual glass of white at her usual chair, she had made a cup of chamomile tea, and was sipping that as Peter regaled Juliette with the details of the global financial meltdown.

Mavis listened to the story she had heard all morning as she continued to iron and as her steak and kidney pie heated up in the oven. In the middle of Peter's tale of banking gloom, Martha interrupted and said to Juliette, 'I'm sure all that's the last thing you want to hear. Tell me about your trip to France. Paris is always so lovely … where did you stay?'

Pssshhh. Mavis turned the iron off at the plug. The pie would be hot. She boiled the kettle for coffee and listened to Juliette describing the interior design of her suite in a beautiful hotel in a street full of shops and restaurants.

'How divine!' said Martha, her heart breaking with envy.

'The banks in France are also suffering,' Peter said, chewing a mouthful of salad that he quite liked; yes, it wasn't bad, the blue cheese, the walnuts; the grapefruit was too sour though. 'This grapefruit is awful,' he said, before continuing: 'In the whole of Europe the banks are in a terrible way. No country has escaped. Nobody expected this; it hasn't been this bad since 1929.'

Martha longed for the space, the wide boulevards of Paris, the freedom. 'Did you go to any wondrous restaurants?' she asked Juliette.

Peter went on softly about those banks in crisis.

After a sip of wine, Juliette, seated at the head of the table between Martha and Peter, answered Martha first and then commented on the collapsing banks so as not to be rude to Peter.

Mavis lifted the crust off her pie and set about extracting the kidney. Muffin stood at her side, looking on in supplicating silence. The pie was more kidney than steak, so, with the kidney gone, it wasn't going to be a very substantial lunch. Before she sat down on the corner chair between the yard door and the garage door, opposite the fridge and flanked by the sink with the drain that always blocked, Mavis scraped saucy kidney into Muffin's bowl. For the time it took for the dog to eat the warm kidney in sweet pie sauce, Muffin was the happiest being in the unit.

Many news bulletins and a rerun of the US vice-presidential debate between Joe Biden and Sarah Palin later, Martha and Peter were in bed. The Kreepy Krauly in the neighbouring unit had automatically come on and, as it chugged around its turquoise pool beneath the stars, it sent loud vibrating tremors up their bedroom wall, which backed directly onto the pool.

They kept well to their sides of the king-sized bed, thanks to modern mattress technology. Over the hard cover of his seven-hundred-page tome on Britain's naval history, Peter glanced across at Martha. She had her reading glasses on, and a book called *Eat, Pray, Love* was propped up in front of her, but she was fast asleep and snoring gently.

After three hundred pages, Peter was tired of being at sea. Tomorrow I'll go to Exclusives and choose a new book, he thought. He got up to turn out Martha's bedside light and, without touching her or waking her, removed her glasses and her book. Back on his side, he settled in and turned off his light.

Dadadadadadadaada went the tireless automatic pool cleaner. Peter closed his eyes. *Dadadadadadadaada.* He saw Sarah Palin winking. He opened his eyes. 'Catastrophic,' he whispered of the sub-prime lending crisis. He closed his eyes. *Dadadadadadadaada.* 'Change,' said Becky Anderson. 'The American people want change; they want reforms.' Change. Reforms. Obama. Taxes. The words, the news, CNN was inside Peter's head. *Dadadadadadadaada.*

Some days he was a Republican, usually to goad Martha, who favoured Obama, but tonight, restless, disturbed, unsettled, trapped by unit life, lonely, he too felt in the mood for change.

*Dadadadadadadaada. Dadadadadadadaada. Dadadadadadadaada. Dadada-
dadadadadaada.* The pool cleaner was relentless and seemed to be getting
louder. Without turning on the light, Peter got out of bed.

Change would require clothes, he thought. He got dressed in the spare
room where his clothes and his sleeping dog were kept. Muffin opened
one eye. In the dog's limited experience, night visitors to his room usually meant that he would be rudely evicted from his warm blankets and
ordered to go downstairs, out into the cold, to wee. He closed his eye
and contracted into a ball.

Slipping on trousers, socks and a pair of shoes, Peter wasn't entirely
sure of a plan; this change was unprecedented in his life. In his head he
had a picture of himself sitting at a restaurant having cocktails with an
unnamed woman; he was holding her hand. He tucked up Muffin even
tighter in the poodle's Woolworths fleece blanket, and took the car keys
to the car parked outside the garage. It had to be that car because the
garage made too much noise when it opened and Peter didn't want to
risk waking Martha. He wouldn't know what to say.

As he closed the front door behind him, Martha woke up. Something's
wrong, she thought, coming out of a fraught dream about Paris.

Dadadadadadadaada. Damn Kreepy Krauly, she said to herself and
turned to look at the man she had as a husband, but he was gone. *Dadadadadadadaada.* And not to the bathroom as she had first imagined: the
bathroom door was open, the light off and there were no sounds of
tinkling urine or running water. *Dadadadadadadaada.*

Careful to stick to the speed limit, Peter, feeling the bliss of liberation,
was sailing along De Waal Drive in the quiet dark of the first hours of
Tuesday. The harbour sparkled. He had Fine Music Radio on and the DJ
was playing midnight jazz. Thoroughly pleasant. Not that Peter was a
great jazz aficionado, but this was 'change'. The specifics of the reform
were still hazy to him, but he knew the streets he should head for as he
turned past the pink Mount Nelson, beautifully lit beneath palms. He was
entertaining two options: cruising the street to find the woman for the
drink, or going to a strip club like the one called Mavericks, which he
had heard about once or twice, but never considered visiting. Wasn't that

how it was done? 'What do you think?' he asked the Fine Music Radio DJ as he waited for the traffic light outside Michaelis to turn green. The lights were against him; he had to stop at the Long Street intersection too. He peered down beyond the Turkish Baths, along the street famous for its bars and nightlife. The picture in his head came to him again: restaurant, woman, cocktails, holding her hand. The hand he could see more clearly than anything else in the vision. It wasn't in a bar in Long Street. That didn't fit his idea. There should be somebody playing the piano.

Green. At the top of the hill he turned right into the road where he knew Mavericks was located. There, the sign, the bouncers, and inside girls from Russia and Poland – beauties who would let him touch them. His old heart, he realised, was racing. 'An adventure,' he said to the Fine Music Radio DJ.

He didn't stop, but continued driving, passing another strip club, the Moulin Rouge. Years ago in Paris, he remembered he and Martha had been to the real Moulin Rouge, for a laugh.

At the street famous for prostitutes, he turned right and slowed to a cruise to appraise the possibilities. He wasn't sure that he wanted to know prices, but supposed he should find out. Wasn't that the next step?

The answer came too late; he was at Long Street already and turning right again, picking up speed, watching the night, the lights, the street pass by from the safety of his metallic-green Mercedes, long past its warranty.

There was that comfortable-looking cigar bar; he could go there and sit at a table with a cocktail and maybe the woman in his vision would simply materialise, sit down, close, with her hand on the table ready for him to boldly reach out to and hold. He inhaled, pulled in his stomach, patted it flat – he was trim enough – and glanced up at his face in the rear-view mirror – he was still handsome, wasn't he? At the last intersection he exhaled, slumped, and had to decide if he should turn right and head back to Mavericks, or turn left and go back home, back to the unit, back to Martha. His shoulders knotted at his neck.

Right. He set the indicator clicking. Up the hill and right again, but this time as he approached Mavericks he was determined: he wanted out of unit-dictatorship; he wanted new life, new freedom. He scanned the street for a parking space. By God, he spotted one right outside! The angels must want him to go to that strip joint. He slipped in, elated, truly excited for the first time in a long time.

But Peter's joy was short-lived, undone by the sound of fury taken out on a hooter. Startled rabbit, Peter looked up into the glare of a rival driver's headlights. The driver was shouting, gesticulating. The car was towering, one of those 4 × 4 monsters. In a show of peace, Peter held up his hands and smiled. He was a gentleman; if the other driver had seen the place first he could have it, was what he tried to communicate, but failed. The driver took Peter's raised hands to be a gesture of dispute and became all the more enraged, shouting, cursing at him. Peter tried to shout back: 'I'm sorry! I'll move, if only you'll let me. You've blocked me in. Just go back, go back and I'll leave. I don't want your place. Go back!' He flapped his hand in a hapless 'go back' fashion, which was totally mis-interpreted by the rival driver as a declaration of war. No matter how hard Peter tried to shout, the man couldn't hear his plaintive apology over his own hooting and venomous shouting.

'Honestly, all I want is to get out of here. Believe me,' Peter said, throw-ing up his hands at the shouting man. It occurred to him that it might be unsafe to get out of his car, to attempt to explain the misunderstanding to this obviously irrational person, who had begun to look very much like a gangster. So much noise had been created that one of the bouncers outside Mavericks ambled over to ask Peter what the problem was.

'Would you please tell that man that I don't want his parking space,' Peter said. 'He can have it, if he'll just reverse so that I can get out of here!'

As swiftly as it arose, the problem was solved. Peter was shaken, though, and no longer in the mood for Mavericks. He turned right into the street of prostitutes again. 'This is a much better option,' he said to the DJ at Fine Music Radio. 'I'll find a nice girl and go to a nice bar, like the Planet Bar at the Mount Nelson. Something genteel, with good music and pleasant decor.'

Oh, but there was the problem of being seen. It was unlikely that any of their friends would be around at this time, but their children's friends might well be. 'Not the Planet Bar, then.'

Long Street came again before he'd even had time to give much consideration to the available women on the previous street. 'Where do people go with prostitutes?' he asked the DJ. 'I don't want to get a hotel room; that would give the wrong impression entirely.' The red light at the intersection halted his progress. Left or right? Undecided, he had stopped between the lanes, not committing to either of the arrows painted in the tar, one urging him to return to the unit, the other directing him to attempt Mavericks again.

Peter looked at his hands on the steering wheel. They were always very dry now, chapped and blotched with liver spots; he'd worked for thirty-five years as an accountant before retiring. Long hours, but he wasn't brilliant enough to make the money Martha had wanted, and then a few bad investments, debts … his nails were thick, difficult job to cut them, but they had served him well, those hands. In the vision he had of the cocktail and the woman, he realised now that he had pictured his hands as younger. The hands in the vision were his hands at thirty-five – unwrinkled, unmarked, strong, full of promise.

He turned right and headed past Mavericks again. Seeing that 4 × 4 in the contested parking spot filled him with a rush of remembered anguish; he'd actually been scared of that insane driver. No, he definitely wasn't going to Mavericks.

Peter continued to circle round town, past Mavericks, past the prostitutes, all the while thinking, and listening to jazz. With each circuit, he noticed some new detail about his city, about the women, and the men, out in the dark, on the streets. He became part of that night. A certain prostitute took to waving, saying, 'Hello, honey,' each time he passed her. Another parking space opened up outside Mavericks, and the guard, who had developed a habit of smiling at Peter, tried with theatrical arm gestures to usher him into the space. Peter just waved 'no' and waved 'no' again when he went by again. The guard laughed and laughed again and again and again. 'Hello, honey, back so soon?' called the woman on the corner, whom Peter was beginning to regard as almost a friend, along with the Mavericks guard. This went on for an hour. Another lap came and there was the guard smiling outside Mavericks, offering a choice of two empty bays, to which Peter waved 'no', and the guard laughed.

But the next time, the woman on the corner had vanished. Nobody called out, 'Hello, honey.' Peter wanted to hear the words once more, so he circled again, four times, but she was definitely gone. Finally, after all that cruising, at the intersection with the Long Street Baths, Peter indicated left and sailed back along De Waal Drive to the unit.

As he crept into bed, he thought it fortunate that Martha hadn't stirred, but as soon as he closed his eyes, she spoke, saying sharply into the darkness: 'Peter, where were you?'

His eyes sprung open. This was momentous: Martha hadn't addressed him for … he couldn't remember when last he'd heard her say his name. He switched on the bedside light and turned to her waiting eyes. Evidently, she had been worried and had imagined all kinds of reasons for his departure in the middle of the night – perhaps one of their children had been in an accident.

In an act of revolutionary boldness, Peter scooted closer to his wife and, before she could do anything about the intrusion, he took her hand in his. He squeezed it, then rubbed her palm and said with delight, 'Martha, my love, I went for a midnight drive, and it was exhilarating. Next time you must come. We live in a beautiful city.' Then he kissed Martha's hand, scooted back to his side of the bed, turned out the light, and, after all the excitement of change, was asleep, snoring, in a moment.

Martha's eyes were wide open and it occurred to her that the bedroom was filled with a lovely peace: the Kreepy Krauly had stopped. In the stillness of pre-dawn, she contemplated whether she ought to be extremely angry or unexpectedly happy. She could feel a trace of Peter's lips tingling on her hand, and concluded that the kiss, though charming, was almost, but not quite, in any way, enough.

susan
mann

Salt

Forgive me. I did not call. I didn't expect to see you, you see. Ever again or at least not so soon. Not face to face and so distant. Besides, it's not quite seven years yet. There are still a few months to go.

Yes, I have an old photograph of you somewhere, with 'Luka, Croatia' scribbled in pencil, fading on the back. I think it's tucked into a book of Sanskrit poetry. And once I saw a picture of you in a British newspaper. I didn't realise how famous you'd become for your driftwood sculptures. Or that you'd married a woman who picked capers.

I took only one shot of you that summer. At the time I wasn't thinking of the future. There's one of me too, in my shorts and T-shirt. You must have taken it the day after I met you, my cheek still red where you struck me. To be honest, I hardly look at either picture, or any others for that matter. Using snapshots to freeze significant moments depresses me. And, anyway, surely the most memorable photographs are taken with the mouth.

It was of course you who told me about the seven-year thing, on that late afternoon in the lighthouse, ebbing and flowing in and out of conversation, only a thin mattress separating us from the dusty stone floor. You said the body took seven years to completely renew itself. 'Every cell?' I asked. 'Yes,' you answered. 'Every cell.' You were leaning back, one leg up and bent for me to rest against. Through the window, cracked and full of cobwebs, and through my kelpy hair, the sun was roasting my shoulders. Thoughts, naked as gulls, were swirling and swooping, now and then vocalised in some vague attempt to hold on to them. As though without words the experience would simply fly away. No matter. The mind could replace thoughts all the time, using words like tiny cages to hold memories and tuck them away, or tiny coffins burying them beyond recall. But the body, you were suggesting, must work for seven years to forget.

My escape to Vis, your island of only three thousand inhabitants off the Dalmatian Coast, marked the end of my first year in England, where I'd won a scholarship to continue studying law, and a place as an articled clerk in a firm of solicitors. My childhood, barefoot and sunburnt, a buchu farmer's daughter in South Africa's Boland, had hardly prepared me for that first frigid English winter. As soon as the summer drew closer, and I had enough money for a ticket, I flew to Croatia, took a taxi to the harbour in Split, and jumped onto the next ferry out. As it chugged towards Vis I breathed in the salt of the Adriatic, a refugee seeking light.

On arrival, I dragged my suitcase along the quay, looking for a room. I remember cicadas ringing out from the dust up on the hills, while boats like white cut-outs lolled on the water. It was the summer of mirages. Beyond all blue, birds knifed across the landscape in the time it took to blink away the glare. Heat steamed up from the pebbles from the sun-whitened sandstone in the alleyways, and seeped through the soles of my slip-slops. A starving cat sliced across the path.

I bought an ice cream. Further down the pathway, two children had set up a low plastic table, covered it meticulously with a cloth and were selling seashells that they'd carefully arranged in categories, and which varied in price from three to five kuna. Much to their surprise, I bought one. An old man cycled past me, a small dog and a newspaper tucked into the basket in front.

I found a room some way up the hill and returned to the quay to rent a bicycle. The next day I rode around the island, through the vineyards, the olive groves, the hills, till the heat of the afternoon rose in my throat and made me nauseous. In the hope of cooling off in the sea, I followed a sign pointing down a steep dirt road surrounded by cliffs, to Stoncica.

There were people on the beach and in the water, someone had a CD player, a little girl had lost her shoe. And in the distance, at the furthest edge of the rocky cliff that protected the bay, I saw a lighthouse. I left my bicycle on the sand and ran into the sea in my clothes. The shore was littered with broken shells and I jumped now and then when my foot touched something sharp, gasping from the cold. I waded out further and further, bouncing up in the shallow waves till I found a little cove where nobody could see me, where I removed my shorts and baggy T-shirt and hung them on a rock.

Time seemed to change its laws for me that afternoon as I floated and splashed and felt the sea wash through my hair. I hardly even noticed the bank of dark clouds mushrooming in the distance, or the sun and the crowds disappearing. It all seemed to happen unnaturally fast. Then, quite suddenly, even the Adriatic grew silent, and I noticed it was growing dark. I made my way back to the rock where my clothes were hidden, and put them back on in the water. I started to swim back, as my T-shirt ballooned all about me. The beach was empty. Everybody had left, except for a very tall man walking out towards me, a piece of driftwood in one hand, the other beckoning me to come ashore.

I shouted out that it was okay, I was fine. But the man continued to beckon.

'A storm,' he cried. 'You must hurry.'

Fat drops of rain started pelting the waves. The island suddenly seemed dense and austere. I did my best to speed up, but the sea's dreamlike resistance frustrated all attempts at reaching the shore faster.

The man shouted something through the wind, but I could barely hear him. As I reached him he repeated, 'A bad storm coming in; you must come with me.' He pointed to the lighthouse. Already the warning shafts of light were falling on the water. 'You can wait there, till it's over.'

'Why?' I questioned.

'Because it's too late for you to go anywhere else,' he replied.

And that's how I met you, Luka. You looked like how I imagine Jesus, with your beard and your stick, knee-deep in the sea. I half-expected the water to part.

You lifted my rented bicycle off the sodden sand and ran it along the path, hurrying to the lighthouse in the rain. I simply followed you, trusting as a disciple. You were still holding your piece of driftwood. The next day you would fashion it into a fish and call it 'Freak'.

You took the bike inside and, closing the heavy door behind us, you pointed upwards. A spiral staircase curled towards the storm. I hurried up the cement stairs behind you – wet and cold, grains of sand rubbing raw my skin under my waistband – noting again how very tall you were. I stood at the door of the circular room at the top and took it all in: on one side your mattress with a blanket thrown over it, on the other your stove. A few paces away the screen you'd made from pieces of wood tied together with string, used to block off the shower and the toilet. There were windows all around blurred with rain, pieces of driftwood of all sizes propped up against them.

'You need to get out of those wet clothes,' you said, passing me the blanket from the bed. 'I'd offer you a hot shower, but I'm afraid it's a bit risky. The lightning conductor is being repaired – summer storms are quite unusual – which means the lighthouse itself can get hit.'

I took the blanket and disappeared behind the screen to remove my clothes. The next few minutes are unclear. Maybe my body has deleted them from memory already. I seem to remember that the salt was stinging the place under my waistband where the skin was raw. Perhaps it occurred to me to rinse it quickly. I think I tried the tap, but I'm really not sure. The only thing I remember is my body arching up, as the force of what felt like a skyful of volts racked through it. I heard screaming all around me; I had no idea who it was, of course. Then your voice.

'It's all right. You're okay. You're alive.'

'What happened?' I asked, struggling for breath. You were wrapping the blanket around me.

'The lightning hit. The pipes in the shower act as conductors. You were shocked.'

'Who was screaming?'

'You were.'

'Me?'

'As I say, you were shocked. Literally. I had to slap you quite hard, I'm afraid, to bring you back.'

I sat on the mattress on the floor clutching the blanket, still shivering. You poured some brandy into mugs and handed me one. I don't remember how much time passed. At some point you asked me my name.

The storm continued to blast the lighthouse, hail like white bullets bouncing off its walls, light and lightning clashing like sabres.

'Like a battlefield,' you said. 'Which is why I'm here in the first place.'

Between the cracks of thunder and the clatter of rain you told me how, after the leaden years of war, you'd longed for peace and solitude. You went to Palagruža where you first became a lighthouse keeper, then to Jadrija. Finally you found Stoncica, or maybe it found you, and it had been home for the last five and a half years.

The brandy warmed me like a filament from inside while you told me all about Vis, and the lighthouse, and particularly its associations with war. How, till recently, the island had been a military zone, without any tourist activity at all. How, during the Second World War, they took the light off this lighthouse and buried it to protect the crystals. How it had been known as a signal station since fires were first lit on plateaus to warn ships. How, before the naval battle of Vis, the telegraph operator had stood in this very room and informed the Austrian command about the arrival of the hostile fleet.

As time went on, I noticed you were cold, and offered to share the blanket with you. Wrapped inside the sound of rain we eventually lay down. Story after story you dredged up from the night to stop me shaking. You told me that the island had many secrets in its soil and its sea, dating back to the Iron and Bronze Ages. That the Greeks had colonised it for a while, and that the large white stone blocks on the quayside go back to that time. That documents dating back two thousand years had recently been discovered, praising the quality of the island's wine. That the fishermen of Vis were once considered the best in the world. Story after story. Each one an opiate. Till finally the storm surrendered to the silence, and I grew aware of my nakedness next to yours. Till the sense of being alive grew stronger than my fear, despite wars and acts of God. Till I reached out and touched the words and made them mine, and your voice became flesh and your words became bone.

'Someone must have died last night,' you said in the morning, looking out into the pristine blue. 'She's always still like that when she's taken some-body. As though her innocence requires a human sacrifice to be restored.' Sure enough, news reached us later that a fisherman had drowned in the storm; his body, and later his red canvas hat, washed up on the shore.

I stayed for the full six days of my break at the lighthouse, and, aside from the brief sojourn to pick up my things from the room that I had rented, I hardly left Stoncica. The weather returned almost seamlessly to perfection. Clear days, fragrant nights. In that short time I learned the rhythms and rituals of your simple routine. Coffee in the morning as soon as the light was switched off, then the daily report, some repairs, more coffee, then onto the beach to collect driftwood, which you carved into sculptures and took to the market. In the evening you cooked fish, fresh from the boats, and sometimes some chard with garlic, olive oil and sliced potatoes. I've tried to recreate it back in London with fish bought fresh at Borough Market, but I can't of course. The real ingredients are always missing.

I didn't hear from you for some time after I left. The weeks went by. And then once again the winter – the darkness, the evenings that begin mid-afternoon, the changes in temperature between the Tube and the street. I imagined you closed up in your lighthouse for days, fixing equip-ment, holding out against the Scirocco and the sea. I wondered whether the lightning conductor had been fixed. One day I received notification from the post office that a parcel had arrived. I darted out in my lunch hour in my terrible tights, woolly hat and gloves to pick it up, and opened it in my office. The piece of driftwood, shaped like a fish, seemed bizarrely incongruent among the chrome and leather and sleet through the windows. I wrote a note to thank you. In it I mentioned I would soon be moving to a flat near Waterloo. I did not include the address.

The following summer, I travelled with some friends to a house in the south of France. I swam in the Mediterranean and read short stories by Guy de Maupassant. I was trying to teach myself French. Most Europeans, I'd discovered, could speak at least three languages and, even if they couldn't, were accustomed to reading literature in translation. It seemed gravely important not to be ignorant. I was also studying for my finals. The groove of my life required the repetition and discipline to complete what I had begun. To flow unhindered in the direction that my career had dictated. To be equal to and worthy of my privileges. To step beyond my history, which from my new – advantaged – perspective I found confusing. I teetered between homesickness for the simple clarity of my youth and judgement of a context that seemed parochial and provincial. So I put your driftwood fish away, lest it evoke impulses stronger than my resolve, or raise questions that would not answer themselves in cities. I only took it out again the other day, after I ran into you outside your exhibition.

You didn't recognise me at first. I look a little different, I suppose, with my cropped hair, linen suit and high heels. I even wear underwear these days. You just stood there, on the riverside by the gallery at Oxo Wharf, while I called your name.

'You don't recognise me,' I said. 'I've changed my hair.'

'I don't know you in such a hurry,' you answered. 'What are you doing here?'

'What are *you* doing here?' I replied.

An exhibition, you explained. Your driftwood sculptures had become quite popular for some reason. You'd been invited to show them off, perhaps sell one or two; it was all a little overwhelming.

Even in my heels, you towered over me. Lean. Remote. Your sun-bleached hair was turning salt and pepper. There were patches of grey in your beard. Metallic.

'Would you like a drink?' I asked. 'A brandy? It's cold outside.'

'I have to go,' you said. 'The airport.'

Then you dug in a canvas bag for some paper and a pen. 'But here's my number. Call me.'

Later that night I looked for you on the internet. Discovered the success that your work was attracting. Read the article from the British newspaper about your home with the spiral staircase and the cliffs that sweep down into the sea. 'The cliffs are covered in capers,' you tell the interviewer. 'My wife picks them and prepares them for us to eat.'

I took the driftwood fish out of the cupboard, like a lost sailor with a compass. I turned it over and over, feeling the roughness of it, touching in the soft wood the texture of writing, where you'd carved a line from a French poem: '*Trop près on brûle, trop loin on gèle.*' These days I'm able to translate it myself: 'Too close, one burns. Too far away, one freezes.'

Words are like lighthouses. People can be too. This Christmas I return to South Africa, miles away, for a holiday. I look forward to seeing my family, and to long walks in the mountains, with or without shoes. I'll go to the beach, swim in the Indian Ocean, allowing my hair – I'm growing it again – to wrap itself like seaweed around my face. Seven years will be over. Only the sea will remember. There will be sun on my shoulders and salt in my mouth. Perhaps I'll call then.

imraan
coovadia

File Under: Touch (Avoidance of, Writers);
Love (Avoidance of, Writers). (1000 Words)

1. I number my paragraphs because I don't want them to touch each other.

2. I am a writer. I have rules about language. As far as possible

   (a) a period should not rub up against a capital letter;

   (b) adjectives should be unemotive, while adverbs are banished to a foreign language, like French, where they do not have the sense to avoid them;

   (c) a paragraph should be surrounded by a one-centimetre frame of white space; and

   (d) a piece of literature should be expressed in an interesting number of units: say, one hundred syllables or iambics, or two hundred and ninety-nine stanzas, or three hundred pages, or three hundred and twenty-nine pages (which is the sum of ten consecutive primes). Therefore this story – including the eleven words of the title – numbers precisely one thousand words. (Count them.)

It bothers me that the *Thousand Nights and a Night*, where Scheherezade wins her life by avoiding conclusions, is one night too long to be a perfectly rounded number. I think Scheherezade should have avoided her own last night. In fact, in the earliest Persian notices, the compilation is referred to as *One Thousand Nights*.

3. Suppose the ten years of my marriage to Salma weren't the happiest years of my life. Suppose that. I am not the type of person who has happy years. My point is that the period with Salma was the characteristic period of my life (just as the characteristic period of a salmon's life is when he swims up the river). I am not revealing secrets when I say that Salma hardly needed to be touched herself … and, which is maybe more unusual, didn't need to be the toucher.

4. Salma, I thought, was an unusual Capetonian. She had cold hands, cold feet that she kept in stockings in bed in June and July, and a kind of cold beauty – assisted by high-heel shoes and cosmetics – which held you at a distance. Salma could have your penis in her mouth but keep you at bay. She was scientific about the procedure, as if she was a carpenter sanding something down. She had a cold, cat-like tongue, as pink as lipstick, and cold lips. The effect of living with Salma was similar to standing inside the door of a refrigerator every minute of your life. Maybe I didn't love Salma (just because her supply of love was so limited). But I couldn't imagine anything different. I didn't want anything different.

5. For the last nine years of our marriage I slept on the gabardine couch in my study while Salma stayed in the bedroom – sleeping on satin sheets, perfuming herself in the bathroom, primping, and thinning out her eyebrows year after year so that by the time she was thirty they

seemed to have been written onto her brow with a ballpoint. Some evenings I could hear her battery-powered vibrator from my post in the study. I was relieved to have a substitute. I feared being sucked into Salma and never returning to myself. Would I have preferred some other way? As a writer I am bound to my problems. So I could never see a psychiatrist who would steal them from me.

6. I would have never separated from Salma – there was nothing to separate from – if not for nature. Nature, who keeps her secrets more cunningly than Salma, made one of her blood vessels weaker than the others, a defect as subtle as a single loose thread in a shirt. The day after she had a minor traffic accident near Rhodes Memorial, when the university shuttle bumped into her from the back, she didn't wake up. She lay in bed until ten in the morning, eleven, then twelve, when I went in to see her and found that she was as cold as a slab of ice.

7. My hands stung from where they had contacted Salma's forehead, then her chest, which was colder than ice and devoid of a heartbeat. It was a crude situation, far cruder than anything I would try in writing. Imagine inventing a character who, because she's emotionally cold, has poor circulation, hands and feet she's always complaining about, and then whose heart stops beating. Laughable!

8. Justice, including poetic justice, is contextual. Salma was as cold as the mussels she liked to eat, but so was her mother and so was the much older cousin who wormed his way into her Wynberg bedroom when Salma was thirteen. Is there also poetic justice for him? And for the man or woman who made him? For the men and women who made them?

9. I married again a year after Salma. I wasn't used to being alone and by myself at one and the same time.

10. Cherysse is a secretary at the university. She had read both of my books and, when she was introduced to me, asked the right questions

about them. (I keep to a strict limit of one question per reader per book.) She has a face that is beautiful, at face value, but somehow reminds me of paper, specifically ricepaper, as if she were an actress in a Japanese movie of the 1930s or 1940s.

11. Above all, Cherysse has the quality that most men – and I have never made an exception for myself where my tastes and prejudices are concerned – like in most women: Cherysse is receptive. Her ricey face glimmers with feeling, with sympathy, whenever I say something. When I am cold, or soaked with rain, she is also cold, and soaked with rain. When I stub my toe she rubs her foot. She is more worried than me about my worries.

12. So, of course, I fell in love with her. Since I find love unendurable, to reduce its intensity, I asked Cherysse to marry me. She accepted. On the first night of our marriage I waited until she was fast asleep. I walked through the flat, where I moved after Salma took the house. It's in Rosebank, as functional as a gumboot. I looked at the dark doorways and staircases, the cars, the one lit bulb dangling on a string behind the entrance. I was saturated in them, in these images, in my own words, like a pickle bottled in its own vinegar.

13. When I got to the couch Cherysse was already there, her eyes wide open and shining in the evening of the room. She had moved. I associated the rich light in her eyes with love. I couldn't stand it. I went back to the bedroom to go to sleep.

z o ë
w i c o m b

In Search of Tommie

TS knew precisely when it first came to him, the conviction. So powerful a feeling it was, like fresh blood rushing rudely through his veins, roaring in his ears, that he knew instinctively. Besides, how else could one know such a thing?

Had there really been no forewarning, or, later, a stray question left simmering through the night? Well, no, none that he could think of. What he remembered was that it had been such a long winter, waiting and waiting for the sun to return while the wind howled, heaven clutching for dear life its old grey blanket of sky. And the rain, that thing that people had prayed for in the summer of drought, just bucketing down in a vengeful rather than bounteous way, so that people – those upcountry dominees on television – surely learnt their lesson with praying. And how, by the way, do you turn prayers round? Would reversing the words not be like praying to the Devil? TS didn't want to think about that old mincing couple, the bickering faggots, God and his Devil; things hadn't come to that yet, although his mother still went on about making his peace with

God before it's too late. As if that would have made a difference. No, it was just the rain, unseasonable weather for November, which drained him, made his chest wheeze so that there was nothing to do but stay indoors. It was then that TS started his reading programme in earnest. Talk about meeting up with the truth in books! There the man was, the vark who had begotten him, skipping cool as a cucumber off the page.

No wonder TS had for so long avoided reading. Because why, it takes you into adventures just as if you have packed a rucksack and set off blindly, without a map, and not even knowing where you're heading. He ought to have remembered that from school, because although Joe called him an innocent philistine it is the case that he had in fact spent some years at high school, that he had read, or struggled to read if truth be told, the great guys. But now that things had taken such an unfortunate turn, when there was so little time left, so little energy for striking out with a real rucksack, he had become addicted to heading off into stories. Let's blow, says the book, and off they go, whoops-a-daisy and hee-yah, into the great unknown.

Next thing, you'll be reading poetry, Joe laughed, then the shit will hit the fan. That's the kind of thing Joe said, and then you had to work out what he meant, because Joe could sometimes talk like the guys in the Bible, in riddles, some of which eventually made sense, and others that didn't, because why, people say all sorts of things. Joe himself may not have worked out what he wanted to say; in other words, he could bullshit like the rest. But when Joe said, You must read this Hallam woman's book, could he have known what it would bring? But he, TS, should've remembered that the old guys with beards spent their time predicting the future, never mind what's going on here and now – those Josephs of old in their amazing Technicolor dreamcoats. But his Joe, and he knew Joe wouldn't be his for much longer – and who could blame him? – his Joe was the very one to decide that TS needed to change things, to do something different, a programme, he said, that didn't sap his energy. That was the first bolt of lightning. He knew in a flash what the reading programme was all about: the books were a substitute, were meant to replace Joe, and TS had to lie down there and then as the blood, the bad blood, drained from his head. Of course he didn't let on that he understood. No point in spoiling the times they still spent together, because Joe was a scream, and still they had a good laugh. Joe was not to be blamed; he'd done his bit, had come and gone just as TS himself had over the years come and gone. Together they had a history, and that is something grand, something to be grateful for, because why, just think of those unfortunate people who flit through lives remembering no one. He and Joe didn't talk about the drugs that were paid for; TS just knew that Joe would always be there in some way or other. The days of head-over-heels were in any case in the distant past, and Joe had always wanted children. Perhaps he would find a woman.

For TS the idea of reproduction was horrible, the thing that dogs or pigs did; he had never had anything to do with women. There was his mother, of course, but he did not like women's bundled-up softness. Or the crying. What he remembered about girls, even Pumla who was his best friend in primary school, was the black dogs' eyes, lolling in liquid for no reason at all.

His mother, a veteran crier, did the same eyes when she talked about his father, the vark. A gentleman, she said, from way up north, a university man who had studied in England, and then her voice would become weird, strangled, so that TS felt responsible for her pain. Actually, he was responsible. It was his arrival that drove the father away, but how could he care about the vark who went off to reproduce himself elsewhere with no care in the world? But, no, he was not allowed to say anything bad about the man. Oh no, his mother would protest, a gentleman he was, an educated man whose first responsibility was to learning. Since she sheltered behind a veil of tears, she was naturally hazy about the details, but what she knew was that when the man went to do some important business overseas, he got an English woman pregnant, so of course that was a new responsibility.

TS had to laugh at his mother's story, her use of the posh word, *ensnared*, which was what she thought the English woman got up to. The word reminded him of visits to his grandparents in the Transkei where he had helped his grandmother make snares for wild animals. He didn't like the skinning, the sound of Gogo's fist kneading the skin free from the carcass of deer or rabbit, while he, TS, held a leg. But Gogo's wild meat stew with a hunk of stiff pap, that was something to remember; they ate and told stories that never mentioned the vark.

When TS thought of that father, ensnared, skinned, swallowed by England, finished and klaar, his mother's broken voice after all these years made his blood boil. As a teenager he had taken to mocking her. Poor man, he'd say, twice ensnared, which he knew would break her heart all over again, but what did he care, how could a person care about women's stupid tears? All her life, she wailed, she had remained faithful to her Tommie, a highly educated man, by now a doctor of some kind, so that TS knew that such nonsense could only be brought to an end by being brutal.

Never again, he said, do I want to hear about that fucker, that fraud, that vark.

His mother wept. Her Tommie would never have used such language. TS kept his hands clenched in his pockets. He smarted at carrying the name of the vark who went about making little varkies, and solved the problem by using his initials. And that was that. Once his mother knew not to talk about him, the man was easily forgotten.

TS turned out to be a good name, especially when he met his first lover at Strandfontein where he spent hours staring out at waves crashing on the sand. That was where Richard found him. Richard drew on the sand with his big toe the name TESS. Embarrassed, TS dragged his own foot across to erase the writing, but really he didn't mind at all. Richard was too touchy, sensitive as they say, and he was no spring chicken; he would have died anyway.

When Joe came along a couple of years later he seemed especially pleased with TS's name.

Ah, the poet, he said, and putting on a sad, pensive look, with finger held to his cheekbone, intoned: I grow old, I grow old, Shall I wear the bottoms of my trousers rolled? Dare I eat a peach?

Just like Joe, turning anything into a rhyme, although the words did ring a bell.

Only a moffie would worry about eating a peach, TS said, and that made Joe laugh.

You should check the poof poet out, Joe said, and TS didn't say that he knew, that it had just come to him: the guy's poems were in the old school anthology.

So, for many, many years TS had not even thought of the vark father, not until this woman's book. It took some time for Joe to persuade him to read a book by a woman. An exceptionally lucid style, Joe said. That was how Joe talked, like the schoolteacher that he was. TS laughed. Yes, he, TS, was a bigoted, sexist pig; he would have no truck with a soggy book – how else would a woman's tears translate onto a page? But Joe insisted that he'd find the story interesting. The woman was a fiction writer, but the book he recommended seemed to be semi-autobiographical, about an absent father. It was the author's name that persuaded TS, or so he said. Chris Hallam could pass for a man. And on the dust jacket there it was: Hallam – that was what they called her.

TS had to confess that he was absorbed from the start, although at first he mistook the tingling sense of recognition for a new symptom of his sickness. What he admired was the cool, matter-of-fact way in which Hallam described the man's failings as a father, scarpering when things got difficult, her own bewilderment at being a black girl in an English town, her mother's garbled story of a wife and son in Africa. TS could not imagine the writer woman crying as his mother did. He studied the photograph on the dust jacket: a slim woman, with short, frizzy hair and big, strong features. A blood relative for sure, no question, and TS all but felt the fresh blood gallop through his veins as he focused on the very grain of the image. The woman looked like him, the same brow, the same mouth. Was that why Joe wanted him to read the book? But Joe said, no, he hadn't looked at the photograph, and when he did, said he could see no resemblance. Which is why he didn't tell Joe that he had written to her. The father from the Venda described in the book, a man who spoke passionately about education, was unmistakably his own vark father; TS knew it in his bones, and, besides, the dates matched perfectly.

The blurb spoke of the woman's other fictional works, including a volume of poetry. She was undoubtedly the daughter of the ensnarer – in other words, she was TS's sister – and he felt a surge of pride for her robustness, the rude health that exuded from her prose. He must have let on in some way, as Joe warned that it was a fictionalised autobiography, something about its postmodernness, which he supposed accounted for the jumping about of the story, the fact that he was not always sure of what was going on. But in spite of that there was the knowledge, the certainty, so that he read the book several times. Just to make doubly sure.

It was only correct that he should write to her; it was the civil thing to do, for was the book not at some level a quest to find her African family? He kept the letter simple; he knew that the author, or Chris as he thought of her now, was a no-nonsense person who would cut through the crap, go straight to the heart of things. Come to South Africa he wrote, after congratulating her on an exceptionally lucid style, I have reason to believe that we have the same father. Some would say that he had no reason whatsoever but, given that there was so little time, given that he would succumb sooner or later, he would not be held back by the un-reasonable demands of reason. Enough for him that the woman struck a chord, that her research on the vark, minimal as it was, was spot on. Besides, if she came, he would get his mother involved, get her to persuade Chris of old Tommie's identity.

Lately he was finding it easier to tolerate his mother; he didn't know how or when it happened, but the crying had definitely stopped. Come home, Mama said, that Joe won't be able to look after you for ever, and it pleased TS that she finally acknowledged Joe. She was old-fashioned, belonged to the bad old times. Keep away from white boys, she used to say, it will only lead to trouble. Now when his mother claimed that she could nurse him back to health, TS didn't mind. She was after all a nurse, even though she had spent most of her working life in children's wards.

It was almost six months later that the woman replied, and, to tell the truth, TS had more or less forgotten about her. For a while he checked the postbox twice a week anyway, and, to speed things up, he told his mother, which turned out to be necessary, since she needed more preparation than he imagined. First, she returned to her old ways by bursting into tears, and said in her churchgoing voice that she knew her Tommie would return somehow, even if it did mean turning up in a book. Then she laid into the author woman, whom she was sure was a schemer like her mother. See how history repeats itself, his mother sobbed, once again a strange girl turning up like a bad penny, this time to ensnare her only son. That threw TS.

But she hasn't even written back, he protested. And please don't start your crying nonsense, he shouted. Which made her cry harder. Was speaking to a mother in such a disrespectful way not evidence of the girl's bad influence? TS had to be tactful. He needed her help, needed his mother to be nice to Chris, convince her with the first-hand stories that he had thus far prevented her from telling. Ever since he could remember her eyes would grow moist, dreamy, and she would start up with: Now your father again, I remember the time when … Then he had to be firm, hold up his hand as if to push back down her throat the story that, like so much poorly digested dinner, rose, ready to be spewed.

No, Mama, TS said, Chris will want to hear your memories, the stories about your Tommie. He felt momentarily guilty as his mother composed herself. He worried that she might disgrace herself with weeping, that the sophisticated English writer would pity and despise her. It was clear from the book that Chris did not especially admire the man, and his mother's sentimental stories might grate. On the other hand, she would of course want to know about his life in Africa, her own African roots. Why else would she have written the book? And then TS remembered that she had not replied.

He explained to his mother. For all the man's carefree times in London, your Tommie must have spoken about us back here in Cape Town, and that is exactly why Chris would want to come. To see you in the flesh; to hear about her father from your own mouth.

Again he felt guilty as his mother brightened up, smiled serenely and said, If you think that's what's needed, my child, then she must come and we'll cook her real African food, offal and trotters with pap. And for her the special treat of brains tied into the little pouch of tripe – you know, the honeycombed part of the stomach.

But no one eats that kind of food these days, TS protested.

It was also your father's favourite, she said, so that's why the English person will enjoy it. TS warned that Chris might well be vegetarian.

Nonsense, she said. And I'll make a whole bucket of ginger beer as well, seeing as you can't take hot drinks. We'll have to get this place fixed up nicely, at least fresh paint for the front room.

Then she stood up and pointedly tied her apron strings as if it were time to get on with the preparations. TS threw his arms around her, not least to steady himself, for a strange wobbliness – perhaps a new symptom of his sickness – seemed to invade his body. She was his old girl, his mama all right. Had he not always relied on her, in spite of her crying, to get on with things, to get things done? As the wobbliness subsided he wondered if he had done the right thing, not telling the writer woman about his sickness. A difficult one that was. She may not want to have anything to do with people like him, and be really angry that he had not told. On the other hand, she was educated, civilised, and telling might seem like piling on the pressure, playing for sympathy.

Chris Hallam could not say why she had taken so long to reply to TS's strange letter. The memory of her dad, the man who had actually raised her, could have been the reason. When he was alive, she would never in a million years have risked hurting his feelings by going traipsing after the biological African father who had deserted her. But her daddy had died of a heart attack two years before, which may well be why she got round to writing the book. She thought of herself as decisive, but whether to write to this TS or not – that she could not decide. For all she knew, he was a fruitcake, or worse, a fraud. He had offered no reason for his belief, and, besides, she felt no burning desire to meet her African relations. To find out whether he was genuine she would have to get into a correspondence that could turn out to be a costly mistake.

Chris had learnt her lesson from a visit to Kenya organised by the British Council a couple of years ago. For months afterwards there were embarrassing begging letters – please would she be so-and-so's friend – and much as she understood that poverty brought with it such humiliation, it was hard to believe that even the two guys who had behaved so professionally as hosts barely waited for her to leave before writing their begging letters. Please would she sponsor them, which meant finding them places at university to study creative writing or medicine or law, any discipline would do it seemed, and then pay their overseas fees which, they pointed out, were impossibly expensive.

She had not been able to eat for weeks. The letters remained on her kitchen table. Frozen by embarrassment, and guilt, she could not reply. It was she, the metropolitan with her cool linen trousers, silk shirts and leather handbag, who had robbed them of self-respect, who turned them into no more than the beggars on the street for whom she found fistfuls of coins and tattered notes. How could they be expected to believe that neither she nor anyone else she knew could afford the exploitative overseas fees? She too had to take responsibility for the shameful recruitment of students in Africa. Now there was the South African claiming kinship, and the further shame of thinking him to be fraudulent, but what else could she think? What if her reply were to set off the indignity of a second letter, this time begging for God knows what? She did not tell her mother about him.

It was an invitation to the Book Fair in Cape Town that brought a decision. That was a valid reason for going to Africa, and perhaps she would fit in a visit to TS and his mother. Shortly before her arrival Chris wrote a brief note to say that she might have a day to spare, that she would be in touch. There was no point in being too encouraging.

But TS was more than happy. The letter was admirable, brisk, entirely in character. Why should the woman get excited about meeting the family of a man who had let her down as only the old vark could?

His mother started cleaning and painting. TS protested; it was quite unnecessary, but he helped all the same, and for all his exhaustion and wheezing found the work surprisingly pleasurable. She made cups of revolting OXO, left to cool and so develop a greyish-blue film that surely was the colour of a corpse. Drink up, his mama ordered, it gives you energy and refreshes the blood. Together they rested outside, in the weak sunlight trapped against the wall, where he became adept at pouring the foul drink into the earth.

Chris had never in her life been so cold. The Cape Town wind howled every day, driving in the rain at a punishing angle, and there was no central heating to be found. She wore her coat indoors and asked for hot-water bottles. On the two occasions that the rain stopped, the days were sunny, summery, but the buildings would not thaw and she shivered indoors. People were friendly, hospitable, but she was disappointed by the division of Cape Town into white, black and coloured cities, no different she imagined from the bad old days. People said that Johannesburg was better, a proper cosmopolitan African city, but the prospect of being even colder was not something she relished.

Then there were the embarrassing tours to the townships, and that made her decide. No need to do anything so shameful when she had genuine, ready-made access to people, although her literary hosts thought it unwise for her to go to Langa on her own. Chris may have been a sissy about the cold, but she certainly was not going to be put off by nonsense about the dangerous townships. Wasn't that also what people said at home about Brixton or Toxteth? She called TS to arrange a visit.

With only a day's notice, TS and his mother were pleased about their early preparations. A pity that the English woman could not stay long enough for something to eat, but once she'd been, once she'd fought her way through the mad drivers, she could come again. When Chris drove up in her rented car, TS and his mother hastily folded away the blankets they'd wrapped themselves in.

It's too cold for ginger beer, the old woman shouted above the television, we'll have coffee and koeksisters. Then, dunking her koeksister in her coffee for a dangerous length of time, she said: You are an angel sent by God. You've brought this family together, and see, Tommie, she's as pretty as an angel too, your coloured sister. TS held up a bony hand. Huh-uh, he said, no Tommying, okay? Don't take advantage. He tilted his head theatrically to examine Chris, and said she shouldn't mind his mama, that she was of the old school.

Chris was puzzled. There was no attempt on their part to find out whether what could be no more than a hunch had any basis in fact. There would after all be very many such men of the same name who went abroad. But they offered no information and asked no questions. Did they have any photographs? she asked.

The old woman had had one, her most precious thing, but it disappeared many years ago. She shook her head sadly. Why would anyone steal her picture? Chris must know that there was nothing, and she clapped her hands emphatically, nothing at all that people wouldn't steal these days. Terrible it is, even in this respectable part of Langa.

Chris's own attempts to tell what she knew of her father seemed to be of no interest to them. She didn't like to say that she had never seen a photograph, that her own mother had destroyed all evidence of the man who had let her down so badly, but they didn't ask. Instead, the old woman said that Chris looked so much like her Tommie, a certain look across the brow that came and went, a fleeting something, but definitely the same eyes, just like her boy, although TS was of course a proper black African.

Chris frowned, stared at TS, who raised his eyebrows in a camp gesture she was unable to read. These people were crazy or plain crafty; there really was no resemblance, but it was too embarrassing to say, especially with the mother so genuinely thrilled, and thanking her for putting her Tommie in a book.

A real gentleman he was, very educated, no wonder the English ensnared him, the mother said, upon which TS held up his hand again. No Mama, he scolded, don't take advantage. You promised not to speak like that.

Then the old woman asked Chris to stand up and walk across the room. Her Tommie had a distinctive walk, which sadly had not been passed down to TS. Chris was adamant. There were surely limits to indulging a proper black African lady. Oh no, she said, I can't do that; it won't be any use. I'm five foot four, small like my mother, and he was tall, wasn't he?

Oh yes, very tall, dark and handsome, but he used to hold his head like you do, a little to the left side. What did he say about your being so light-skinned?

Instead of saying that she did not remember her father at all, that he had left when she was three, Chris said, Actually, I'm not usually so pale;

I go quite dark in the summer, but the thing is we haven't really had a summer this year. I mean – there hasn't been much summer as yet. Later, in August perhaps …

What possessed her to talk such nonsense, to capitulate to these crazy people? It was as if she had walked onto a stage to deliver learnt lines from a surrealist script. Whatever would she say next?

The mother wittered on about Tommie's cleverness, his ambitions to be a doctor, not the sort who could do anything about sickness, which was more the pity since they could do with help in that house, and she nodded towards TS. But TS, who seemed to have lost interest in the visit, had turned his attention to the television. Chris wondered if he was disappointed in her. She had deliberately dressed down in an old grey jumper and frumpy skirt and, instead of a handbag, carried her keys and purse in a Woolworths plastic bag. Perhaps she did not look exploitable. Well, if she didn't look the part, so be it, and she rose briskly, thanking them for the coffee and cake sisters, at which the old woman laughed and made her repeat after her: koeksisters, which sounded no less silly a name for a doughnut. Next time, she said, it will be nice tripe and trotters, proper African food.

Chris fished out her keys. Well, she said, short of tests there'll never be any way of knowing for sure—

Oh no, my child, the old girl interrupted, don't say such things. It's enough that you're here. That is proof enough for us.

TS looked up from the television, smiled, nodded, and Chris wondered what their next move would be. What on earth did these people take her for? It was downright insulting. Would they also wait until she'd left the country?

Then TS swung to his feet, and, grabbing a jacket hanging over the chair, said briskly, Let's blow. Without a word to his mother he led the way.

And where, Chris said after shutting the door, are you blowing to, and how will you get there?

We, he corrected. We're going to Sea Point. You've got wheels haven't you? We're going to see Joe.

Chris did not know why she gave in. They drove in silence, except for the directions, which he gave wearily, sullenly, as if it were she dragging him about town against his will.

Joe came to the door fastening his belt, tight under a bloated belly. He buttoned up his cardigan. The place is in a mess, he said. He threw his arms around TS, which triggered a coughing fit.

Are you looking after yourself, he asked, taking your medicine? It's orange juice for you, darling, he said, as he opened a bottle of red wine.

Of course, that was it: the poor guy was ill, probably dying. Chris chided herself for not having realised, for not paying attention.

Let me introduce you properly, TS smiled. This English woman, he boasted, is your famous writer, Chris Hallam, and now, wait for it – and he paused dramatically – she just happens to be my sister.

Joe winked at Chris. That's African talk, he said, all sexy black women are his sisters. What a little skelm you are, TS, getting up to all this behind my back.

But TS said, No, really, look, I found this just yesterday. And from his jacket pocket took a photograph that once had been severely scrunched up. See, it's our father, yours and mine.

Not the guy you call the vark, Joe shrieked. Pig, he translated. Chris won't want to have anything to do with your porker.

The man in the photograph was slim and tall like TS, and, as the mother said, had passed on his eyes, the entire brow area, to his son. TS stood over Chris, jigged her shoulder excitedly. Never mind the pig business, that's another story. Come on, he said, triumphantly, you didn't think I'd have proof, did you, hey?

Joe laughed, shook his head in disbelief. The guy's no oil painting, that's for sure. You'll be pleased to hear, Chris, that you look nothing like him. Ou TS here's gone crazy; the varkies have jumped clean out of their pen.

But Chris said, Hmm, well, let's see.

Hunched over the photograph, she stepped to the window. The light was dying. On the choppy sea spread before her, a pale moon lapped at the crest of the waves. Was it the tenderness of the light that made her straighten up and turn around?

Ye–es, she said, looks like my mum's picture – same guy – taken not so long after this one, I'd guess.

She placed a hand on TS's shoulder.

What the hell, eh, she laughed. Just as long as you make sure, my brother, that I don't have to eat authentic African offal.

byron loker

Your Stop

In London that day I came to find you. I had come back from the job in
Minnesota and, with weeks until the flight to Cape Town, I was stranded,
so I came to find you and tell you how I felt about you. I caught the train
up from Brighton, where I was staying, with the intention of visiting the
old places I had lived in. More than anything, really, I came to see you.
You were living there then.

   I walked down Regent Street in the rain, barely noticing it, and I could
hardly remember to breathe in and out on account of all the things on
my mind, the weight on my shoulders. I walked east towards where you
worked, the famous perfume shop. You had told me in a letter where
you were. I had written to you from the States a few months before, the
only love letter you had yet received from anyone, you would later tell
me. Before we left on our travels I had tried to convince you to come
over to the States with me. I said I could arrange a job for you there. You
seemed to entertain the idea, briefly, over the table at the coffee shop in

Cape Town. I had put my hand on yours and you had returned the gesture, but I could tell your heart was drifting elsewhere.

Walking down Regent Street I passed the Disney Store and the insult of it caused me to cross over to the other side of the road. I could manage only one block at a time, needing to stop and think about things, to wonder whether it was any good to try to find you. You weren't expecting me. I stopped at the edge of every block and stood under an awning or in a doorway out of the rain and tried to remember to breathe in and out. There was nowhere else I wanted to go though, except the old places, but I didn't think I could afford the nostalgia, or the pain: I had long before lost a great love in London and the memory of it still weighed on me. I didn't want to lose another if I could help it. I know now there is no helping it, but at the time I thought it was within my power.

I still knew my way around the city so well, which surprised me, and I found the street where you worked; it was a long way from Regent Street. I found the store, but I passed by, unable to enter, ready to call the whole idea off.

We had almost made love in April, earlier that year. We had arranged to meet on the beach that day. From there we had moved to a bar and then another and then the Cuban restaurant where the waitress presented the bill in a cigar box decorated with ballpoint scratchings by the restaurant's patrons. 'To see the world in a grain of sand and hold infinity in your hand,' had been your contribution to the box. I drove us in your car back to my bachelor flat and we sat on the couch and I lit a cigar, which you also wanted to smoke, but when you inhaled, it made you nauseous. I took it from between your fingers and kissed you and you let me. I wrapped us up together in the duvet from my bed and we took off our shirts and we kissed. You said I had soft skin and I said I wanted to count each freckle on your body.

'You're just trying to get into my pants,' you said.

'You're not wearing any,' I said. You were wearing a denim skirt.

'My bikini pants!' You laughed. But then you sat up and you said, 'I can't do this.' You sat over me, looking down at me. You touched my chest and arms and you said, 'You have very soft skin.'

You left me then. You went into the kitchen and poured yourself a glass of water and I came in and you were sitting on the countertop. I tried to take the glass from you so I could kiss you again and you let me kiss you and the glass dropped to the tiled floor and smashed. 'I'm so sorry,' you said.

'That was my fault,' I said.

'I have to go,' you said. I was drunk and you led me to my bedroom and lay down on the bed with me. You had put on your backpack. You went away and came back with the duvet from the couch and spread it over me and kissed me a last time. I begged you to stay but you said, 'I can't. Watch out for the broken glass on the floor.'

A bell tinkled. 'May I help you, sir?' the woman behind the counter said, not convinced about calling me sir.

I asked for you and the woman behind the counter said, 'She's not in. She called in sick today.' She made that sound like my fault.

I nodded and said, 'Thank you,' and left through the tinkling door and stood outside in the rain once more.

I called you from a phone booth on the street and you answered.

'I'm in London,' I said. 'Are you okay?'

'Yes!' you said and we arranged to meet in Covent Garden.

I walked there and arrived half an hour before you did. I stood near the Tube station and watched for you. I knew I would see you because you are tall, taller than me, something of which I am ashamed. There were so many people. I thought I saw you three or four times and each time I nearly called out, but stopped when I saw that it wasn't you. Then you arrived in the crowd like sunlight through a break in the clouds and I watched you moving. You were there to see me, but you looked lost. I moved into the crowd to greet you. We hugged and started talking and walking until we stopped because we realised that we are going in the wrong direction; you wanted to take me to Neal's Yard.

You took me to Neal's Yard and we ordered lunch in a bright-coloured café: sandwiches and salads that cost too much money, coffee and, for you, peppermint tea.

'Your hair's different,' I said. 'I like it.'

'This is more its natural colour now. All those years of dying it, and now it's more back to its natural colour.' Your hair was redder, not blonde any more, straight, down over your shoulders. I had fallen in love with you simply by looking across a lecture theatre and seeing you. You were wearing a baseball cap then.

We talked, and I wish I had kept each of your words. They fell through my fingers like the raindrops. If I had saved them, I would put them down now on this page like jewels in a display cabinet. Perhaps I was too busy then collecting other treasures: your pale-green eyes, your white, expensive teeth when you smiled, your breath when you spoke. You had a boyfriend somewhere, in another country then. There had always been a boyfriend. You were devoted to him, I can see it now.

When we left the café you took me to your favourite shop in Neal's Yard. It sells glass trinkets and fairies and pieces of rainbows and lightning. Then I took you through the rain down Neal Street, cobbled and too narrow for cars. At the end of the street I took you around the corner and down Shaftesbury Avenue to the pub where I had worked in the years when I lived in London, years before I knew you.

I took you to that pub and we shared one of the long wooden benches at a table tucked around the corner beyond the far end of the bar. I'm in a photograph high up on the wall behind that table. It was taken one night after closing time when we would stay back and drink until the sun came up the next morning.

You drank lemonade and I drank Guinness. I told you about the times I had had when I worked in that pub, and when I proposed another round of drinks you told me that there was nowhere else in the world you would rather be. We sat there and talked for a long time. We left because you were worried about missing the last train back to where you lived in zone 6. I sat next to you in the Tube carriage and we didn't say anything for a long time until we reached Angel Islington Station where I needed to make a connection to Victoria, for the last train back to Brighton. The train stopped and I didn't move and still had not said what it was I wanted to say to you: that I was there for you. You placed your hand gently onto my thigh and said, 'This is your stop.'

julia
smuts louw

Paper House

His hands and feet, Mia had decided at last. It was in the hands and feet, and perhaps also, no, definitely also, the way that he hunched forward, elbows on his knees, forming an awning of focus over any object or project that held his attention. Always soft and sure, never hurried. Physically, this was where it lay, the similarity between the two men: Matt and Sam.

'May I ask why you did it?' Matt said.

'I don't know,' said Mia. It was the truth.

That posture: the bones of his neck curved down, his shoulder girdles rolled forward. She had considered, both before and after his death, attempting to draw Sam sitting that way – a line drawing, not a painting – but had never been able to bring herself to do a single stroke. The possibility of making a mistake at any point was too oppressive.

'You really don't have to do that,' said Mia.

Matt was fixing her Zippo for her. It was a second-hand one that a colleague had passed on to her, and she had never bothered to look after it, although she had bought the necessary things: the flints, the wick, the fuel. She had struggled to light a cigarette as the confession ended and the air lay empty and girded between them. The grind of the thumbwheel had been the only sound in the room until he held his hand out, palm up, and said, 'Here.'

Mia had hoped he would shout and storm. She had feared tears. What she had not expected, and what she now realised she should have expected, was this: this inward turning of the watchful eyes, and the calm, and the walls going up. And, to her horror and shame, no surprise whatsoever.

'Just the once, was it?' Matt said.

'Yes.'

'And you don't know why you did it.'

'I don't,' she said again.

He nodded.

Matt finished threading the new wick with a confident hand, as if he had done it a hundred times. He turned the lighter over. 'It goes into the batting?' he said, pointing to the lighter fluid.

'Yes.'

He refuelled the lighter, ignited it, snapped the lid shut over the flame, and held it out to her. Mia took it. She no longer wanted a cigarette.

Deprived of his one distraction, Matt rose to his feet and turned away from her. The task had given him an excuse to look down, at his hands, and not at her neck. Before she could will herself not to, Mia reached up a hand to touch the daisy chain of love bites around her throat. The marks were getting worse before they got better, as bruises do.

Matt's hand went to the vulnerable skin at the nape of his own neck, mirroring her. He was comforting himself, Mia knew, and Matt didn't.

He had been running his hands over things ever since he entered her kitchen. The table. The counter. The neighbour's cat, who had leapt down from the wall to greet him. His own knees, his clothes. Everything but her he touched.

'I'm so sorry, Matt.'

She had apologised. Now he would hate her.

'Mia,' he said.

No, now he would leave her. 'Yes?'

'I have to go.'

'I understand.'

Mia gave it ten days, hoping she would hear from him. She spent the ten days wandering doggedly through the house in Tooting, as if she hoped that some corner of its modest dimensions would yield up a miracle, or at least an answer. She would have to vacate the premises soon. Helena, her sister, had gone back to South Africa, and their lease would expire at the end of the month. Mia would have nowhere to go.

When the ten days had passed, she went to Lambeth to fetch her things from Matt's flat. She chose a time of day when she could be fairly certain he would be at work. As she found out when she let herself in, she needn't have bothered. Matt's flatmate, Davy, was there, playing Xbox, and he told her that Matt had put in for leave at his insurance firm to visit his people up north.

'How long's he gone for?' she asked. Davy said he didn't know. He had left a week ago.

That took the wind out of her. For seven of the ten days she had been mis-imagining him.

Mia had brought two boxes along, but only found enough of her stuff to fill one.

'Davy?' she said, kneeling at the bookshelf by the bottom row of DVDs. 'Davy!'

'Wait, wait.'

'I'm in a hurry.'

'Now look, you made me lose a life. What is it?'

'Have you seen my *Buffy the Vampire Slayer* DVD box set?' She had brought it here to introduce Matt to the series, but they had never got round to that in the end.

'Oh, was that yours? I lent it to a friend.'

'You knew it was mine.'

'I didn't think you would mind.'

Mia rolled onto her hip and crossed her legs, abruptly exhausted. Behind her, Davy rose from the couch and came to stand behind her, leaning his knees into her back.

'Stop that,' said Mia. 'Where are my DVDs? Can't you call your friend?'

'I'll get them for you later.'

'I need them now.'

He toed her box. Toothbrush. Clothes. A book. 'You and Fletchy on the out and out, then?'

'It's over.'

'Aw. Thought as much. He was moping around with a face a mile long. What happened?'

'I'd prefer not to talk about it,' said Mia, marvelling for the hundredth time at the differences between men and women. Matt and Davy lived together; it was almost two weeks since she had done what she had done and Matt had left her, and Davy, apparently, knew nothing of it.

'Come on, tell Uncle Davy.' He began to knead her shoulders. Mia winced at the contact and shook him off.

It occurred to her that it was just like Matt not to say anything about it. Not because he was embarrassed that his girlfriend had been unfaithful to him, but because he wouldn't want anyone to think ill of her. Oh, the sheer, hopeless decency of him. She would not show herself the same courtesy.

'I slept with the king of the fairies,' she said.

There was a monkey's wedding in Tooting when Mia emerged from the earth: rain and sun together. Despite the load of the box in her arms, she walked the rest of the way to Southcroft Road rather than take a bus. She wanted to feel the water on her skin and to breathe in the smell of hot tar-dust that the rain would release from the street.

A half-mile into her journey, the bottom of the box came apart and her belongings fell to the ground. A ceramic incense burner – a gift from Helena – broke into three pieces. Mia knelt to gather the shards and everything else. Two people passed on her side of the road, and neither offered to help her. She wanted to spit in their faces.

There was too much to carry in her hands. Mia shoved what she could into her handbag and put the rest back in the soggy box, holding one hand beneath it to keep the folding flaps in place. A bus passed her; she was not quite close enough to the bus stop to be reckoned a commuter and didn't have a hand free to hail it. Mia wanted to spit on the bus, too.

Soaked and encumbered, she arrived at number 68.

At the door was Matthew Fletcher.

In her kitchen, Matthew Fletcher.

His parents were well. His brother was well. His sister-in-law was well. The baby had said his name.

Mia said his name. She asked him why he was there.

He had helped her carry her things indoors, careful not to touch her hands as he took the box from her. He put it down on the kitchen table now. 'This ...' he said, holding up a third of the broken incense burner.

'I've just been to yours,' Mia answered. 'Davy said you'd gone up north.'

Matt dropped the piece of ceramic back into the box. 'I came back,' he said.

Mia nodded.

'I came to apologise,' he went on at last. 'For leaving. I really only intended to go for a couple of hours, and walk a bit, and think. I'm sorry it turned into more than a couple of hours. I came to say that. And to tell you that I'm not going to leave you again.' His greatcoat was laden with rain like the pelt of an animal; the lenses of his glasses were dappled.

His face so familiar, she could feel the smooth, wet bones of it beneath her palm, although she had not touched him in weeks and did not touch him now. The watchful otter's eyes she had suffered under. He was looking down, his mouth stiff, almost grimacing. She would release him, relieve him. But he had not finished.

'Listen,' he said. 'I've put down a deposit on that place in Angel. The one we looked at. I'm going to move.'

'You are?'

'I'd like you to move there with me. If you still want to.'

'You ... would?'

He paced soundlessly to the sink, dried his face off with a dishtowel, and then turned to face her again, his hands on the back of a chair. If he was going to look her in the eye, he wanted the table between them.

'Mia. I know about Sam. Your sister told me.'

'What? Helena told you about Sam? Sam Loudon? When?'

'Just before she left. When I took her to the airport. She didn't mention his surname.'

'What did she tell you?'

'That you loved him.' He paused. 'That he was killed. That he was shot, and that you were there. On a mountain. That's right, isn't it?'

Mia drew a chair back and sat on it. Matt stayed on his feet.

'You see, Mia, I know why you did it,' he said. 'I know you were trying to hurt me before I could hurt you. And I know that it's because you love me. And I love you too. So I'm going to prove you wrong. I'm not going to leave you. And I'm not going to let you leave me.'

There it was again: not a question, not a request, not even a suggestion.

Mia felt duped, as if it were he who had deceived her. Why didn't you tell me you were strong, she wanted to say. Why did you lead me to believe that you were weak?

'I'm not him, Mia,' said Matt. 'I'm not Sam.'

'I know,' said Mia, in a small voice. That much she had known for some time.

The distance between them was suddenly beyond bearing, and Mia realised it was she who would have to close it. She rose from her place and went to him, leaning forward into his chest with her arms folded across her own. She did not exhale until he had curled himself around her and lowered his mouth into her hair.

Together they moved into the flat in Angel which Mia had once set her heart on.

It was more than Matt had wanted to spend, but he had clung to the memory of the flushed smile she had thrown over her shoulder when they first came to look at the place.

Now she moved through it like a ghost, or a refugee, or the ghost of a refugee, pausing in doorways as if she suspected the rooms of having altered themselves in some small, devious measure since she last set foot in them. It was Matt who arranged for her things to be fetched in Tooting; Matt, even, who arranged her easel and all her equipment in the second bedroom, where once she had pointed to the tall windows and evoked for him, with animated hands, how the light would fall.

Mia was not doing work of any kind during this time. She had completed her last commission – set-dressing for an off–West End production of *A Midsummer Night's Dream* – at the end of April, and showed no signs of looking for a new project. Matt would have been happy to support her, if it meant that she had decided to concentrate on her own work, her real work. But the stretched canvas he had bought and placed on the easel as a house-warming gift remained blank.

She complained that she could not sleep. Matt knew this wasn't so: she talked very often in her sleep now. Before first light she would turn towards him, her lips and fingers seeking him out like some purblind forager, her words loud enough to wake him.

It's a paper house, she murmured one night, the back of her hand curled against his flank.

It was a theatre term, he was almost sure. A play where the tickets were given away free. He supposed she must be dreaming of her work on the stage production, that feral thespian crowd.

He forced himself to think the name: *Oberon*. Perhaps she was dreaming of him. The thought barely pained him; he could not muster a sense of betrayal. He knew then that the cause was lost.

A paper house, he repeated to himself. To Matt the image it called up was literal, and in concert with his deepest misgivings. Their salvaged love, the redeeming power of his grand rain-soaked gesture, was a fiction he could not sustain unaided.

How could he explain it to her? Was there some way to set her free without abandoning her?

He had made it impossible for her to leave him, as he had made it impossible for himself to leave her. Not only had he promised Mia, he had given his word to her sister, Helena, the day he had driven her to the airport to catch her plane back home to South Africa.

He and Helena had long since halted in the Heathrow parkade, and Helena's check-in time was upon them, when she had finished telling him the story of Sam: this dead boy, this first love, the phantom rival of whom he had been unaware all this time. He had been killed, shot, on a mountain road in Stellenbosch, at the end of his first year of university.

Mia had been with him at the time. The two of them had been sitting on the hood of his BMW, having a difficult conversation which, had they ever finished it, might have left Mia with a broken heart. But then a man with a gun appeared and changed their priorities.

Had the man wanted only the car, Sam might have kept his life. But he had wanted the car with Mia in it. In the moment that Sam launched himself from the bonnet towards the stranger, he had shouted at Mia to run. And so she ran, stumbling pell-mell through the dark towards the safety of the campus below; falling blind on the narrow footpath when the report of the gun split the darkness above.

Although it had happened long before he met her, in another country, relief at Mia's survival had surged absurdly through Matt with each exhalation as he absorbed the story. 'She cut her teeth on it,' Helena had said. 'Back then, understand, Mia was so … *niksgewoond*, it was like the whole world had failed her, when Sam died. She was barely eighteen. Everyone, I suppose, has that experience once, that first time, that day the world breaks faith with you. You know? For me it was when our father left, but Mia was very young …'

'That word,' Matt interrupted. 'I've heard it before. What does it mean?' It was a word he had overheard Mia using to describe him, on the phone to a friend in Cape Town, when they were still relatively new to each other. 'The thing is, he's so flipping *niksgewoond*,' she had said, a smile in her voice. 'It makes me wonder …'

Helena's thoughts had already hurtled past. 'Which?' she said.

'*Niks* …'

'Oh. I couldn't think of the English word. Maybe there isn't one. Naive, I suppose, is the closest. Literally, it means "not used to anything".'

Matt took this in with an impassive nod. He could see how Mia might have reached that conclusion. It could have been worse.

'What I'm basically saying,' said Helena, 'is that I think, for some reason, she's only beginning to deal with it now. Or I should say rather, she's only just beginning to *fail* to deal with it now. Now that she's found you.'

'Now that she's found me?'

'Don't you see?'

He swallowed. 'I suppose I do.'

Matt didn't like to think that he had caused instability in Mia's life, on any level; still less that he had been oblivious to it. Just lately she had seemed different, it was true. Distant. But certainly not on the point of any sort of crisis. He had never thought of Helena as a woman who tended towards melodrama, though, and was willing to believe that there might be more to it: factors, symptoms that she was hesitant to delve into, or that Mia had kept hidden from him, or that her sister could see and he could not.

'I just wanted to ask you,' said Helena, 'please, just … take care of her. You're the only person in a three-hundred-mile radius that I trust to do what's best for her.'

Matt knew what she was really saying: prove me right. Don't fail her. And he knew what would set her mind at ease.

'I mean to marry her,' he said simply. 'In time. If she'll have me.' He smiled. He had wanted it to be good news, in itself, whenever it came to that point. But Helena was in need of reassurance, and he had been glad to be able to provide it unstintingly.

She had smiled back, and kissed him on the lips, because he was as near as made no difference to family, now. Then she had left at a trot for her plane.

The clock blinked three. Mia's breathing had slowed, and Matt was waiting patiently for the muscles of his back to ease and his thoughts to dissipate in response. There would be no messages ferried to him from her sub-conscious, at least for the next hour or two.

He had lain a long while in darkness, watching the clench and flinch of her small form beside him and listening for news of her faltering passage through the dreams she would not remember.

We rarely have the privilege of knowing beforehand when it's going to be the last time. But, that night, Matt knew.

It's a paper house, he thought. He was merely staying so as not to leave.

Lying on new sheets on a bed in Angel, Matt thought back to the morning of his eighteenth birthday, lying in the rain in a field of daffodils in Cornwall. He had just finished high school, and had thought to start a backpacking tour of Europe by working as a picker. Every day they began before dawn, and almost every day it had rained. He still woke occasionally from languageless dreams of bulbs and stems and wet yellow in the darkness.

For the duration of that month, he had assumed he was miserable. He was away from home, he slept in a shack, he was terrified of his Oxford scholarship, he had nothing in common with the Poles and Lithuanians who picked many more daffodils an hour than he could, he had had his heart bruised by a tow-headed girl who forsook him to become an air hostess.

But Matt remembered it now as a time of perfect contentment, or rather, perfect containment, a self-containment and self-sufficiency he had taken for granted and assumed to be an immutable property of himself. There in that field, and in the few years before and after that field, his strength had depended on nothing other than the continued bounding of his heart in his chest. His employer's obtuseness and his mother's diabetes and his father's retrenchment and a half a dozen disappointing love affairs had taught him otherwise, and he had become not bitter, but deeply fretful at the growing certainty that he would never be able to knit his boundaries together again.

With Mia, he had wished, for the first time, to give it away freely – this sovereignty he had guarded so jealously and for so long. He wished to be vulnerable to her; he wished for them to be interdependent.

He had wished to be trusting, and naive, and unused to anything. And unused. He had not noticed when she started becoming not so much a chosen weakness as the source of his power.

Only apart from her had he begun to feel himself whole again; apart, he had become convinced he could return. He would stand against her, she could lean against him. They would be equal halves.

But it was not, after all, fear that had driven her from him. It was fear that had kept her by his side.

Matt woke again in the small hours with a memory of petals and soft black earth behind his eyes, and, wondering what had roused him, he became gradually aware of Mia's voice whispering once more into the darkness. He heard the sibilant tails of hushed yeses and, turning, he saw her sitting half-upright in the bed, propped on her elbows, staring into nothing, and answering nothing's questions.

'Mia,' he said, 'Mia, who are you talking to?'

'It's quite all right,' said Mia. 'You needn't worry. It can't get out, you see, it's trapped.'

He realised she was dreaming, and knew enough to talk her out of it gently. 'Who is trapped?' he said.

Mia turned her face towards him, her unblinking eyes dry-red. 'Mia!?' she said.

For all it was dream-talk, this was enough to send hollow shudders roiling across his skin; to hear her addressing herself in bewildered panic.

'Run,' she said.

She murmured once or twice more, words or just noises, he wasn't sure. Then her elbows folded beneath her, her shoulders sinking towards the mattress. Within thirty seconds her breathing slackened, but her eyes remained open, the lids at half-mast. Matt reached out a careful hand. Very gently, with thumb and forefinger, he drew them closed.

jonny steinberg

Sheila

When I first heard news about you, Sheila, I was locking my bicycle to the bicycle stand at Esporta Gym off Woodstock Road. It was a little before lunchtime. From my pocket an SMS hailed me, and it was from Lomin, and he said: 'Sheila out of surgery and doing fine.' I snapped my cellphone shut, slung my bag over my shoulder, and strode into the gym as if there were spurs on my heels and my bike were a tethered steed.

It was Friday, about noon, a time when I share the swimming pool with middle-aged ladies of leisure. They are commuter-belt housewives; their husbands left for the City early in the morning to earn a lot of money, their children are grown and out in the world, and they, meanwhile, join me in the swimming pool and stand there talking to one another very loudly and with paramount confidence, without ever actually swimming, it seems.

In the changing room, I took off my clothes, put on my Speedo and stood on the scale. I was a satisfying 75 kg. An image of you came to me momentarily: you were still sleeping in your bed in the ward; you had not yet come around; the ribs they had broken to get to your heart would in six weeks' time be healed. And then the image vanished and you returned to the place from which you had threatened to wobble and tilt during the uncertain morning hours: you have neither body nor face there, but are simply the tunnel through which I move.

I swam, and it was me and my breathing and the water and the solitude of swimming. And then my biceps and pectorals began labouring and I felt and fought their weariness: this jealous, grim business of exercise.

It was now about 12:40 p.m. in Oxford, which made it about 2:40 p.m. in Johannesburg, and I did not know that by then you had already been to the brink of death, and that the things they had to do to keep you from dying were so violent that your body had lifted clear off its bed thirty times, Sheila; thirty times your heart stopped beating and they shocked it back to life.

They wheeled you from the ward back into theatre, stopping every few metres to shock your heart into beating again, and they put you back on the heart-and-lung machine and opened up your chest all over again, and when they saw your heart the right side was sick and blue.

Showered and changed, I rode through the grounds of King Edward School, where the boys at rugby practice carried their backs ramrod straight, as if balancing steel rulers under their jerseys along the length of their spines. And then I was back at my desk up in the attic at the African Studies Centre, and I was, I soon discovered, still in command of the chapter I was writing. I anticipated the feeling of shadows having lengthened without my noticing.

The phone rang, and it was Lomin.

'There has been a complication,' he said. 'The operation went well, but when they were resuscitating her in the ward she began to fibrillate like she had done after her angiogram, but much worse this time. She is back in surgery. They are doing a bypass.'

I said okay, I understand, and do you know when she is expected to be out of surgery, and on hearing my voice I discovered that I was crying. It so surprised me, Sheila, did that crying, that it seemed to come from somebody else, and I knew at once that everything had changed a great deal, and that I needed to move with great caution.

'It will be okay,' Lomin said, as if issuing an instruction. He had thought carefully before choosing his words.

Several weeks earlier, Sheila, you had been to see William Kentridge's production of *The Magic Flute*. You had lapped it up, you and Carol; you had left the theatre in a state of ecstatic excitement. Now, as you lay there with your blue heart under these other theatre lights, the Queen of the Night came to you. She was quite massive and overwhelming; she had on the same brilliant white dress she wore in the final scene.

'What was she doing?' someone asked you.

You thought for a moment. 'She was just doing her thing,' you finally replied.

She was ignoring you, Sheila. She was too powerful to need even to acknowledge your presence. You had no choice but to follow her. She was taking you somewhere. You did not want to go.

As for me, I stared for a long time out of the window, at the tips of the rooftops and the tops of the trees and at the chimneys. And then I turned back to the monitor on my desk and looked at the paragraph on the screen. I began to read. What a few minutes earlier had been a shaping chapter, a very promising chapter, standing up around a strong spine of purpose, had collapsed, the words spluttering around the screen like gasping fish. In that moment, I wondered quite genuinely whether there remained an author to reassemble them, for it came to me in a flash that I had only ever written because you had been watching me all the while.

I swivelled in my chair and used the momentum of the swivel to kick the wall very hard, and I examined the black smudge my kick had made. Staring at it, I saw myself coming back here many years from now, finding the smudge still there, then sniffing the room for residues of this moment. I turned my back on the smudge, and found that my mind had filled with the men who on Sunday afternoons wander the hallways and darkrooms of the gay men's sauna on Shoreditch Road, naked but for short white towels around their waists. They are truly motherless, Sheila, for in those rooms they have no history, no quiddity; the eyes that seize them are taking in only flesh and a few simple signs. How do they have the strength, I wondered, to venture forth so narrowed, so shorn, so unseen?

Were you to die now, I thought, how long would it take for the news to reach me? Ten minutes? Fifteen, maybe? With each passing moment, I had no way of knowing whether I still had a mother. But I could always be fairly confident that I had had one ten minutes earlier. I began an exercise, an experiment, surreptitiously, a little shamefully, like a dog creeping up on a plate of food he knows very well is for his owner's guest. I began to see whether I could resurrect the chapter that lay squirming and shapeless before me. And I found, quite quickly, that who I had been before I left for gym was quite easily retrievable, that at least for a few moments at a time, I could still write pretty much what I would have written had I been oblivious to what was happening to you. And then the chapter collapsed again before my eyes, as if utterly exhausted by the task of remaining erect, and I turned to the wall and cried.

I went on like this for some time, Sheila, writing for a while, crying for a while, my work standing up, falling over, and then rising once more. It came to me with great relief, every time I managed to write, that whether dead or alive you were still capable of watching over me, that the gap between who you were inside me and the reality of you out there was sufficiently wide. Sufficient for what? I grew restless. The skin on my shoulders itched. I was, I discovered with growing unease, resenting you. How could the frailty of you out there so upset the certainty of you inside me? If I could still keep writing without knowing whether you had died, then, perhaps, Sheila, you were expendable. I felt myself tugging away from you, wanting to be free of you. But I could not hold on to the cruelty of that struggle without my skin burning.

I pulled myself away from my desk and cried once more, primarily, I think, from the shock of glimpsing my own hardness.

That night I was to have dinner at the home of the historian William B and his wife Troth, whose house abutted a meadow at the edge of Iffley, a good twenty-five-minute bicycle ride from my place. Cycling into town, my phone rang, and it was Carol, and her voice seemed close, so very close, as if there were a fleshy, pulsing cord connecting our phones, a cord buried safely beneath the earth of Western Europe and the length of Africa. Between us lay the shared trauma of near motherlessness, and in my speech I detected a subdued hysteria. Within twenty minutes or so we had convinced each other, with the help of a smooth-tongued doctor who had spoken to Carol sometime earlier, that our mother was safe. Yes, she had nearly died just a few hours earlier, but she was out of danger now. More than out of danger, in fact; she was better than ever, for she had a brand new heart, a good and a strong one, whereas this morning she had had a heart on the brink of failure.

Cycling up Broad Street that night, I fancied the idea that central Oxford was a large and fabulous film set lit up by a medley of bright floodlights. The people on the streets and on the pavement were extras, chatting among themselves between scenes; any moment now, a loud-hailer would send them back to work. The footfalls of the people I passed echoed against the cobble with the clop of donkeys' hooves, a sound that somehow reinforced the idea that we were on the streets of some pre-fabricated scene, one that might be torn down tomorrow. Beyond the edges of this floodlit set, I imagined, the rest of the world lay in darkness.

I made my way up Iffley Road, and even this section of the journey momentarily found its place in the scene. The road was a kind of back-stage area, I imagined, a long tadpole's tail of bright light squiggling off from the main body of the actual film set. It was here that technicians fiddled with their equipment and carried things back and forth, servicing the main action.

William B and Troth were very warm, and they had a houseguest, Luvuyo, from Alice in the old Ciskei. He and I shared anecdotes about the suicidal, half-crazed drivers on the treacherous road between Alice and Fort Beaufort. At the dinner table, Luvuyo remarked with genuine surprise that he had been sleeping ten hours a night since arriving in Oxford, to which William responded, his voice full of self-mockery, that he and Troth were too driven to sleep that long.

I wanted to climb inside the warmth of the house, to curl up and sleep in the sound of the banter. But as the evening passed, I felt myself being poked, gently at first, a little tap-tap-tap, but then with increasing force. I had used the lights of this town and the pleasantness of this house to shut out the fact that my mother was in a coma, that although she had survived today, she may not survive tomorrow, and that even if she did live, what had happened to her was so brutal and so damaging that she would in all likelihood never be the same.

And so the following night I was on a plane bound for Johannesburg, my antidote against the long hours a detective story by John Banville writing under the pen name Benjamin Black. I hated every moment of the book. The working-class men seemed too working class, the lugubrious men too lugubrious. And besides, Sheila, the incessant murmuring of your coma-thoughts seemed to have found me more than a mile above the ground, and they kept interfering with the words of poor Benjamin Black, such that I could make sense neither of what he was writing nor of what you were dreaming.

And then I was in Carol's house, how I got there now obliterated from my memory, and when we made eye contact the mutual recognition was too much to bear, and we both looked away.

Next we were heading north along the M1, then curling around westwards on the concrete bypass, and then we were descending the stairs to the cardiac unit in the basement of the Sunninghill Clinic. And then, Sheila, we were standing over you.

My eyes recalibrated each time I blinked. At times you seemed to be sucking with great hunger on the pipe that reached down your throat and into your lungs, as if you were willing yourself back to life. That is the story some of the nurses would tell us in the coming hours and days: that you were a fighter. But then I would blink and something very different appeared. The heft of your breathing was coming, not from you, but from the machines. They were lifting your diaphragm up, dropping it down, lifting it up. You yourself, Sheila, had little to do with your breathing, for you were closer to death than to life. Your face was callow and lifeless and had lost its shape. The flesh under your skin seemed to have curdled; were I to touch it, I'd expect to feel lumps. Your eyelids, which just moments earlier I had imagined were shut tight in concentration, were shuttering nothing.

I stood as close to you as I could and placed my palm on your forehead. Then I brushed your cheek with the backs of my fingers, before settling my hand on your forehead once more.

I am not sure for how long I stood like that, a minute, maybe more, willing you back to us with my hand, when the transgression of what I was doing made me recoil. Conscious, you would never allow somebody to touch you that way: not your mother, not your husband, not your children. You had never, for as long as I have had any recollection of who you are, been a receiver of nurture, a requester of help, a person in need. This simple gesture of care, a healthy palm on your sick forehead, you would not countenance.

The idea of you as my mother, which I had held closer and more intimately in the last two days than ever before in my life, exploded into shards. In its place I saw *you*, not my mother, but *you*, and I wondered, were you to make it through this ordeal, how on earth you would recover your health all on your own.

elleke boehmer

The Father Antenna

On Sunday afternoons the stocky man in his safari shorts stood in the middle of the canna-lily patch, wires dangling from his raised arms, aiming the two metal frames in his balled fists to the northern sky.

The child could never tell what made him do it, even in later years. Was it duty or personal honour, or some hard-bitten determination to force the hot continent to embrace his wife? Was it even, perhaps, a sinewy and grudging love? What was it that persuaded her father to stand out in their garden in all weathers, holding aloft two antler-like antennae, so that her mamm might listen to Radio Nederland Wereldomroep during the cultural broadcast on Sunday afternoons?

Her mamm had, after all, *never-never*, at *no* point, wanted to come and live in this green and greasy Durban, this godforsaken, civilisation-bereft neck of the tropical woods. So she assured all possible comers, at the least pretext. She had been dragged kicking and screaming, the child often heard her say, to this cockroach-infested *kontje* of a country. And in the end it hadn't been the husband-to-be's promise of a Dutch delicatessen (what, *one* only?), his more-or-less wishful talk of the flower market downtown (those terrible heat-blackened blooms), the tennis club (*too* competitive), or church-hall recitals (to an out-of-tune piano) that had persuaded her to stay on. It was also not the mention of Radio Nederland Wereldomroep, not then, that gave her the strength to persist. At a time when long-distance radio reception was a wavering affair, this promise would have been, even for the child's ever-hopeful father, a claim too far.

No, it was none of these things that had persuaded her mother, but rather Mamm's own father, who delivered a firm, two-part instruction. First her papa told her that the crabby, acculturated Nederlander who had proposed to her, and who had gone ahead to make a new life in far-off Africa, was despite appearances a solid, reliable sort. No matter that he couldn't sing or dance, that he had a tin ear and was unable to sustain a rhythm or hold a tune. No matter that he couldn't read music and that even his voice was unmusical (it was the first thing she'd noticed about him). No matter all of this – the man had honest eyes, while singing and dancing men, by contrast, were not to be trusted. Secondly, her father meaningfully added, after any war there was a dearth of decent husbands for respectable girls, so she should be grateful for the offer she had so poutingly received (he was her bird in the hand), and try to make do.

'And so it came that I'm here,' her mamm always ended the story of how she fetched up in this dismal wasteland in the tropics. '*Zo is het*. In those days we obeyed our fathers.'

For a while her mamm did try to give it a go and she did make do. The delicatessen shop sold excellent imported Speculaas, it was no lie, and the municipal library was a godsend, a precious godsend, where they invited 'busy-bee' readers to write short book reviews for the foyer noticeboard (though she generally felt too shy to post hers up). The mail boat did, as promised, take a mere two weeks to sail from Holland, three at the outside, and you learned from your string of defeats at the too competitive tennis club to abandon polite European-style play and slam the ball at your opponent from the baseline. It was possible to grow used to soft-soaping the mildew off your beloved piano's keys before playing, and to stuffing a sock in your mouth to try to suppress your screams at the sight of the city's mouse-sized cockroaches. It was even possible to accept that black people *chose* to avoid eye contact when you met them on the street and weren't simply (though this remained your suspicion) hating the very guts of you as they passed.

But despite all her efforts, for her mamm the process of day-to-day survival – the survival of her European heart, *mijn kern, als het waren, mijn ziel* – stayed tough. Africa's pressure on her soul felt like the insistent hand of some resentful foster-child, clammy, unloving, yet inescapable. She felt she had nothing to give this foster-child – not even her music; Africa cared nothing for her music – and there was nothing she might ask of it in return, though it pressed itself on her without respite.

The sweltering summers were the worst. It made no difference how many letters home the mother wrote or tennis games she played. As each blue-sky day submitted to the next, so her depression darkened. Summer holiday mornings began with her eyes welling with tears. By noon, at the most minor of prompts, a slow washing machine, dusty footprints on the carpet, she was in full voice. She demanded of the empty air (or her daughter sitting on the kitchen step covering her ears with her hands) why, just why, this hideous place denied her all comfort? Was it impossible to set up even an occasional opportunity of real culture? To offer just a little solace? She asked for so little, *no more* than a *concert* now and again, a *kwartetje*, just a small European ensemble, that alone, along with proper instruments, cleaned, tuned and tastefully arranged on stage, *comme il faut*.

By Easter time, the depression had harried her into exhaustion. The mother lay on the settee, mostly quiet, reminiscing sometimes in a strange, throaty voice about the spring beauty of Easter weekends back home, when, as she said she could *never* forget, Bach's Matthäus-Passion was performed in Amsterdam's Concertgebouw and the soloists wore corsages of pale spring flowers. The vast, expanded choir had been drawn from various local choral groups, including her own, the Singers of Scheveningen. Every year since she was eighteen she had participated, she said softly, and the last year before leaving she had made a distinct impression on the choirmaster. He had complimented her on her low notes, and even smiled at her from his dais when, raising her chin as high as she could, she had formed them.

And then, all of a sudden, on an Easter Sunday, there was a break in the mother's imprisoning darkness. Perhaps a mail-boat letter had carried a tip-off, or it was pure coincidence that brought Mamm to dusting the dark-veneer Philips radiogram that late March afternoon, her inevitable tears mingling with the Mr Min polish she was spraying onto its surface. Whatever it was, she worked with a fury, as if some invisible force were powering her arms.

The child's father in those days was a closet follower of sports broadcasts, so he often had the radiogram almost inaudibly switched on and listened at the appropriate times with his ear pressed to the woven plastic speaker. The child did the very same with the Saturday hit parade, muffled for the same reason, so as not to bother Mamm. The Philips was switched on that afternoon, though her mother could not at the time have known it. Pop music and sports other than tennis were far outside the realm of what counted for her as civilisation. Then, at the moment she bent to polish the glass dial in the front of the radiogram, her duster accidentally flicked the tuner that switched the stations from FM to short-wave, and, in the same instant, the cloth knocked the volume knob as well. The resonant contrapuntal of Bach's St Matthew Passion, that exact music, filled the room like a miracle. The child would never forget how her father's collection of pewter mugs hummed on their display shelf as the sound first struck.

Her mamm straightened up slowly. She looked down at her daughter in disbelief, as if she were a long-lost relative who had returned home without warning. She did not immediately stop her usual weeping, only now she was smiling through her tears and before too long singing along with the choir. Drawn by the music, her father stepped in from outdoors and stood stock-still beside his daughter, as if the slightest movement might break the magic spell that had so wonderfully been visited upon them. Later, when it turned out that the concert had been live, broadcast live on Radio Nederland Wereldomroep from Amsterdam via Hilversum – yes, the very place, her one-time singing ground – the mother could only shake her head, reduced to silence. There must be a God, after all, she finally breathed, there must be. Certainly this discovery would rescue her from the doctors with whom her husband had already threatened her, more than once. The three-hour Sunday programme from Hilversum could have been designed for her, its music radiating in a great spreading fan of harmony across the vast African continent.

Ich bin Gottes Sohn, the tenor on the radio intoned, striking open the moment on which he held his final note as if time were a flint, and the sound a napping blade.

'All the way across Africa,' Mamm gulped through her tears. 'Can you believe it, the sound coming all the way through, and still so pure?' The father and the child silently made eyes at one another, barely believing their good fortune.

In the days that followed, the father maintained his amazed silence. He and the child tried several times to rediscover the Radio Hilversum station setting, initially without success. 'Nothing doing, nothing doing,' he whispered, his calloused thumb rolling the dial. The child could tell he was up to something then, because he suddenly began talking to the neighbours. Most days he no more than grunted if he spied them over the fence. But now he borrowed from the neighbour on their right-hand side a drill bit that was larger than those in his own tool box and used it to bore a hole through the sitting-room wall, in the corner where the radiogram stood. Through this he threaded the radiogram's antenna wire. From the other neighbour, Mr Simmons, a part-time handyman, he bought an old antenna and then, when that was put in place and hooked up to the wire, borrowed a big steel contraption said to be a cow pacifier, and moulded its looped arms into longer, frond-like shapes. This he rigged up beside the first antenna as its back-up. A system was now in place. Together the family waited for Sunday.

At three o'clock exactly that Sunday, at the moment Radio Nederland came on stream, the child's father stepped outside into the canna-lily patch, where the reception was clearest, and raised his two antennae to the sky, the blue veins bulging in his scrawny forearms. At the same moment, Mamm switched on the radio, but avoided the least touch to the tuner. The father claimed to have set it minutely, to the micro-kilohertz, and no one other than he might now mess with it.

But what success! What magic! At that very same instant the warm clear sound of Radio Nederland Wereldomroep, those three precise words, announced themselves. They had pulsed through the dry air of the Sahara, so the child imagined it, and down the Great Rift Valley, and over the Zambezi and Limpopo rivers, and round the blue arc of the sky above their heads. And finally, she thought, they came beating along the high, braced antennae in her father's hands, and so through his body, and here into the sitting room. Through his liver and lungs the pulse went, through his guts and sclerotic veins and bones, and then became transfigured into spoken words. The price of a barrel of oil was rocketing to record levels, the Radio Nederland newsreader informed them, but it was as if he were singing Bach, so elated was Mamm's expression.

A sudden yelp. Her father'd had to rub at the sweat collecting on his nose and for a moment had lowered one of the antennae. The mother's anxious face was pressed to the window. Where the newsreader's voice had been, she cried, a high-pitched buzzing now assaulted her. The station had been lost, irrevocably lost! The father raised the antennae again, strain-ing even higher, and the child stretched tall behind him in a vain attempt to prop up his elbows. Mamm's face again came to the window. The connection had returned, but was very crackly, she gestured. It wasn't to be helped, the father shrugged back. Go indoors, he instructed the child, and tell your mother that at any given moment there is bound to be a tropical thunderstorm somewhere in Africa; it is to be expected. The string of sound connecting us to Europe will have to be snagging at some or other point.

But the message did not dislodge the mamm's bogged-down spirits. For the time being, she was crestfallen and determined to stay that way. She was appalled to think of tropical storms at any time, she said, and least of all as crashing into her radiogram in the form of this horrible roaring static. The child thought of how that same static had thundered silently through her father's body only moments before they all heard it, and wondered whether he felt it in the slightest, and how he stood it if he did. The loudness of the thrumming.

The father, though, was not so easily put off. A snag of stormy static wasn't about to scupper his efforts to give his wife and so himself an island of sanity on a Sunday afternoon. Trial and error across the next few weekends showed that as long as the antennae were held high at the moment of switching on, and then maintained in the aloft position throughout the broadcast, Radio Nederland's reception continued clear from start to finish, regardless of the intervening storms.

So the father's afternoon antennae watch became a fixture. Particularly if there was a concert or a recital, Bach or Schubert especially, but even Mozart, he committed himself to his garden post for a full three hours. It was the child's job to keep him supplied with liquid refreshment, always cold beer, the only time that he was allowed it, and occasionally, if his arms grew very tired, she would take a chair to stand up behind him and support his elbows in her palms. Years later she retained the clear picture in her memory. Her father out there in his mauve polyester shirt, sweated through or soaking wet with rain, his comb-over dishevelled, shifting himself up higher if Mamm so much as murmured from indoors that a burr of static had spoilt a favourite chord.

What drove him? He had always hated sunshine and was indifferent to music. He winced when the shrill arias on Radio Nederland pierced the walls of the house and reached his ears. All that Mamm loved about old Europe – its complicated manners and traditions – he resented. And yet every Sunday he stood there for those three hours at a stretch, in silence, at peace with himself, a small smile of contentment playing around the lips to which his daughter lifted, ever so gingerly, the long glasses of cold beer he loved.

ivan
vladislavić

Lullaby

I saw them at the airport, the woman and her young lover, but I would surely have forgotten them by now if everything had ended well. You know how it is: unhappy endings sharpen the memory. So many things snagged in my mind afterwards, details that would otherwise have slipped away in the torrent of experience that courses through each of us without leaving a trace. One of their suitcases had split during the flight and the baggage handlers had sealed it with yellow tape. It was an old-fashioned case, not the hard mussel-shell you're advised to use these days, a battered brown-leather carryall stuck with labels showing palm trees and hula skirts, like something out of *Casablanca*. The boy, the young man, wrestled it off the clanking conveyor and they laughed about the tape: the chevrons made it look like the scene of a crime. Their second bag went by, a backpack full of zippered pockets, clips and slings, and he chased after it, squealing with laughter again, and nearly knocked me over. The suitcase must be hers and the backpack his: luggage and gear. Two styles of travelling, two versions of the world. He tugged a wisp of red from the gaping case and pinned it against his hipbones, a lacy thong, barely there, and she snatched it away, pretending to be embarrassed, and buried it in her shoulder bag. Quite a bit older than him, I thought, but young enough to show those slivers of belly and back between T-shirt and sarong. Half the passengers were in Hawaiian shirts and Bermudas, signalling that their island holiday had already begun. The couple sharing my row had ordered G&Ts for lunch. In my suit, even without a tie, I felt like a grown-up among the kids, and it was a relief to get out of the terminal and into a taxi.

My hotel was on the edge of Grand Baie. I knew the Coconut Palm well, a comfortable, touristy place close to a good beach and half a dozen restaurants. The exclusive resorts are more beautiful, but what's the point when you're on your own? Mr Appadoo at reception greeted me by name and asked how the new range was moving. Little touches like this make you feel at home, whereas chocolates on the pillow and the bedclothes turned down remind you that you're not.

'You must join us for sundowners at the Sandbar,' Mr Appadoo said.

'Thanks but no thanks. I'd rather take a dip, clear my head.'

I was in no mood to break the ice with a gang of sun-deprived Europeans, self-basting Germans straight off their sunbeds, and Brits so pale they glow in the dark, all behaving like teenagers on a field trip. Been there, done that. They would let their hair and a few other things down before the evening was over. After the first free drink on the terrace there would be a string of others you had to pay for. Inevitably, someone would discover 'Dancing Queen' on the jukebox or one of those anthems for binge drinkers. I get knocked down, but I get up again.

I went to my room, meaning to change for a swim, but an invitation card on the dressing table waylaid me. It showed a cocktail glass with a tipsy straw and a stream of bubbles that spelt out *Willkommen! Bienvenue!* The cartoon had the same outmoded charm as the leather suitcase at the airport. I did not have to be in Floréal before noon the next day. Perhaps a drink would do me good. On an impulse, I changed into shorts and a T-shirt and headed for the bar.

The Sandbar was no more than a handful of wooden tables under thatched umbrellas scattered along the beach wall. *Stehtische*, the Germans call them, tables for standing at. Stairs went down to the sand; the sea was as flat and blue as a swimming pool, and so close you could leave your sandals on the grass and hotfoot it across to the water. Harry the barman had a counter with a sea view so that he could double as lifeguard. He knew some moves with the cocktail shaker and some jokes about Tom Cruise. He remembered my name too.

Under the umbrellas, a dozen people were swirling about, moored to their drinks on the tables like boats to bollards. A spume of coconut butter and rum drifted downwind. The ice had not just broken but melted. In a rising tide of accented English the odd phrase of Italian or German bobbed like a cocktail olive or a lemon wedge. The whole place was charged with the reckless energy people from a cold climate generate when they feel the sun on their arms and sand between their toes.

The complimentary cocktail was an extravagant thing in a hollowed-out pineapple, mainly rum and strawberry juice, I thought, with melon balls afloat in it like mines. Looking for a quiet corner, I went onto the terrace beyond the last umbrella, and there I saw them again, the couple from the airport, sitting on the same side of a table in the lee of a windbreak, pressed together, looking out to sea. They had their faces turned to the afternoon sun and their backs to the noise. Her hand was on his neck, rubbing the bristles against the grain.

Nearly every coincidence has a dull explanation – the airline and hotel bookings had probably been packaged by some agency – and I was only mildly surprised to find that we were in the same hotel. I was curious though. On another day, I would have left them there alone, but I went closer. It was enough to hesitate on the edge of their privacy.

'Would you like to sit?' the woman asked.

'Are you sure? That's kind of you.'

They made place for me at the table by shifting apart, separating into two distinct people.

'I'm Martha from Rotterdam,' she said, putting out her hand. 'And this is my son Eckhart.'

'Eckie,' he said. The boy had a fierce handshake and a goofy smile. I imagine it matched the one I kept pasted to my face to cover my confusion. Mother and son? The possibility had not crossed my mind, but now the likeness seemed obvious. They had the same thick blond hair, the same full-lipped mouth. I introduced myself.

'Are you enjoying your holidays?' she asked.

'I've just arrived. On business rather than pleasure, I'm afraid, although you wouldn't think so to look at me.'

'You must have a bit of fun too.'

'Well, I'm going to reward myself with a weekend of loafing when the work is done.'

'What kind of work?'

'I'm in the rag trade, as we call it. Accessories mainly. We have a factory in Johannesburg, but some of our ranges are manufactured here.'

'Rag trade!' he burst out.

Almost everything I said made him laugh, a disconcerting high-pitched snort. I very soon began to wonder whether he wasn't a bit, well, *slow*. He was too bright-eyed for a man of eighteen or twenty. Twenty-two? The fact that I couldn't place his age seemed telling. He had a rough-and-ready masculinity, and he was drinking like an old pro and rolling his own cigarettes expertly from a packet of Drum. His chin was covered with stubble, his neck bulged from a white T-shirt – he'd clearly been working out – but his eyes were childishly innocent. He wouldn't sit still. He kept squirming around on the bench like a child who wants to go out and play. When he knocked over his drink, a fat pineapple like my own, he looked distraught. His lip actually quivered. A bit slow, I thought, definitely. That would explain the easy physical warmth between them, the way he nuzzled at her neck and put his arm around her shoulders, left his hand to curl over her breast. And perhaps it also explained why she received these attentions with no sense of impropriety, of a boundary crossed or sanction violated.

Eckie went in search of a refill.

'And what do you do in real life?' I asked.

'Real life?'

'What business are you in?'

'Oh, we're just on holidays,' she said with a laugh that ran deeper than her son's. 'We travel together when we can.'

'Is this your first time here?'

'Yes, we found it on the internet. You've been before, I guess.'

'Often. I like to stop off on my way to Europe. I'm lucky to have a good excuse.'

'Then you must give us some advice about the beaches.'

'There are great places to snorkel. Do you dive at all?'

'She won't go in the water,' Eckie answered, coming up behind her.

'And he won't come out.'

'A water baby,' I said.

'Water baby!'

He put down a tub of Bombay mix and went back to the bar. I asked again what she did for a living, but she wanted to talk about the best places to snorkel, to eat crayfish, to buy presents. This is what holiday-makers do: they indulge themselves. They do not want to be reminded of home. When she asked how long I would be staying, I wondered if there was an invitation in the question. She had not mentioned a husband. I looked for a wedding ring and noticed that she wasn't wearing one.

The party grew as new arrivals checked in and guests came back from their outings. So many Germans, but also Scots, Italians, Swedes. The very pale blondes all seemed to be wearing red cotton pants. The small talk and flirtatious laughter grew louder and hotter until it was a roaring bonfire.

Eckie scampered about, overexcited and glowing, talking to everyone, making a collection of new friends and swizzle sticks. But he could not keep away from her. Every few minutes, he would be back to lace his fingers into hers or lean against her. I liked her neck, the way the tendons showed under her skin as she turned her head, but when he rested his face in that brown curve I thought: impossible. She has a lover already. Metaphorically speaking. She loves the boy too much.

I had another drink, in a glass. The sun slid to the bottom of the sky like a sodden cherry. I was about to excuse myself, when a gust of music and laughter reached us from over the water. A catamaran was coming in, a beautiful white craft with sails furled, running on its engines. The coloured lights strung along the deck were luminous in the dusk, and in that charmed web small figures could be seen dancing. I recognised the

Parakeet. I'd done this cruise once before, and I planned to do it again when the work was out of the way. It was touristy, of course, a packaged day trip to one of the islets off the coast, but delightful too. They would moor the cat off a beach strewn with dead coral – it was like walking on bones – and the crew made a barbecue while you snorkelled and sunbathed, and then they fed you fruit and grilled fish and rum punch under jury-rigged canvas. Castaways with catering. Perfect.

When the *Parakeet* drew closer, the dancing became wilder, as if the day trippers wished to show the landlubbers how much fun they'd been having. The captain, a piratical kid in a headscarf and dreadlocks, brought them close to the beach, almost in among the swimmers, and then swept out in a wide circle, extending the trip by five minutes, marketing his services. Even before they'd cast anchor, some of the more boisterous dancers plunged into the water and swam for the shore. The others milled around on the deck, showing off their sea legs, waiting to be ferried in on the dinghy bobbing at the stern.

A strange tension crackled between the new arrivals on the terrace and the old hands on the boat. The tourist's timescale is finely calibrated: a single day is the difference between innocence and experience. The people on the boat seemed browner, saltier, happier. We watched them with envy as the party at the Sandbar faltered. The catamaran had reminded a few among us that there were meals to eat and brochures to read, and they began drifting off. My thoughts turned to my plans for the next day. I said goodnight to Martha and Eckie and went to my room.

I saw them again sooner than I expected: in the morning they were on the shuttle bus to Port Louis. They were heading down to Black River so that Eckie could go parasailing. Tomorrow, he said, they might do the catamaran cruise, and the day after that snorkelling. And then there was walking on the ocean floor in a diver's helmet. She caught my eye while he prattled on and quirked the corner of her mouth as if to say: indulge him, he's young.

Nearly every seat was taken – tourists on the way to one attraction or another, I discovered as they swapped notes. In Triolet we picked up a housekeeper carrying a bucket full of brushes and a feather duster, and

I felt a twinge of solidarity with this woman who also had a job to do. I was going to the factory in Floréal.

I sat behind Martha and Eckie on the bus. Something about the heat and the closeness, the sense of being confined among strangers, made me overly aware of their presence. It was almost as if I were seeing some magnified version of them. I remember looking at the sea chart of her freckled shoulders and the bite marks on the earpieces of her sunglasses. He was wearing a cap, and a tuft of hair like a shaving brush stuck out through the hole at the back. I imagined that the passenger behind me, a German woman who couldn't stop taking photographs, was paying the same exacting attention to the back of my head, watching an enlarged bead of sweat run down inside my collar.

Before long we fell into a drowsy silence. Even the German's shutter blinked and closed. On the long, straight road out of Triolet, Eckie's head dropped and jerked a couple of times, and then he leant over and laid his head on his mother's shoulder. She put her arm around him and drew him close. She let him sleep that way for half an hour, scarcely moving so as not to wake him. It struck me as a kind of sacrifice.

When the bus stopped on the outskirts of Port Louis to let off the housekeeper, Eckie awoke with a start. Sleep had wiped the features of the man from him entirely: his face was as soft and round as a boy's. He stretched and yawned. Then we saw it. Perhaps he noticed it first or perhaps I drew his attention to it by leaning over the seat for a closer view. In any event, we looked at it together. On the soft, freckled flesh of his mother's shoulder, where his head had been resting, was a perfect impression of his ear. He cried out in amazed delight. She dipped her shoulder to see what was causing the excitement. It was strange. The shape of his ear, perfect in every ridge and whorl, seemed to have been carved on her body. She rubbed at it, as if she could smooth it into her skin like a dab of suntan lotion, but it persisted in clear relief. Soon everyone was admiring it and laughing, amused or intrigued. The blood rose in Martha's neck. I cannot say why, but this odd, displaced organ embarrassed her. I cannot explain my response either: I was filled with revulsion, something close to nausea.

It took five minutes to fade away, slowly losing its definition like a waxwork in the heat. Once the commotion had passed, Martha and Eckie began to joke and giggle quietly, both of them flushed and radiant. He kept running his fingertips over the carved skin, discovering his own flesh in hers, again and again. When the image was almost gone, he bent down to it and whispered a secret into her body.

Soon afterwards, they got out. I was relieved. I put aside the briefcase I'd been holding on my lap, stretched my legs into the empty space, and tried to think about other things.

You know that I saw them again. We haven't had the unhappy ending yet.

The following afternoon, I was reading on the verandah when I saw the *Parakeet* coming in. It was earlier than usual, but that only occurred to me afterwards. What struck me at the time was the silence. No reggae or chatter, just the chug of the engines and the passengers hunched on the deck. The simple explanations – bad weather, spoilt food – did not cross my mind. A dark stain in the air made me go to the railing and watch the boat come closer, lying heavily in the water, or so it seemed to me. There were no showy zigzags or loops; it nosed straight in among the swimmers, the captain cut the engines, and his mate threw the anchor overboard.

Then a sound rose up from the deep and flayed the skin from the backs of my hands. Keening. I understood for the first time what it meant. It was coming from a woman in the bow, and I saw that it was Martha, slumped over a bright, shrouded shape. The wailing died down into choked sobs. They broke into the sunlight one by one, ragged and raw, like creatures torn out of her on a hook.

All along the beach, people splashed out of the water, knees up, as if a fin had been spotted in the shallows. I saw Harry the barman running down to the boat.

The passengers came ashore. Some of them went away at once, others clung together on the beach, talking among themselves and then to the people getting up from their deckchairs and towels. Martha still sat in the bow with the captain beside her, weeping quietly now, while the sun clanged on every surface.

I should go and speak to her, I thought, comfort her. We've made a connection. But I couldn't face it.

When Harry came up to the hotel, I followed him to the Sandbar and found him pouring rum into a dozen glasses on a plastic tray. He told me the story. The *Parakeet* had anchored off Coral Point as usual. While the crew prepared lunch, the snorkellers did as they always do, floating out into the water at the end of the beach and letting themselves be carried back on the current. I remembered it myself: you hardly needed to swim, you just lay on the tide, drifting, suspended between two worlds, with the sun on your back and your face pressed through the surface of the water into another dimension. No one knew whether a spiteful current had turned Eckie in under the boat or whether he'd decided to swim through there on his own, and it made no difference. He'd been caught in a tangle of lines between the hulls and drowned. By the time his absence was noticed, it was too late. The captain dived in and cut him loose, and they hauled him onto the beach and pumped his chest for an hour. Even after they'd gone on board and turned the boat towards home, they went on trying to make him breathe.

But what about Martha? I asked. Didn't she see that he was in trouble?

She was sleeping, Harry said. She had sat down in the shade against the dunes, watching Eckie in the water. I imagined him floating on the current, rolling over now and then to find her on the shore. 'Look at me! Look at me!' She stretched out with her head in the shade for a moment, she said, just for a moment, and she must have dozed off. When she awoke, the captain was already in the water with the knife in his hand and the boy's body dragging. She thought her son had been murdered.

The boy's body. I could not picture it. It was easier to imagine that it was a prank, that he would cast off the shroud of beach towels and jump up, squealing with laughter.

An ambulance came. Two men in floral shirts waited on the grass, while another in a white suit went down to the water's edge, stepping carefully so that sand did not get in his shoes. The captain and his mate brought Eckie's body ashore on a board and the other men put it in the ambulance. The captain carried Martha ashore in his arms like a child. Her silence was vaster and denser than her weeping. Everything fell into it.

I did not go to Blue Bay or anywhere else. I finished my work and in the evenings I sat on the verandah with a book on my knees. The *Parakeet* was anchored nearby. The newly arrived holidaymakers, unaware of its freight, and some of the old ones, eager to make the most of the time left to them, swam out to the boat and splashed around it. Behind the counter at the Sandbar, Harry went on cracking ice and slicing limes.

The overnight flight to Frankfurt was packed and I wished I was flying business class like a grown-up. The penny-pinching would have to stop. Watching the backpackers stuff their bags into the overhead bins, I wondered what Martha had made of Eckie's rucksack. Could she figure out where everything went? Perhaps the travel agent had sent someone to help her, a guide or counsellor. They must have trained professionals for a situation like this. Or a sister might have come to support her. Did she fly home with the body? What do they do with a coffin? It must go in the hold with the luggage.

The safety film unnerved me. 'In the unlikely event of a loss of pressure in the cabin, oxygen masks will drop down automatically from the panel above you.' I imagined what it would be like to face death here, the sheer suffocating terror of it, the struggle for air, the release of bladder and bowels. The cartoon figures on the screen, mincing stiff-legged towards the emergency exits or reaching calmly for the dangling oxygen masks – 'Make sure your own mask is properly secured before you help children and others in need of assistance' – were meant to reassure. These beige dummies should be less alarming than actors, who were real people, after all, but they had the opposite effect on me. They looked like horror movie zombies. The living dead.

I ate the little helping of Moroccan chicken with the little knife and fork. I drank two little bottles of chardonnay.

There was an empty seat a few rows back, and after the trays had been cleared away, I thought of moving for the elbow room, the chance to put my head down for an hour or two. I remembered those stories about passengers on doomed flights who swapped seats with a stranger and were miraculously saved when the plane went down. But what about the others who were saved by staying where they were? There was no story in that. And there was no lesson in it either. You lived or died. Luck could not save you, and neither could love.

As soon as the lights were dimmed, I covered myself with the baby blanket and tried to sleep, but I was too near the galley. A procession of people looking for water or whisky kept pushing through the curtain, bumping against my shoulder.

In the small hours, when I had begun to despair of sleeping at all, a voice reached me. It was a young mother in the next row. She had an infant in a bassinet secured to the bulkhead. I'd noticed her earlier because she kept getting up to look into the crib, to adjust a blanket or run a hand over the child's head. Now she was singing a lullaby. I did not recognise the language, but I understood it well enough. Baby language. You speak it too.

The cabin was quiet. Under the lit signs that said 'Do not smoke' and 'Keep your seatbelt fastened' nearly everyone was asleep. The baby was sleeping, but its mother went on singing. Just as she needed to reach out and stroke the edge of the crib with her fingers, she needed to reach out with words into the soft shell of his ear. For a moment, I saw an aeroplane full of little children asleep in their adult bodies, under youthful muscle and middle-aged fat, behind beards and breasts. Babies. The long, grey nursery droned into the dark. I pulled the blanket up to my chin and the consoling babble washed through me.

maureen
isaacson

Love in Lalaland

Before it happened, I was about to buy a man, a bird and a saxophone. Made from wire, these items were to stand in the entrance to the embassy. A bullish clasping of my shoulder and a handcuff snapped around my wrist put an end to the transaction in the craft market and to the freedom I had taken for granted.

One of the snarling policemen who took me captive confiscated my identity documents, although I was entirely within my diplomatic rights. It is not easy to maintain one's dignity with dogs salivating at one's ankles and the menacing voices of an unfathomable law breaking around one's head.

As I was steered into a yellow police van, I lost sight of my seven female companions, who had been allowed to accompany me by the generous concession of my husband, the ambassador.

Dear husband, he must be demented about the plight of his beloved wife, whom he chose not only for her looks and charm but for the articulation of compliance that the women of our class have perfected.

Of what use are my virtues now? I am incarcerated in the Way Station; a grimy isolation quarter that the inmates call 'Lalaland'. They refer to the slovenly female officials as the 'O's'. To think that these women, who bore the brunt of this country's lunatic oppression until ten years ago, now do unto others as they were done unto!

My imprisonment is significant. It surely means that there is conflict at home; I am a martyr. Our country's relationship with our host is tenuous at best. Bilateral trade is on the cards: they want our oil; we want their wine. But our embassy's presence here is conditional on our observance of the international nuclear non-proliferation treaty, to which we have only recently subscribed. It is also dependent on peaceful domestic relations. For our current leadership, the overwhelming concern is the rapidly rising power of the military. If there has in fact been a coup, which we have been anticipating, our privileges will be confiscated.

I shudder to think that my miserable routine in this desperate place of waiting may be a preparation for the subservience to which I will be subjected at home. Every day, after morning 'meal' (a square block of corn porridge and black tea), we are sent to Queue. We line up in the quadrangle outside Office Block, where the ministry attends to 'home affairs'. Like everybody here, I anxiously await the moment I will be allowed to proclaim my innocence.

I have been here for twenty-one days. And every day I have been turned away by the authorities. No reasons are offered. Some women say they have been here for as long as one thousand days; many say that they have lost count.

I grow increasingly anxious about dear husband's whereabouts. I have not heard from him since the day of my arrest. He supported our new president's grand plans to restore our nationhood when the revolution forced the invaders out of our country. But he worried privately about the forces of darkness that continue to make their presence felt.

Our president has made our national identity a priority: 'We must know who we are and we must honour our traditions,' he says. He is yet to say something about the subjugation of women in our society. Optimistic comrades believe that he plans to address the ongoing violations against women for alleged 'sex crimes', such as adultery. We who belong to the Mission, an underground organisation, believe this should happen before all else. If you have heard of the cable floggings in our country and the rape of women by men they are later forced to marry, it is thanks to the Mission. We target all perpetrators – not only our own countrymen but those invaders who have raped our women as well as our land. Most of these have left, but we are ever watchful.

Before the last invasion ended, a Mission comrade was abducted by a soldier. He was dressed in Levi's jeans, the mufti of his country. Fellatio in the back of his car over, he drove my dear comrade to 'McDonald's', a fast-food outlet that his countrymen deposited on our soil. Inside, the comrade was obliged to order burgers with potato fries. The invader forced her to sit down and eat her portion. 'Now I feel right at home,' he said.

The soldier never made it home that night. Accidents happen. The Mission makes sure of that.

My husband, who is a 'liberal' and is among a handful of men who encourage women to study, must nonetheless never know about the machinations of the Mission.

As the days grow longer in this dry, alien place, my longing for the certainty of his physical presence becomes increasingly intense. As I sit here, I can see him before me, his grey hair falling softly across his dark brow, his shoulders bent from writing. His scent never leaves me; his aura is impressed upon my own. Our marriage, arranged by our fathers ten years ago, is companionable. I put this down to the age gap. We are now both three weeks older than we were when I was apprehended. At fifty-six, he is twenty-six years older than me, to the day.

Our intimate relationship reached a plateau soon after we wed – a passionless zone in which a certain sensual comfort nonetheless prevailed. How I crave the sensation of his firm hands on my head as I fall asleep on my narrow prisoner's mattress in Lalaland.

I am grateful for the respite provided by Shower Block in Zone One. Some days, when my aching for touch becomes unbearable, I allow myself to stumble gently against a naked body, as if by accident. In this moment I feel almost alive, as I go about the real business of the day – cleansing my body and washing the clothes (olive-green muslin dress, several matching undergarments) that were 'on my back' when I was arrested. Apparently the limited budget of this institution makes no provision for prison uniforms.

I am utterly alone here. The women, wrapped in their individual misery, pay no attention to me.

M is an exception. She arrived two days ago, her black eyes and warm skin still fresh from the world of traffic fumes and orgasms. Her clothes are patterned in the bright 'continental' traditional style; her long dress, worn over trousers, clings snugly to her strong, firm form.

She is attractive! She is taller than me, and darker. Her movements are crisp and efficient. Her sense of purpose is unusual in Lalaland; her confidence is compelling. This is remarkable, considering that – as I will learn later – she has fled from a bloody civil war in her country, where rape and pillage have turned the capital on its head. I will learn, too, that she is a journalist who has travelled widely, reporting on regional conflicts for an international newspaper.

But allow me to relate first things first:

Yesterday, I 'fell'; the underside of my arm brushed tentatively against M's thigh, which bore the weight of my fall. In her eyes there was a sense of recognition and horror, as if she felt in my flesh the desolation that awaits us all in this place.

Our meeting has relieved me of the burden of isolation. Same-language speakers are cruelly separated. Here in Residential Block we are catalogued, filed, stashed away like yesterday's news, cunningly divided and ruled. For innocents such as myself, the punishment is criminal.

Sometimes I talk to myself. I repeat: *The future is in our hands*, exulting in the lyrical sounds of the vowels of my own language. I am among the few women linguists in my country. I have a doctorate; my specialisation in the origin of languages provides me with a key. The lingua franca used by the O's is a bastardised version of the language of the superpower bomb-makers who have destroyed what little we have in our country. I understand far more than I admit. *Good 'n yew?*

Prior to M's arrival, my only friend was the sun. At dawn, I continue to accept its pale overtures; later, its powerful rays dry my precious single-outfit wardrobe. My illegal comrades are late risers, but I am vigilant anyway. Without my clothes, what am I? These garments set me apart from the fashionable young women, who in this part of the world wear trousers that grasp hips, buttocks and pubis, as if in anger.

The information afforded by the intimacy with my fellow women captives is excessive; I see it all. Beneath the tapered, buttoned blouses, I see awkward brassieres, made from synthetic material and underscored by wire. As below, so above: such harsh underwear underscores harsh attitudes.

The body is a skilful autobiographer; in the postures of some new arrivals to Lalaland, I see the frustration of women who are accustomed to love. I witness, too, the dull solitariness of those who have become accustomed to living without it. The lonely ones stoop; the lines of their face harden.

I am compelled by the shapes of bellies that have been stretched by childbirth, an event I may never experience. It is not yet the time for you to bear children, my husband told me in the first of our ten years of marriage. But you will soon be too old to sire our child, I warned. He ordered the doctor to prescribe the birth-control pill.

Our understanding of pharmacology is advanced; the Pill's side effects of thrombosis and stroke have been eliminated. They (men) do not want us (women) to be born; *give me a male child and I will give you the future* is every new husband's song to his young wife. Yet when we women are old enough to do their bidding, the men want to keep us alive.

When I arrived at Lalaland the doctor spitefully said: 'Stop taking the Pill. What use will it be?'

It is M's third day here. My instincts were correct. She is lovely! Early-morning light softens the desolation of Shower Block as the wind waves our garments to dryness. This is not her first stay in Lalaland. During her last visit to this country she worked as a researcher for a radio station. She was arrested, detained and brought here without warning. Several months later, she was told that she was to be deported by train. It took two weeks for the train to arrive.

'Every morning I would prepare myself for the journey,' she tells me. 'Every day, nothing happened until eventually five hundred of us were loaded into police vehicles and deposited on the station platform. We were made to line up before a row of soldiers and policemen. A male "O" (called in for such operations) screamed his orders: "Sit down and look down!"'

So much for tolerance in the Promised Land for which my husband holds high hope! I run my fingers lightly through M's hair; I twirl strands tightly together; I let them go, as if releasing a bird into the air.

M continues: 'When we had all been counted, the police and soldiers ushered us onto a number of trains. "As you were!" shouted an official. "Be seated! Heads down! Stay!"'

'Like dogs,' I whisper.

'Like dogs,' says M. 'Then the counting began again. They forced us to look down, at the space between our legs. The scenery was out of bounds for us, in case we "jumped". Two friends, who did in fact jump, walked for days through the open veld that is inhabited by lion, elephant and leopard, desperate to return.'

I must protect M. I resolve to do all that is in my power to help her, once this is all over.

M explains, as if to an intelligent but ignorant student, that the neighbouring countries in this region are no longer able to support their own people. Economies crash, wars erupt, limbs are hacked; strong winds and fires sweep away makeshift houses. Governments make promises.

I am afraid to take our conversation further, although I do feel that I can trust M. She listens as well as she speaks; in her presence I feel that I am heard and seen. This experience arouses feelings akin to love. We sit close together on the wooden bench that digs deep ridges into our thighs and into the cushioned flesh of our buttocks. Hair, hands, skin ... all meld in a blur of feeling.

When M tells me I am beautiful, this inspires in me a confusion of emotions – an unidentifiable fear and a wrenching tenderness. How many women has she embraced in this way?

Our washing is our only witness; our washing guards us without prejudice until it is sufficiently dry to cover our bodies so that we can arrive in time for morning meal. My mind is curiously free of its usual fears and my dread of the colder days is less intense today.

M says that foreigners are hated in this country. The locals believe that they have come to steal their jobs, women and cars. 'Have you ever stolen anything?' I ask. My irony escapes her and she is indignant, offended almost.

I am nonetheless impressed by M's forthrightness, and by her worldliness. A woman like herself could undoubtedly be useful to the Mission. Still, I will need proof that I can truly trust her before I can broach the subject.

I speak instead of my love for the Russian writer Leo Tolstoy, whose novel *Anna Karenina* I was carrying in my bag at the time of my arrest. The O's confiscated it when I arrived, forcing me to rely on memory. My request to 'borrow' it, if only on Sundays, has been ignored. Fortunately, I have memorised several passages. I plan to recite Anna's monologue of despair when her affair with Count Vronsky has ended, before she throws herself under the wheels of a moving train.

Modern tranquillisers may have averted many tragedies, but I can think of no instances where medicine has served literature. Tolstoy had no use for a zombie; his Anna was willing to die for love.

The subversive sense in this pre-revolutionary Russian novel strikes a direct chord with what my husband indulgently refers to as my 'romantic heart'. I yearn to experience such passion, for which he is entirely without aptitude. Fortunately, my husband's predictability makes subterfuge as simple and as essential as breathing.

Another week has passed; another lifetime of bureaucratic lies. At Queue, we women are under surveillance as we slouch, each under the weight of her own pain. In order to avoid separation, M and I dare not look at each other. Her warmth permeates my being. Surely she wonders about my origins?

The motto of the Mission is carved into my brain: *Women are the soul of discretion*. I edit my life story for M's benefit as I watch her prepare for another day of inaction. For a few lingering moments, the dour, celibate atmosphere of this place is obscured by the movement of my beloved sun. It highlights the way M's cotton dress cleaves to the smooth, supple lines of her long body, as it warms her neat breasts. When M turns to smile at me, her eyes reflecting my desire, I wonder: for whom am I to be the substitute?

The sun moves gently over her body as she sits, first on her haunches, later cross-legged, hands on her knees, resigned. My absorption in her leads to thoughts of my husband. Naturally, I think continually about what may have become of my tall, imperious spouse. My husband, with his determined chin, is a fastidious man, whose barber clips his nose hairs every Tuesday. I cannot fault his appearance. He is always impeccable in his nakedness, always striking in his fine white suit, his red fez.

Distance and my meeting with M have intensified my feelings for him and have helped me to define them. These are feelings of a niece for a beloved uncle, a daughter for her father. I *care* about him.

Four days later, it is now two full weeks since M's arrival in Lalaland. She is beginning to open up about her home in 'the rurals'. Twenty people depend for their survival on the money she earns. M and her family, once strong supporters of the incumbent president's liberation movement, fell out of favour for resisting the militarisation of the state. She understands very well the threat that casts its shadow over my own country.

We have eaten our evening meal (chicken stew, which includes the pre-plucked fowl feet and beaks I am unable to ignore, as well as cabbage pulp and bread and bitter black tea). We have received and discarded our compulsory 'vitamin pill', which is in fact a blend of recognisable narcotics. Its side effects are potent: one minute you are in Lalaland; the next you are at home in your own country, listening to the voices of supplication in the morning souk. Your mind jumps: now you are enjoying your last minutes of freedom in the Promised Land. You are thrust back to the place where you were at the time of your arrest, amid hand-woven reed mats and baskets at the craft market.

You become agitated: why are these men about to arrest you? Your husband is a friend of the government; your papers are in order. Is there no respect for diplomatic immunity? Have you really done something wrong?

On the only occasion I actually swallowed this compulsory 'vitamin pill' these questions danced around my head. I wanted to apologise for my perceived trespasses, but what were they?

This is not the pill I would diagnose for the suicidal Anna Karenina.

How sad it is that women are born to suffer. I am moved to learn that M has left her two small children in the care of her family. She has never taken the contraceptive pill, she says. She is forced to rely on 'condoms', although she is aware of the dangers to which western women are exposed through their usage.

Despite the medical advancement in contraception, our masters have kept this form of contraception from us.

One morning M tells me: 'I have a surprise for you.' She has smuggled in a packet of these soft rubberised shields. She removes one from its tight wrapping and stretches it, never taking her eyes off me. Her husband wears one when they have sexual intercourse. Is it not uncomfortable for him? And for her? Why does he wear it? Is he unfaithful?

M reads aloud from the package insert: 'ComeOn is the world's leading trusted brand.' This message is translated into several European languages: *ComeOn ist die weltweit führende Kondommarke, der Millionen vertrauen. ComeOn, la marque leader de préservatifs …*

Instructions on the insert warn against the slipping and sliding of condoms up and down the penis during lovemaking, to the extent that they can fall right off! My God.

'Don't make me laugh!' I say.

The days are shorter now, and there is a chill in the air. One week passes and then another. It is exactly four weeks since M arrived, ushering in desire amid the waiting and fear.

Today we have visitors. A team from the state-owned national television and a reporter and photographer from the so-called 'independent' press wish to report on life behind the high walls of Lalaland.

The O's have donned fresh military-style uniforms and undertake an early-morning inspection in Shower Block at the time that M and I usually enjoy our morning tryst.

The inspection is performed in a desultory fashion and completed long before morning meal. The breakfast menu – for the first time since my arrival written on a blackboard – includes a choice of one egg, hard-boiled or fried. I shall not describe the one that was slapped onto my plate.

I have allowed my long black hair to fall loosely about my shoulders and my eyes are circled with the pencil of kohl I have saved for 'emergencies'. It is imperative that I attract attention to myself so that someone in the outside world – and hopefully my husband and my countrymen – can see what has become of me. Perhaps M will recognise some of the journalists or vice versa?

Well, the eggs were wasted because it is 11 a.m. and the media people have not turned up. Or perhaps they are being kept waiting at the gate – a common occurrence, according to M.

'Tea time,' shouts the most officious of the officials, who knows full well that there is in fact no 'tea time' in this place. We greedily receive some 'Zoo biscuits'. These are plain cookies, frosted with a variety of abstract, brightly coloured sugar animals.

The bowl containing the biscuits has been placed on the table in the room where we have been waiting for four hours. Is it my imagination or is the room becoming smaller? There is no air in here. The tension in the room smells like stale breath. It makes its home in my solar plexus. I am struggling to breathe and to contain my impulses. I do not know whose idea it is to rush for the bowl of biscuits, but I am at the front of the pack seized by a hunger so ravenous that we are prepared to fight 'to the death' for an 'animal biscuit'.

I use the expression advisedly. But the television journalists, who arrive as the brawl breaks out, will be less restrained in their descriptions. In the midst of this savage fight, as we inmates rip blouses and hair, as we scratch faces caked with saliva and chewed biscuit, faces smeared with blood and mucus, I experience release. Suddenly, a knife flashes in the hand of a fellow inmate. Where did she find it?

Her eyes dance wildly, the knife creates a river of blood in the throat of an 'illegal foreigner'. Amid the confusion of screaming, the perpetrator plunges the weapon deep into the woman's chest. I am close enough to hear her breath come in short gasps as she repeats the action three times.

She stands back, as if suddenly afraid of the knife that remains inside the bloody chest.

She is dragged away by two O's. Above the bloody screams of the victim and the prisoners, I hear a journalist say: 'No better than animals; no wonder they are in here! This place is too good for them.'

He is talking into a machine that I assume has recorded the pandemonium. Then I hear him say: 'At least one woman has died at the Way Station. This event took place just before midday, in an unprecedented fracas caused by a simple bowl of sugar-frosted Zoo biscuits.'

An official says: 'They do not usually react in this way to the daily tea-time confection. But we are always on guard against such behaviour among these people.'

By the time I realise that I will be implicated in this terrible event, which was, in fact, a murder, it is too late. Oh my God, where is M? I have not seen her for some time. Where is she?

'Do you think the full moon had anything to do with it?' I ask M later, in our moonlit cement meeting place.

'Oh, the tea treats are an old tactic, surely you see that?'

'Of course,' I say, although I see it only now.

M and I are standing at opposite ends of the courtyard of Shower Block. I am aware of the distance that separates us. Is she?

M says that the culprit has been incarcerated in Strong Block. I am trying in vain to visualise the face of the deceased. M says that she sometimes sat beside me in Queue.

She asks: 'Is it shock that makes you appear so calm?' I smile through an angry sneer that I cannot conceal. Come and try out some public justice sessions, I want to say. I am thinking of the handectomies I have witnessed, the standard punishment meted out to a woman for varnishing her nails or wearing rings. Why do they do it? I can hear the screams of the women 'sex criminals' as they are flayed. I want to tell her: Come and see how the ordinary men, even the 'democrats', punish our women for doing less than what you and I have done. No, I am not calm.

Two days after the murder, Lalaland is still in mourning. The atmosphere is charged with an occult weirdness. It is as if the soul of the murdered woman has infiltrated the borders of our lives, as if the shock of her death will never leave this place. Will the various gods to whom we all offer our prayers grant forgiveness? We beg for this in the same way that we beg for our papers, and our right to a peaceful life outside these walls.

It is clear that beneath the strict regard of the O's, their anxiety is soaring. This gives me the idea.

'Are you mad?' M asks.

'It is easiest to do it when they least expect it,' I say.

When I make my way to Office Block at 3 a.m., I do not care what anyone thinks, not even M. Using a weapon I have fashioned from my combined sandals, I bludgeon the sleeping guard on the head, certain that she will not waken for at least twenty-four hours. I slide my hand into her pocket and succeed in retrieving a bunch of three keys as well as a waterproof torch. Ah: the first key I try opens the information office.

Inside the office, I flip through a batch of files until I find my surname. This is almost too easy! My long, meaningless wait for word from the authorities led me to underestimate the order of this system. Inside my file, I find my blessed identity document. Here I am!

Now I see something else. What is this? A photograph of myself that must have been taken on my arrival. It is of the self that I remember ... the way I used to look ... but wait a minute, there are some fellow inmates: the photograph has been taken here, in Lalaland ... in the airless room. It must have been today! I am pleased to see that my looks have not been devastated by my experience in this treacherous place ... And here is an envelope – it contains several requests from my husband to visit me and all have been sent from within the country. He is possibly nearby!

Also inside my file is a photograph of an unknown man with a shaven head. His crouching, naked body is lit by a harsh light. What is this doing in my file? My God! *My God!* I recognise my husband's crooked little left finger, which is lifted to the blindfold that covers most of his face. What is going on?

Also, what is this? Daily Report One contains a detailed and accurate synopsis of my conversations with M. I have literally spoken to nobody else in this place. The report includes my evasions and my reconstructed curriculum vitae. It concludes: 'A matter of time before full confession about the Mission.' I am devastated to learn in this way that the front has been penetrated.

The report has been signed by M, in small, well-formed handwriting, evidence of her determination. What did I expect? Certainly I had no idea that I would be doubly trumped by an intelligence superior to my own.

'How could I have been so damn stupid?' I am almost shouting.

'You have done a pretty damn good job of being damn stupid,' says the voice that has touched me as no other has in many months, if not years.

M, fully clad in the neatly pressed camouflage uniform of the O's, is standing in the doorway. 'It is fortunate for me that you are very pretty too,' she says. 'As I have said before, you are quite beautiful, really, which makes my job so much more pleasant. Back to Shower Block! Now! Let's go!'

willemien brümmer

A Cat of Many Tales

With the kitten in her arms she looks like a spectral image from his past. 'Happy birthday, Dad,' she says.

His daughter, Mia, with the same delicate features as his mother: the fine nose, the thin lips, the eyes looking as if covered by plastic wrap.

The kitten has a ridiculous golden bow round its neck and a dull black coat which still needs to be licked into a shine by a mother. For a moment he is scared of even touching the animal. 'Thanks for the good wishes,' he says, pressing the button to slide open the front gate for Mia.

He suppresses a yawn, weary after wrestling with formulas all day long. For the past few days the article he has been working on just hasn't been flowing. Hesitantly, he offers Mia his hand, never sure about how to greet this daughter of his.

'Your mum has gone to the shop to buy food for tonight. Would you like to have a drink in the meantime? Brandy? Sherry?'

He leads the way along the garden path, straight to the drinks cabinet in the corner of the dining room. Only when he breathes in the reassuring smell through the wood does he remember the limp little creature in her arms. 'Your … your mum should know what kind of food to feed it. Would you like to call her on her cell?' He turns round, mentioning it casually. 'I'm not sure she'll have time to look after a cat too. You know how busy she is these days.'

Mia presses the kitten against her chest. 'I didn't bring the cat for Mum. I brought it for you.' Her voice is shrill, with a raspy edge. 'It's *your* cat, Dad.'

He notices the tremor in her lower lip, her mouth pulling downward. Her head is turned away from him, as always when she's crying. He remembers, once again, the scene in front of the Labia cinema several years ago. She was barely sixteen at the time, and his wife had insisted that he and Mia see a film together.

Even before the final credits started rolling up the screen he walked out ahead of her to the Benz parked in Orange Street. The film had upset him and set his thoughts jumbling. He was angry with Mia, with his wife, with himself. The portrayal of sorrow has always made him feel helpless.

As she reached the car a few minutes later, he pressed the central locking button, starting the engine just as her hand touched the door handle. He looked her in the eye, shifted gear into reverse, and pulled back. It had started raining lightly, and he still remembers her mouth, half-open in surprise, the drops on her skin. Her curious little knobbly shoulders, hunched against the cold. Something about her vulnerability drove him to pursue the crazy game.

He drove forward along Orange Street and watched her in the rearview mirror, walking after the car like a dog programmed to follow him. Only at the turn-off to Rheede Street did she stop, her arms folded around her body.

She hesitated, then ran into the street. Cars came sweeping past her. A feeling of irredeemable guilt and anguish and love rose up inside him. He could barely breathe. He turned round and stopped beside her.

Until now, that evening has stood between them like a mute creature in a box.

He sees the kitten digging its claws into her wrists. 'Mia,' he says, approaching carefully and pulling the small black feet from her white skin. There are tiny red scratch marks next to the turquoise vein running from her hand down to the crook of her arm. He wets his handkerchief, wipes off the blood.

He searches for her eyes, although she is looking down at the floor: 'Thanks for my kitten.'

He goes upstairs to the linen cupboard and takes out an old white towel. In another cupboard he finds a basket.

Back with his daughter, he puts the kitten in the basket, and folds the towel over it so that only its little face is visible. Mia dribbles some milk into a saucer for the creature and he pours brandy for the two of them. She seats herself on the edge of the easy chair in the lounge, as if she cannot quite believe that the chair will support her weight. She sits exactly like his mother, her calves primly crossed. As he has done so many times in the past, he once again wonders how it is possible for two people to look so alike.

He thinks of the last few times when Mia came to visit him and her mother. Sometimes, if he'd had enough to drink, he would tell the two women anecdotes from the past, but more often than not there was only a silence heavy as black syrup. During the days that followed he would always feel depressed. All he could think about was the conversation that had not taken place.

She smiles stiffly as she often does when they are together. 'I think the problem is that you no longer tell me stories.'

Years ago, when he came home from the university, he always used to sit down on the yellowwood rocking chair in the kitchen. Then Mia would shyly put out a small hand so that he could pick her up and sit her on his lap. Even though the stories always concerned dogs or monkeys or little bears, they both knew that they were really about their family.

He takes a mouthful of brandy and feels the muscles in his stomach relax. For the first time in years he can feel something inside him loosen up.

'You see, a cat still means a lot to me. Have I ever told you about my mother and the cat?'

She nods. 'Yes, I seem to remember something like it, but I'd like you to tell it to me again.' Her voice sounds almost urgent.

He thinks back to the dark *voorkamer* of his parents' house in Beaufort

West, his mother's bedroom door closed till late every morning. The two white servant girls, Anna and Ria, in whose bedroom he was expected to take his afternoon naps. Even when he was a baby he never slept with his mother.

He wonders where one begins: with the great flood of 1941 when his mother had the deluded impulse to open the doors of the house *Eindelik* for the water to come in? Afterwards nothing was ever the same again. Or with George Arliss, his mother's pet turkey, always strutting in their garden, his wings spread out like those of an angel? Or should he begin with the institution in the city to which his mother was taken when he was in primary school?

He takes another sip of brandy. 'You know, in my youth there was precious little real contact between my mother and me. My mother wasn't really the type to cuddle children.'

As always, he goes a long way back to round up the story. 'She had the comfort of white girls to look after me. Occasionally she took me with her to Krynauw's grocery store in the upper village, or the fruit and vegetable shop in Donkin Street. Sometimes she took me to the Good Hope Café. On Sundays she and my father would have a drink in the lounge and my mother would pour me some lemonade.'

The words stick in his throat. 'My mother was a kind person; she loved me in her own way, but …'

He tries again: 'In those days ladies used to be very restrained in their bodily movements. She never really played with me.'

His daughter nods, as if she already knows the story by heart. 'And the animals?' she asks.

He has told her about the animals before: the cats were always around, the most important of the pets. George Arliss following his mother into the house and attacking the mirror. If *he* didn't go to town with her, George Arliss hitched a ride. Sometimes the turkey stuck its head out of the yellow splintered celluloid rear window to gobble at passers-by.

'There was a kind of bond between my mother and our animals that was quite amazing. It was as if my mother understood them better than …'

He sighs. 'I suppose it makes sense. There's nothing one needs to explain to a dog or a cat or a turkey.'

He does his best to contain his emotion. 'In our house I remember the cats sometimes sleeping on my mother's bed, but in later years she wouldn't allow it any more. She must have started sleeping badly. Some nights she would read until late, and there were nights when she ...'

His daughter nods and he knows there is no need to finish the sentence. She has always been fascinated by her grandmother's story. He isn't sure why he wants to tell her, but he suddenly feels that it is imperative for her to know about his childhood game.

'In the end my father asked the greengrocer to take George Arliss away, because the bird had become an embarrassment to him. As the man bundled the turkey into a bag, my mother fell sobbing into his arms. After that we still had the cats. In those days I never had much to do with them, but one thing I still find difficult to forgive myself for was that one afternoon I took the cats ...'

For a moment he closes his eyes. 'I terrorised the cats. In the cottage at *Eindelik* ...'

He can still see the cottage in the backyard behind the house, the stovepipe he'd set up against the edge of the baby bed where Spotty and her litter lay. One by one he had pulled the kittens from their mother's teats and sent them sliding down the cold stovepipe until they ended up in a mottled, mewing heap at the bottom. He even chucked one of the kittens into the brown toilet water, and then ran off. He still doesn't know whether Spotty managed to save the little one.

He looks down at his hands. 'Boys can be terribly cruel. I never told anyone about it, not before I'd grown up. Gradually your mum taught me about being humane.'

Strangely enough, Mia doesn't look shocked. 'Aren't love and cruelty part of the same thing?' is all she says.

He nods, remembering the time when as a young man he returned to his parents' home in Beaufort West. It was his first weekend pass in the early spring. In Donkin Street the pear trees were blossoming and in the driveway beside their house there was wisteria on the pergola. His mother was standing on the side stoep, a whorl of cigarette smoke in front of her eyes. As always, she was still in her dressing gown. With one hand she held on to a pillar, and her face looked puffy. Even before he could swing the heavy rucksack from his back, he tried to detect whether she'd been drinking.

'Hello, Ma,' he said, climbing up the stairs of the stoep and inhaling the smell of late, sad nights: Gilbey's and Flag cigarettes. He can't say why, but he reached out to her more rudely than usual, his army boots trampling heavily across the green-polished stoep. When he felt her bony fingers in his, he became aware, for the first time, of how much stronger he was than she. He could almost feel her bones crack in his hands.

His mother must have known what he was thinking. She swiftly moved away from him, back into her room. It was only after Mia's birth that he knew his mother had forgiven him.

Mia is still perched on the edge of her chair. In the meantime the kitten has climbed from its basket and jumped on her lap. Its whole body is reverberating with purring.

'As you know, your grandma was a heavy smoker, and the habit was starting to take its toll. She contracted emphysema, which tended to make her short of breath, particularly in winter. In the fall of 1957 she was admitted to hospital, and we realised that we wouldn't be able to pull her through the winter months.'

Mia nods as if she wants him to go faster. 'In that time I received my first invitation to speak at an international conference. This was in Germany, and at first I didn't feel like going, but it came at a decisive moment in my career. Your mum kept on encouraging me. She even offered to spend some time every day with your grandma in the hospital.'

Even so he felt during that July in Germany that he had forsaken his mother. He doubted his abilities as a scientist, wondering if he would ever manage to discuss his work from a foreign podium. He missed his wife, and Mia especially.

He looks straight at her now. 'I remember how, when I left for Germany, your mum was holding you on her hip as she said goodbye to me at the airport. When I left through passport control it was as if a door had slammed shut behind me. It felt as if I was being torn apart.'

He is suddenly finding it difficult to breathe. 'That winter while I was in Germany, my mother's condition gradually worsened. Your mum spent hours in the hospital with her, and often she had to pass her an oxygen mask. The only times when my mother became alive was when your mum read out my letters to her.'

He is having trouble controlling his voice, even though he knows the story so well. 'On Saturday, 19 July, your mum received another letter from me. Your grandma wanted her to read it to her, over and over. After the last time she …

'She went into a coma.'

That evening he couldn't even recall his mother's face any more, she'd become so remote. The talk he was supposed to give at the conference just wouldn't take shape. Like ghosts, the formulas kept whirling through his mind all night.

'In the early evening I walked to the dyke house of a colleague to try to telephone your mum. After a long struggle the telephonist informed us that a cable in the sea had broken and that it would be hours before communication could be restored. I left the house and in a state of total bewilderment I set out on the kilometre to the inn where I stayed.'

He still cannot trust his voice. 'I believed that my mother … I knew she was at her last.'

He remembers the clouds of fog swirling against the dyke in the twilight. At that time he believed they were coming from the south. There was a faint tingle in his ears, a kind of throbbing in his temples. He heard a cat mewing from the same direction where the clouds were coming from.

'On the way to the inn there was a tortoiseshell cat. I called it. She came to me at once and I caressed her.'

He smiles. 'The cat refused to leave me. She kept following me for at least half a kilometre. I only realised that she must have a home to go back to when I reached the inn. I patted her goodbye and closed the front door behind me, but she kept on mewing outside. I opened for her, and she followed me into the front lobby, but then took fright and I put her out again.'

He looks at the kitten, purring and purring on his daughter's lap, as if this action is the most important thing in the world.

'I wanted the cat to follow me to my room, but I saw that she was afraid of the place. I knew it was most unusual for a cat, especially a female, to wander so far from home. It happened three times that I had to let her out. After the third time I was already halfway up the stairs when the cat started crying so desperately that I turned back and took her very tightly in my arms. She abandoned herself to me like a child. In the room I immediately returned to my work, the cat resting on my lap.'

The kitten gets up slowly, sniffs its way to Mia's knees. There it jumps down and aims in his direction.

'Very soon all my anxiety about my mother ebbed away. I kept on working well into the night until I felt satisfied. Around midnight the cat became very busy on my lap. She was wriggling and milling around, taking small, stiff-legged steps and forming high-pitched little sounds in her throat. It was quite a while before she settled down again.'

He looks up at Mia. 'I felt more at peace than ever before. That night, with the cat at my feet, I fell into a deep and dreamless sleep. The next morning the cat was still there. I got up. She stretched herself, calmly jumped on the window sill and went off over the flat roof.'

His daughter has come to sit beside him. She lifts her hand, rests it on his shoulder. 'And then, Daddy?'

'I'm sure you can guess what happened next.'

'The phone. Mum called.'

He nods. 'Your grandma had died … just after midnight.'

He remains silent for a long time, knowing it isn't necessary to go on.

She looks straight at him. The plastic film has disappeared from her eyes.

'The cat,' she says. 'The cat came to bring a message.'

Note: The events in this tale are fictitious, but the account of the cat in Germany is taken from an anecdote by Guillaume Brümmer published in JC Kannemeyer, Langenhoven: 'n Lewe *(Tafelberg, 1995).*

— Translated from the Afrikaans by André Brink

alistair morgan

Living Arrangements

Someone, I don't know who, is living with me in my house. The clues of this person's existence are subtle – a sip of milk here, a slice of bread there – but nonetheless detectable. Such is my concern that I have taken to measuring and weighing some of the items in my fridge before I leave for the office in the mornings. In the evenings, when I return, I weigh and measure the same foods. The evidence is there in plain view: the mature cheddar cheese I keep in a Tupperware tub is considerably lighter; the half-loaf of wholewheat bread is now a quarter-loaf; the level of orange juice has dropped; there is one less apple in the bowl and, even more telling, the roll of toilet paper in the bathroom is noticeably slimmer. All the signs point to the presence of a ghostly parasite in my house.

I have lived a simple life. I never married and have, therefore, at the age of fifty-eight, never had to compromise my domestic realm for a husband, children or grandchildren. It is a neat, pet-free household and any irregularities are easily noticed. My house, which is in a quiet southern suburb of Cape Town, is modest, with two bedrooms (one, actually, as the second is a study-cum-sewing room), a lounge, a kitchen and a bathroom. There is also a small attic, although I haven't been up there in years. The last person who went up through the trapdoor in the passage ceiling was an electrician I had called out to lower the thermostat on the geyser (my little contribution to power-saving). Yes, I know what you're thinking: if anyone is hiding in my house then the attic would be the logical place to start searching.

Well, I have my reasons for believing that this is not likely. First off, I don't own a ladder (as I said to the electrician, the only ladders in this house are the ones in my stockings). It would be difficult, no, impossible, for a person on their own to lift themselves up to and down from the trapdoor, which must be at least twelve feet above the floor. Secondly, the walls and ceiling around the trapdoor are painted white, and any footmarks or dirty handprints would be clearly visible. Finally, there is a latch and a large padlock, which is always locked, keeping the trapdoor firmly closed. So, no, the attic is not under any suspicion for aiding and abetting a hidden person. And I do believe it is the singular – person, not persons – as the amounts of food that go missing are so negligible that I can't see how more than one man or woman could possibly survive on such meagre rations. Unless it's a child.

Once a week a charwoman cleans my house. Her name is Patricia and she has worked for me for nearly twenty years. On the days that Patricia is in the house no food goes astray. I always leave food out for her and not once has she taken so much as a bite out of anything other than what I have put aside. I haven't told her about the phantom resident for fear of alarming her or perhaps giving her the impression that I suspect her of taking the food. Nothing could be further from the truth. It does, however, mean that whoever is in the house must stay in hiding until after Patricia has gone, although I normally return home just as Patricia is leaving, so there's really no opportunity for them to emerge at all on these days. On weekends I am, of course, at home a lot more, although I still go out for a few hours at a time – either to the shops or a movie. And then there's bridge club on Saturday evenings and tennis on Sundays. That leaves plenty of time for my Anne Frank to come out and do some scavenging.

Whether or not this person, my stowaway, actually leaves the house I cannot say. How would they get back in if they did? Although I suppose there is a Yale lock on the kitchen door, which they could easily leave unlatched, and the key for the security gate hangs from a hook on the wall between the door and the sink. I haven't set the alarm in years as I always forget the code, and the security company soon tired of all the false alarms. So it's not exactly Alcatraz.

The situation has remained this way for some weeks now. I have searched in all the rooms and all the cupboards without finding any concrete evidence of my invisible houseguest. At times I've wondered if I am not experiencing the early signs of dementia. Occasionally I have friends over for tea and once or twice I have considered telling them of my suspicions. But something always keeps me from confessing. I fear, perhaps, that if I do speak out then this will all become terrifyingly real. The police will be called. I will be offered places to stay. People will question my ability to live on my own. None of which I want to happen, as you can imagine. Because, you see, the thing is that I find it strangely comforting to know that I am not alone in my house. And I have no reason to fear for my safety, as whoever is in my house has had ample opportunity to do whatever they want to me. No, this person, like any reasonable parasite, realises that to harm me, the host, is to harm themselves.

In the evenings I sit in the lounge and sip my sherry, which fortunately has not been touched by my houseguest. What a relief they're not drinkers! I turn on the radio and gently let the activities of the day replay in my mind. If there is something that I wish to share with my visitor, I do so simply by talking aloud. There is never any form of reply, but I'm sure that I am being heard. I carry on these conversations as I prepare my dinner, and later while I am eating. Afterwards, as I watch TV, I like to comment on the evening news, just as any well-adjusted person would, given what's going on in the world today, never mind what's happening right in our own backyard (the things people do to one another!). In this way, talking aloud, I feel as if I am at least benefiting from the presence of my unseen guest. Once I even caught myself chatting to them as I walked down the aisles of Pick 'n Pay, asking if they felt like meatballs or fish. If only you could have seen the stares!

Now I find myself leaving out sandwiches or leftovers in the mornings.

I cover the plates with a dishcloth and when I come home the food is gone and the plates and utensils have been washed and dried and returned to their respective cupboards and drawers. Even the plates and cups that I used are washed. It's like magic. And I've also come to notice their likes and dislikes. For instance, one evening I saw in the dustbin two slices of bread with horseradish sauce on them. Of course the rare roast beef filling was gone; however, I now make sure never to put horseradish sauce on their sandwiches. But, aside from minor discrepancies like this, I must admit that our experiment in cohabitation seems to work rather well.

I cannot say what has woken me. Normally I sleep right through until my alarm goes off at six-thirty. But the clock says it's only twenty past two. Last night I was abnormally tired. It's been a long week – the law firm where I work as a conveyancing secretary is often more frenetic towards the end of the month – and so I went to bed a little earlier than usual. And now here I lie, wide awake and alert. While my eyes are still getting accustomed to the dark, my ears pick up a faint sound. Soft breathing. It's so faint I have to lift my head off the pillow to make sure it's not the wind moving through the trees outside. No, it's definitely coming from somewhere inside my bedroom. I sit up in bed and cock my head to one side. No doubt about it, I can hear very slow, very peaceful breathing. I turn my head and listen again. I could swear it's coming from under the bed. I feel like laughing. How could it be coming from under my bed? That's something only a child would believe. But I can even hear a slight rattling of mucus in a nasal passage.

I switch on the bedside lamp. The breathing stops almost immediately. Then I lean over and peer into the gap beneath my bed. I see a pile of blankets. Staring right back at me is a small brown face. There is a shrill scream, although I can't say if it originates from the face under the bed or from me. I leap out of bed and scuttle to the corner of my bedroom where I have a green Old Mutual golf umbrella standing against the wall. I hold it in front of me with both hands and swing it from side to side.

'Come out from under there!' I shout in the fiercest voice I can muster. 'Come out or I'll call the police!'

Slowly, like a chrysalis emerging from a cocoon, a scrawny little body crawls out of the blankets under the bed. It's a woman. She pulls herself along the carpet until her whole body is in view. She's clothed in an assortment of old and torn dresses and tracksuits. And then she raises both her hands, palms facing me. We blink at one another for several seconds. She looks confused and disorientated. I can see that her hands are shaking. I'm sure she can see that mine are too.

'Who are you?' I demand of her.

'I am Honorata.' Even though her voice is not much more than a sheepish whisper I can tell that her accent is foreign.

'Where are you from?'

'The DRC,' she murmurs, as if this is something to be ashamed of.

'DRC? The Congo?'

'Yes.'

'What are you doing here in my house?'

A shrug.

'How long have you been sleeping under my bed?'

She stares at me blankly.

The cheek of it! And sleeping inches away from me too! Literally right under my nose! And yet I feel foolish questioning her like this. She knows that I know she has been in my house because I've been leaving food out for her. I've even been talking to her. Have I not therefore condoned her presence in my home up until now? She is right to be confused. I am the one who has reneged on the deal, not her.

We continue to stare at one another until she lowers her gaze and I lower the umbrella. She is crying softly now.

'Okay,' I say to her. 'It's okay. Come on, it's the middle of the night. I'm going to make a proper bed for you on the sofa in the lounge. You can sleep there tonight. In the morning we will discuss what to do. All right?'

She nods and gathers the blankets from under my bed. I get a sheet and a spare pillow and pillowcase from the linen cupboard and try to make as reasonable a bed as I can on the couch. As I lay her blankets down I notice that they smell of the same washing powder and softener that I use. I suppose this should not surprise me. With a gentle 'thank you' Honorata climbs beneath the blankets and turns on her side. She pulls the blankets right up over her nose, so that only her eyes and forehead are exposed. For a moment I wonder if she's expecting a bedtime story. She is, after all, only the size of a child, yet her face looks at least thirty.

Once I'm back in my own bed I cannot sleep. My mind is awhirl with all the possibilities and permutations that now confront me after having come face to face with Honorata. It's a pretty name. Unusual. But perhaps in the DRC it's very common. Eventually I must've fallen asleep because when my alarm clock goes off I'm still in the depths of an incomprehensible dream. I'm not sure why, but I look under my bed before getting up. There's nothing there. So, was this all imagined in my sleep? I put on my slippers and dressing gown and go through to the lounge. Sitting upright on the couch is Honorata. Next to her, neatly folded, are the sheets and blankets, on top of which is the pillow. She looks as uncomfortable as I feel.

'What do you do in the day while I'm out?' I ask her, after making us tea and porridge. I'm sitting next to her on the couch or, rather, her bed.

'I try to find some work.'

'And how do you get in and out? The kitchen door?'

She affirms this with a nod.

'Then you hide away before I get back?'

'Yes.'

'Well, obviously you don't need to hide any more. There's food in the fridge and ... oh, never mind, you know your way around here well enough. I'm going to work now. Tonight we will talk and we will find a solution for our living arrangements.'

I reach for her empty porridge bowl, but she holds on to it.

'I just want to wash it,' I say.

Still she doesn't let go.

'Suit yourself then.'

At the office I am constantly distracted, so much so that one of the senior partners asks if I'm feeling ill after I have to retype a letter three times for him. No, I'm quite fine, I tell him, although it's fair enough to say that I am feeling ill at ease. Things were more straightforward before I met Honorata face to face. It was easier to accept her presence when she was invisible. I don't know why, but that's how it is. I did not have to see her, or hear her, or touch her, or look into her eyes and wonder what they have witnessed. But tonight when I get home she will be there, staring at me forlornly and wondering what I'm planning to do with her. It's all too much responsibility; it really is. And yet I can't just ask her to leave. Where will she go? What will she eat? But then what will Patricia think if she finds out that I have a foreigner living with me, while after twenty years Patricia is still no more than a servant in my house? The situation is simply not tenable.

When I get home Honorata is still on the couch. It looks as if she hasn't moved all day. She cannot raise her eyes to meet mine. And I cannot get out the words I had carefully planned as I sat in the traffic on the M3. Let me first cook her some dinner, I think to myself. At least she can leave on a full stomach. I end up talking to her about my mundane day while I prepare a lamb stew. But it's exactly like before, because she never replies. She stays put in the lounge, on the couch, staring at the carpet.

I set a place for her at the small table in the corner of the lounge. It's so intimate that our knees knock together as we eat. If she doesn't have anything to say at least she has an appetite: she almost licks her plate clean. And I must admit that it's pleasant to have one's cooking appreciated.

After dinner we share the washing up. And then a great wave of tiredness washes over me and I can barely keep my eyes open to watch the news. Honorata and I haven't even discussed what we are going to do about our situation. But perhaps it can wait until the morning when my mind is clearer. And, anyway, what can be done so late at night? I put out a towel and a new toothbrush for her and then excuse myself for the evening. Later I hear her running the bath. It's a comforting sound: warm water splashing as someone stirs it around the tub. And then there's silence as the taps are turned off, and I imagine Honorata lowering herself into the steaming water with a pleasing sigh.

'Goodnight,' I call out, before switching off my light.

Morning comes and still I have no desire to evict Honorata. I make us porridge and again we sit next to one another on the couch to eat it. I'm struck once more by how comforting it is to have someone to share a meal with. It makes me wonder who's feeding off whom. She's not much of a talker, but I can more than make up for her silence. I find myself chattering away about nothing in particular until I realise I'm going to be late for work.

In the evening, on my way back from the office, I stop off at Cavendish Square and buy groceries and, on a whim, a cardigan for Honorata. I think of buying her underwear too, but, no, that might be getting a tad familiar. God knows the woman could do with some more clothes though. I'd give her some of my old ones, but I'm at least two sizes too big for her.

When I arrive home she isn't there. Her bedclothes are carefully piled on the couch, the kitchen is spotless and her towel is hanging on a rail in the bathroom. I pack the groceries away in the kitchen and then remove the price tag from the cardigan before folding it up and leaving it on her pillow. But something doesn't feel right. Everything is far too neat and orderly, the house far too silent. Of course I realise that this is how it always was before Honorata appeared. This is how we have lived up until now. And yet the lack of her presence is disconcerting. Nonsense, I tell myself. Since when have I been so sentimental? I pour myself a sherry and start preparing a dinner of chicken breyani.

Forty-five minutes later it's ready. Still no Honorata. I busy myself by laying the table and opening a bottle of red wine. I'm pretty certain she doesn't care for drink, but so what? I feel like wine tonight. I put the breyani in the warming drawer of the oven and watch the news. Then the weather. Then some over-the-top American nonsense that the world could really do without. I pour another glass of wine. So that was Honorata, I mutter to myself. I take the cardigan I bought for her and hang it up in my cupboard. I'm sure Patricia will appreciate it. Then I dish up a single portion of dried-out breyani and sit down next to Honorata's empty place at the table. I raise my glass of wine in a silent toast. Good luck to her wherever she is now. No hard feelings. It's not like I was expecting a thank-you note or a bunch of flowers as a sign of appreciation or anything. I shovel the breyani into my mouth and wash it down with more wine. And then, still chewing the last mouthful, I go through to the kitchen and start washing up.

I'm just wiping down the counter when I hear the security gate being unlocked. The kitchen door opens and there stands Honorata. I nod at her and continue wiping down the kitchen surfaces. I expect she's wanting her dinner now. But I just carry on cleaning up and then take my glass of wine into the lounge. Well, what does she expect? This isn't a bloody hotel.

I sit staring at the TV without taking any of it in. My glass is empty again. Honorata comes into the lounge and stands at my side. I'm too annoyed to start a conversation with her. She fumbles in her pocket and pulls out a handful of nickel and copper coins. She offers them to me with both hands.

'What is this?' I ask.

Honorata lifts the coins closer to me, as if asking me to smell them.

'But I don't want your money. Where did you get it anyway? Begging? Is that where you've been? Standing at a stop street begging? Look at that money: it's filthy. Put it away and wash your hands. It's quite unnecessary.'

As I say this I raise a hand in order to emphasise my point, but it catches Honorata's hands and the coins go flying all over the carpet. Honorata backs away towards the door.

'Oh look what you've made me do now,' I say, putting down my wine glass and getting on my hands and knees to pick up the coins.

Honorata watches expressionlessly as I crawl around on all fours until I've retrieved every last coin. I give them back to her and then head for the bathroom to wash my hands before going to bed. It takes me a long time to fall asleep. It must be the wine. But it's also a profound feeling of unease that has crept into bed with me and refuses to let my mind wander off into the safety of the subconscious. Disruption, that is what this all is. Utter disruption. Everything was fine before. But now I am made to feel awkward in my own home. This will not do. It will not do at all.

In the morning I leave the house without having breakfast. At work I am a glowing example of efficiency. I keep my conversations with colleagues brisk and to the point. My mind must not be swayed from the tasks at hand. My curtness raises a few eyebrows, but I refuse to be distracted. I work straight through my lunch hour and at precisely five o'clock I leave the office. By five past I'm in the thick of the rush-hour traffic on the M3. Half an hour later I'm home. Honorata is sitting in the lounge watching TV. Before I even put down my bag I deliver my verdict. Honorata listens without taking her eyes off the soap opera on TV.

'We cannot live like this. The only way is if we never see one another. I am going out to a movie now. When I get back I don't want to know that you are here, or that you even exist. If you can do that then we won't have a problem.'

But when I go outside to my car I don't have the slightest inclination to drive to the movies. Instead I sit in the driver's seat with the car keys on my lap. The sun has long since slipped behind the mountain and the daylight is rapidly seeping away. The noises from the exterior world are pleasantly muted inside my car. Even my neighbour's dog's barking is muffled and distant. By pushing the remote button on my car keys I can lock and unlock the car doors automatically. I listen to the reassuring metallic 'clunk' of the locks slotting closed and then open and then closed again. Satisfied that I'm safely locked in, I tilt back the seat and make myself comfortable.

nadine gordimer

The Third Sense

The senses 'usually reckoned as five — sight, hearing, smell, taste, touch.' — OXFORD ENGLISH DICTIONARY

He's the owner of one of the private airlines who have taken up the internal routes between small cities and local areas the national airline, flying at astronomical heights to five continents, hasn't bothered with. Until lately, that is, when their aircraft with full-length sleeper beds and gourmet menus haven't succeeded in cosseting them against falling profits. Now they want to pick up cents on the local routes' discount market, enter into competition with modest craft flitting to unimportant places on home ground.

But that wouldn't have anything to do with this night.

Could have been some other night (Tuesdays he plays squash) if it didn't happen to be when there was a meeting of private airline owners to discuss their protest against the national carrier's intention as a violation of the law of unfair competition, since the great span of the national wings is subsidised by taxpayers' money. She didn't go along to listen in on the meeting because she was behind time with marking papers in media studies from her students in that university department. She was not alone at her desk, their dog lay under it at her feet, a fur-flounced English setter much loved by master and mistress, particularly since their son went off to boarding school. Dina the darling held the vacant place of only child. So intelligent, she even seemed to enjoy music; The Pearl Fishers CD was playing and she wasn't asleep. Well, one mustn't become a dotty dog lover, Dina was probably waiting to catch his footfall at the front door.

It came when the last paper was marked and being shuffled together with the rest, for tomorrow; she got up, stretching as she was instructed at aerobics class, and followed the dog's scramble downstairs.

He was securing the door with its locks and looped chain, safety for their night, and they exchanged, How'd it go, any progress, Oh round in circles again, that bloody lawyer didn't show – but the master didn't have to push down the dog's usual bounding interference when the master came home from anywhere, anytime. Hullo my girl – his expected greeting ignored, no paws landing in response on his shoulders. While he was questioned about the evening and they considered coffee or a drink before bed, you choose, the dog was intently scenting round his shoes. He must have stepped in something. As they went upstairs together, he turning from above her to repeat exasperated remarks about why he was so late, how long the meeting dragged on, the dog pushed past her to impede him, dilated nose rising against his pants' legs. Dina, down! What d'you think you're doing! He slapped the furry rump to make her mount ahead. She stood at the top of the stairs in the hunting dog's point stance, faced at him. Dina'd never been in the field, he was not a hunting man. Some displaced atavistic tic come up in an indulged housepet.

While they undressed they decided for coffee. Dina didn't jump on their bed in customary invitation for them to join her, she was giving concentrated attention to his discarded pants, shirt, shoes. Must be the shoes that perfumed his attraction. Doggy-doo, Eva said, Wait a minute, don't put them on the rug, I'll run the tap over the soles: Michael laughed at the crumple of distaste lifting her nose, her concern for the kelim. In the bathroom, instead, she wet a streamer of the toilet roll, rubbed each sole and flushed the paper down the bowl: although there was no mess clinging to the leather a smell might remain. She propped his shoes to dry, uppers resting against the wall of the shower booth.

When she came back into the bedroom he'd dropped off, asleep, lying in his pyjama pants, the newspaper untidy across his naked chest: opened his eyes with a start.

Still want coffee?

He yawned assent.

Come, Dina. Bedtime.

As a child enjoys a cuddle in the parents' bed before banishment to his own, it was the dog's routine acceptance that she would descend to her basket in the kitchen when the indulgence was declared over. Tonight she wasn't on the bed with master, she got up slowly from where she lay beside a chair, turned her head in some quick last summons to sniff at his clothes lying there, and went down to her place while Eva brewed the coffee.

They drank it side by side in bed. I didn't make it too strong? Looks as if nothing could keep you awake tonight, anyway.

There were disturbed nights, these days, when she would be awakened by the sleepless changed rhythm of the breathing beside her, the inter-rupted beat of the heart of intimacy shared by lovers over their sixteen years. He had put all their funds into his airline. Flight Hadeda (her choice of the name of ibis that flew over the house calling out commandingly). Profits of the real estate business he'd sold; her inheritance from her father's platinum mining interests. Those enterprises of old regime white capitalism were not the way to safe success in a mixed economy – politic-ally correct capitalism. Such enterprises were now anxiously negotiating round affirmative action requirements that this percentage or that of holdings in their companies be reserved for black entrepreneurs with workers becoming token shareholders in stock exchange profits. A small airline, dedicated to solving something of the transport problems of a vast developing country, had patriotic significance. If Michael and his partner are white, the cabin attendants, one of the pilots and an engineer are black.

Isn't it an honest not exploitative initiative on which they've risked every-thing? She knows what keeps him open-eyed, dead-still in the night: if the national airline takes up the homely routes its resources will ground the Everything in loss. Once or twice she has broken the rigid silence intended to spare her; the threat is hers, as well. There is no use to talk about it in the stare of night; she senses that he takes her voice's entry to his thoughts maybe as some sort of reproach: the airline is his venture, way-out, in middle-age.

The coffee cups are on the floor, either side of their bed. She turned on her elbow to kiss him goodnight but he lifted a hand and got up to put on the pyjama jacket. She liked his bare chest near her, the muscles a little thicker – not fat – than they used to be; when you are very tired you feel chilly at night. Climbing back to bed he stretched to close the light above. His sigh of weariness was almost a groan, let him sleep, she did not expect him to turn to her. Let the mutual heart beat quietly. Before moving away for private space they mostly fell asleep in what she called the spoon-and-fork way: she on her side and his body folded along her back, or him on his other side and she curved along his. Of course he was the spoon when enveloping her back in protection from shoulders to thighs, her body was the slighter line of the fork, its light bent tines touching the base of his nape, her breasts nestled under his dorsal muscles. This depended haphazardly on who turned this or that side first, tonight he rolled onto his right, approaching deep sleep giving him a push that way. The gentle impetus reached her to follow, round against him. The softness of breasts in opposition to the male rib cage and spine is one of the wordless questions and answers between men and women. In offended vanity which long survives, she never forgot that once, in early days, he'd remarked as an objective observation, she didn't have really good legs; her breasts were his admiring, lasting discovery. In bantering moods of passion she'd tell him he was a tit man and he would counter with mock regret he hadn't ever had a woman with those ample poster ones on display. In tonight's version of the spoon-and-fork embrace she always had her closed eyes touched against his hair and her nose and lips in the nape of his neck. She liked to breathe there, into him and breathe him in, taking possession he was not conscious of and was yet the essence of them both. These were not the sort of night moments you tell the other, anyway they half-belong to the coming state of sleep, the heightened awareness of things that's called the unconscious. None of his business, secret even from herself that she enters him there as, female, she can't the way he enters her. Or it's just something else; the way you would bury your face in that incredibly innocent sensuous touch and smell of an infant's hollow under the back of its skull. But that's not a memory which persists from the distant infancy of a fifteen-year-old whose voice has broken. She moves her face, herself, into the nape as she does without at first meeting the skin, not to disturb, the touch of the lips to come after the gentlest touch of her breathing there. –

She's sniffing. She's drawing back a little from the hollow smooth and unlined as if it were that of a man of twenty. Comes close again. Scenting. Her nose drawn tight, then nostrils flared to short intakes of whatever. Scenting. She knows their smell, the smell of his skin mingled with what she is, a blend of infusions from the mysterious chemistry of different activities in different parts of their bodies, giving off a flora of flesh juices, the intensity or delicacy of sweat, semen, cosmetics, saliva, salt tears: all become an odour distilled as theirs alone.

Scenting on him the smell of another woman.

She moved carefully out of bed. He was beyond stirring as her warmth left him. She went into the bathroom. Switched on the light above the mirror and forced herself to look at herself. To make sure. It was facing a kind of photography no-one had invented. It wasn't the old confrontation with oneself. There was another woman who occupied the place of that image. Smell her.

She, herself, was half-way down the passage darkness to the bed in the room that served as guest and storeroom when – despising that useless gesture, she went back. In their bed she lay spaced away from where she would allow herself to approach, scenting again what she already had. Rationality attacked: why didn't he shower instead of dozing bare-chested and then climbing into bed. Yes, he'd got up and put on the pyjama jacket; in place of the shower's precaution. He showered when he came home after squash games. Was it really from the squash courts he returned, always, Tuesday nights.

It wasn't that she didn't allow herself to think further; she could not think. A blank. So that it might not begin to fill, she left their bed again as carefully, silently as the first time, and in the bathroom found his bottle of sleeping pills (she never took soporifics, a university lectureship and the take-off and landing of a risky airline enterprise did not share the same 'stress'). She shook out what looked like a plastic globule of golden oil and swallowed it with gulps of tap water cupped in her hand. When she woke from its unfamiliar stun in the morning he was coming from the bathroom shiningly freshly shaved, called, Hullo darling; as he did 'Hullo my girl' in affectionate homecoming, to their dog.

Eva and Michael Tate lived the pattern of the working week, seven days and the next seven days differentiated only by the disruption of Michael's alternations of tentative hopes and anxiety about negotiations with the national airline that might bring not a solution for Flight Hadeda's survival but a bankruptcy as its resolution. 'That's no exaggeration.' He rejected her suggestion that as negotiations were lagging on, this was surely a good sign that the government was at last having doubts. After all their rapping of the private sector over the knuckles for not taking enough responsibility in new ways to develop the infrastructure ... Beginning to listen to the private airlines. 'Government could have just gone ahead and granted licences to the national after that window-dressing democratic first meeting with all of you. Why didn't it? I think it's tip-toeing round a compromise.'

He had pulled his upper and lower lips in over his teeth as if to stop what he didn't want to say.

There were also words she didn't want to say.

She did something out of her anger and disbelief, that disgusted her. But she did it. She called the squash club on a Tuesday night and asked to speak to Michael Tate. The receptionist told her to hold: for her, an admonition not to breathe. The voice came back, Sorry, Mr Tate is not here tonight. 'Sorry' the regret a form of colloquial courtesy personnel are taught.

Eva read in bed and the dog's indulgence, there with her, was extended. Music accompanied them and she did not look at her watch until the dog jumped off and made for the stairs. Michael was back. And early. Down, Dina, down! They were in the bedroom doorway, the dog with paws leapt to his shoulders. Dina's come to accept what she scents as part of the aura, now, of the couple and the house, she does not have to recall the atavism of hunting instincts.

Eva does not remark on the hour. And he doesn't remark that he finds her already gone to bed. Perhaps he isn't aware of her. She's never experienced coming home to one man from another, although she once had a woman friend who said she managed it with some sort of novel pleasure.

'Win or lose?' Eva asked. The old formula response would be in the same light exchange; a mock excuse if he'd been out of form, mock boast if he'd played well – they knew Tuesdays were for keeping fit rather than sport; avoiding the onset of that male pregnancy, a middle-age belly.

'I think I'm getting bored with the club. All my contemporaries working out. Most of us past it.'

She tried to keep to the safe formula. 'So you lost for once!'

He did not answer.

He'd gone to the bathroom; there was the rainfall susurrus – he was taking a shower this time. When he came back she saw him naked; yes, nothing unusual about that, the chest she liked, the stomach with the little fold – no, it's muscle, no, no, not fat – the penis in its sheath of foreskin. But she saw the naked body as she had seen herself in the bathroom mirror that first night when she and the dog scented him.

He spoke, turned from her, getting into pyjamas. 'It looks worse every day. There's a leak that's come to us. Adams knows one of their officials. They've had approved a schedule of the routes they intend to take up. Analysing cost structures if bookings are to be taken only online, cut out the travel agents' levy on passengers.'

'But you can do the same.'

'We can? Travel agents feed us passengers as part of overseas visitors' round-trip tours. We can't afford to ditch them.' He came to the bed.

'Aren't you taking Dina?'

Recalled to where he was from wherever he had been, he put his hands on the dog's head and the two went to the stairs. When he reappeared he got into bed and did not lean for the goodnight kiss. The alternate to his reason for avoidance could be the despairing abstraction: distrait. As Michael turned out their light he spoke aloud but not to her. 'Hadeda's down. Scrap.'

For the first time in sixteen years there was no possibility of one comforting the other in embrace. She said in the dark 'You can't give up.' She didn't know whether this was a statement about Flight Hadeda or a bitter conclusion about where he had been, this and other nights.

They did continue what the new millennium vocabulary terms 'having sex' not making love, from time to time, less often than before. This would be when they had had a night out with friends, drinking a lot of wine, or had stood around at her duty academic celebrations when everyone drank successive vodkas, gins or whiskys to disprove the decorum of academia.

So, it was possible for him to desire her then. Hard to understand. She's always refused to believe the meek sexist acceptance that men's desire is different from women's. When they went through the repertoire of caresses real desire was not present in her body; for her, as it must be for him, desire must belong with another woman.

She was looking for the right moment to come out with it. How to say what there was to be said. The 'Are you having an affair' of soap operas. 'You are having an affair'; restating the obvious. 'You're making love to some woman, even the dog smells her on you.' Away with euphemisms. When to speak? At night? Early in the morning, a breakfast subject? Before Patrick came home for the holidays? What happens when such things are said. Would they both go to work after the breakfast, take their son to the movies, act as if the words hadn't been said, until he was out of the way back at school.

The night before Easter she was taking from the freezer a lamb stew that was to be the last meal together before it was spoken. What she would find the right way to say. When he came home he closed the livingroom door behind him against the entry of the dog and strode over to turn mute the voice of the newscaster on the television.

'I'm shutting up shop. Just a matter of selling the two jets, no-one's going to be stupid enough to buy the licence. Fat hope of that. Adams and I have gone through the figures for the past eighteen months and even if the national thing weren't about to wipe us off it's there – we're flying steadily into loss.'

The brightly miming faces were exchanged on the screen while he said what he had to say.

'But we knew you'd have to rely on our capital for at least two years before you'd get into profit, it's not the same issue as the national one.'

'The competition will make the other irrelevant, that's all. Why wait for that. Sell the planes. Won't make up the loss. The overdraft.'

'It'll be something.'

There were images dwelling on the dead lying somewhere, Afghanistan, Darfur, Iraq.

'For what. To do what.'

He's been a man of ideas, in maturity, with connections, friends in enterprises.

'You'll look around.' That's what he did before, set out to change his life from earthbound real estate to freedom of the sky.

He lifted his spread hands, palm up and let them drop as if they would fall from his wrists while the screen was filled by the giant grin-grimace of a triumphant footballer. 'How are we going to live in the meantime.'

'I don't bring in bread on the corporate scale, oh yes, but there's a good chance I'll be appointed head of the Department with the beginning of the new academic year.'

'It'll just about pay the fees at Patrick's millionaire school.' That school also, had been the father's ambitious mouldbreaking choice for their son; if it was now a matter of reproach, the reproach was for himself, not a sharp reception of her provision of an interim rescue. Despair ravaged his face like the signs of a terminal illness.

She did not say what she had decided was the right time and the right words to say.

She saw he managed to eat a little of the lamb as some sort of acknowledgement of her offer.

Eva recalled that time, the Tuesday when he came home from the woman and said about his fellows at the squash court where he hadn't played with them – Sorry, Mr Tate is not here tonight – he was getting bored with the club, 'All my contemporaries working out. Most of us past it.'

Past it.

Too late. In middle age the schoolboy adventure of Flight Hadeda, even that night in unadmitted faltering, and threatened by the national carrier he had no means to counter. Inside Eva, sometimes softening; the failure accepted, perhaps he had been too tired, stressed's the cover-all word, to make love.

What other way to reassure, restore himself. Not past it; proof of the engendered male power of life, arousal to potency: by another woman.

Eva never confronted Michael with the smell of the woman scented on him. She did not know whether he saw the woman some other time, now that he had given up the Tuesday night squash club; when or whether he had given up the affair. She did not know, nor return by the means she and the dog possessed, for evidence.

anne
landsman

Imprints

Our children were gone for four weeks. The previous Saturday morning, my husband James and I had taken our nine-year-old son, Adam, and his eleven-year-old sister, Tess, to 66th Street, between Broadway and Amsterdam in Manhattan, to the spot where the buses bound for Hidden Valley Camp, Maine, pull up. In a sea of excited children and anxious parents, we had watched the counsellors check our children's names off a list and load them and their trunks onto two separate buses. We had tried to see their faces through the glass, wave one last time before they drove away but they barely noticed us, happily reuniting with old friends.

I felt light as a husk, both free and empty at the same time. In the days that followed, James and I fell into our summer camp routine: lots of movies, dinners out, leisurely breakfasts on the weekends. He's an architect, and has long weekdays filled with job meetings, testy contractors and nervous clients, as July and August are busy months in the construction business. My summer days are more open-ended; I write and I teach and the summers are generally slower, less structured. The city itself is slower, a membrane of humid air cloaking faces, buildings, sidewalks. The streets empty out, even the dogs are enervated, listlessly shuffling behind their owners. The sky grows sullen, and every few blocks you can find a street vendor selling little paper cups of shaved ice, coloured bright yellow, strawberry pink, electric blue, or rainbow.

That July, I couldn't help noticing children wherever I went. Children in strollers with ice cream on their faces, children going off to day camp in Central Park wearing bright-green T-shirts, children in the post office holding their mothers' hands, babies in Snugglies strapped to their fathers' chests, babies in sunhats with chubby, bare legs, toddlers tantrumming in grocery stores, children in the park, on the bus, on the subway trains. Of course I missed my Adam, my Tess, but these children I encountered, and often stared at, were much younger than them. They reminded me of Adam and Tess years ago, in earlier summers. I could still feel the sweaty imprint of the Snuggly's straps on my back, what it felt like to carry a baby against one's chest in the heat. I could still remember how sticky their hands could be, and the cool, perfumed smell of the wipes I used to clean their faces. I remembered that very hot June when Tess was a newborn, and how she was most comfortable lying over my shoulder like a sack of small potatoes. Thinking about those early days of parenthood took me back to Adam's birth, and what it was like to touch the white vernix that he was covered in before the nurse took him away to wash him. I remembered the soft, miraculous feel of it, like nothing I had ever touched before, or have ever touched since.

One steamy afternoon, in this stupor of freedom and longing, I walked over to the library on 100th Street to return overdue library books. On my way out, I noticed a sign pinned up on the noticeboard asking for volunteers to help out at the Claremont Riding Academy in their thera-peutic riding programme. The person to call was Richard Brodie and I found myself writing down his number on a scrap of paper, not quite sure if I was going to follow up or not. 'You're just avoiding rewriting your novel,' I could hear an inner voice scold. But then, another voice, equally compelling, reminded me how close the Claremont Riding Academy was to my heart. It was the last public stable left in Manhattan, a relic from a time when there were scores of them all over the city, housing the horses that lived and worked here. A plaque on the wall proclaimed it a city landmark, and there were special pulleys that lifted hay up from street level to the second floor. The interior was anything but glamorous: a tiny, dishevelled office smelling of horse and cat overlooked a small arena with pillars interrupting the flow of the space. I had watched my horse-loving daughter learn to ride in this awkward, cramped place, my heart in my mouth as she learnt to manoeuvre her horse between the poles and other riders. It was just ten blocks from where we lived and I often found myself walking past the timeworn brick building to watch the horses in the ring, or out on the street on their way to the bridle path in Central Park, just a few blocks away. Claremont was a haven in the midst of the bustling city, a brief glimpse of nature as well as a reminder of a bygone era when there were no cars on the streets.

And then there were the children Richard Brodie described when I spoke to him on the phone that evening. All had disabilities of one kind or another, and were led on horseback by the volunteers, one person at the head, and two on either side of the child in the saddle. He described how valuable it was for them to have this experience, and how it helped them both physically and psychologically. With Tess and Adam away, I had the time and space to reach out, connecting with children who had needs far more complicated than theirs, who encountered obstacles I could barely imagine.

The afternoon I had signed up to volunteer was particularly humid, particularly unpleasant. As always, the stinking piles of rubbish on the sidewalks, the baking tar, the trapped dinginess of a sweltering metropolis were visceral reminders of my earlier summers in South Africa, where the smells were infinitely sweeter, and the sounds of the ocean were never too far away. Over the years away from the scent of fynbos and the sight of Table Mountain's tablecloth, I had learnt to escape the grinding heat by ducking into air-conditioned movies, sipping iced drinks, and succumbing to the general lethargy.

But walking into the Claremont Riding Academy that afternoon was no respite. It was like stepping into a dusty oven. I'd been told to wear long pants and boots and already I could feel the fabric sticking to my legs, my feet soggy in my sturdy hiking boots. The small riding ring – measuring seventy-five by sixty-five feet – was teeming with volunteers. I was shocked at first by how many people there were, but then remembered that it's always like this in New York City. Millions of people live here, and they show up in droves for movies, plays, casting calls, art museums, the annual boat show, the cat show, the St Patrick's Day parade. Why not to volunteer for this most worthwhile of causes? But it did start to resemble a casting call as we waited to get picked to walk with the horses around the ring, each of us wearing a sticker with our name handwritten on it.

The sight and smell of the horses, the plumes of dust rising from their hooves as they gently ambled around the ring, took me back to my own childhood, and my riding lessons on a farm in the shadow of the Brandwacht Mountains with a group of girls and my teacher, Mrs Moffett. Although I didn't take lessons for very long – Mrs Moffett and her family moved to another part of the Boland – the creak of leather and that unmistakable scent of animal kindness had left a lasting impression.

When my name was called, I stepped forward to take my place next to Rigatoni, a chestnut gelding. A boy who had trouble coordinating the movements of his arms and legs was helped into the saddle, and we began our walk around the arena. I was positioned on the boy's right side, my hand loosely gripping one of the saddle flaps in case he lost his balance. The boy was beaming, clearly not bothered by the oppressive heat, the crowds of strangers, the horses who loomed large in this low-ceilinged space with its poles and exposed drainpipes. Three horses were in the ring at once. We made several loops, many of the horses just walking, one or two attempting a slow trot. A partially sighted girl was starting to learn how to post, as the main instructor, a young woman from Australia, cheered her on. I quickly forgot how uncomfortable it was in the heat and the dust. I was completely caught up in the swirl of faces, personalities, nationalities, disabilities, possibilities, as the riders changed places and the three horses in the ring went back upstairs via a ramp, and fresh ones were sent down. The horses were a motley crew – some off the track, some that had been abused, others that moonlighted at the Metropolitan Opera and had appeared in *La Bohème* and *Carmen*. There were Quarter Horses, Paints, ageing thoroughbreds, ponies. The humans were equally diverse, from all sorts of backgrounds, speaking with many different accents. And the children who wobbled above us, their faces lit with joy, were at the centre of it all.

As the afternoon wore on, the crowd of volunteers began to thin. I found myself lingering, not yet ready to leave. Out of the corner of my eye, I saw a dark-haired boy in the office with his mother. Like all the children who had ridden that day, he was going through the process of being fitted for one of Claremont's much used helmets. He must have been ten or eleven, with the smouldering good looks of a boy in a Caravaggio painting. I could see that he was having some trouble, and it looked as if he was resisting trying on the helmets, his hands raised to his ears in protest. Because this was all happening behind glass, it was as if I were watching a child's full-blown tantrum with the sound turned off. I could see concern crossing the Australian instructor's face as she left the ring to join the boy and his mother. It wasn't safe to have a flailing, angry child in the midst of a group of horses, and I could tell she was taking this outburst seriously. The short, heavy woman who had been in my little group leading Rigatoni mentioned that the boy was autistic and non-verbal, and that he'd come to the class before. It was better for him to come later in the day as too many people and too much noise bothered him.

He finally came into the ring, the gentle instructor holding both his arm and his hand, leading him as one would a very nervous horse. His helmet, the chin strap still undone, sat on his head at a rakish angle. His mother, a tall, handsome woman with a broad smile and bright eyes, stood near the entranceway, on the periphery of the circle. An adult – possibly one of the volunteers – attempted to fasten the strap under his chin. It wasn't clear whether the buckle had caught him or whether the sensation of something against his skin was unendurable, but the boy rolled his head to the side and bit the person standing right next to him. I could hear him gnashing his teeth, see his limbs flail with rage. He seemed electrified, as if the helmet were attached to a thousand electrodes. Everything in the arena slowed down, the way I had seen it happen on the rare occasions when a horse threw a rider.

All of us knew that it was important not to frighten the horses, who are prey, not predators, and always act accordingly. Even the person who had been bitten barely moved. The instructor approached the boy again, walking with him, talking to him soothingly. She carefully helped him up onto a palomino. I'm not sure if it was Mozart or Django, Patches, Blossom or Bambi. I had long ago lost track of which was which. The horse stood quietly as the boy ground his teeth and sat awkwardly in the saddle. I had no idea what was going to happen next. Was the boy going to bite the horse? Would the horse buck, rear, or take off with him? Then the boy started to lean towards the horse's ears. I was sure he was going to pitch forward, land in the soft dirt. I was standing on his left side in case he toppled over. The horse began to move, led by the heavy-set woman. The boy slowly laid himself against the horse's long neck, his arms clasping the animal. His body, which had been rigid with alarm, slowly relaxed, and a smile spread across his face. His teeth were white and even, and long lashes shaded his eyes. I walked next to the boy and the horse in awe. As we passed the entranceway where his mother was standing, I caught a glimpse of her face. She was radiant, bursting with pride. The horse ambled slowly, carrying her precious son, who rode with his arms still wrapped around the horse's neck.

After the class ended, I walked home from the Claremont Riding Academy in the waning afternoon light, past the street vendors selling flavoured ices, past dogs and their owners dawdling in the heat, tears blurring my vision. I was crying because I had seen bottomless love on a stranger's face, and I recognised that love. I could still feel the imprints of my own children's hands, the spaces they had hollowed against my collarbone. I still remembered the drape of my daughter's body against my shoulder, and what it felt like to touch the soft vernix pooled beneath my son's eyelids just seconds after he was born. I understood the mother's joy at seeing her son's smile because I had watched my own children with those same eyes, as they took each new step into the world.

I also knew what it was like to feel the wordless comfort of touching an animal – patting a dog, feeling the warm nose of a horse, the silky trail left by a cat winding itself between one's legs. These are the still places, the islands without language, where the beat of another creature's pulse softens us, gentles us, tames us.

liesl
jobson

Nymph

The waiter at Mezzaluna shows you to a rickety seat at a yellowwood table on the uneven stoep. Across the road is a boutique with burglar bars on the windows, wrought-iron curliques, with semicircular rays expanding towards the glass edge. In the middle, the metal curves form a sunrise. A man on a red bench sits in front of the window, obscuring the solar centre of the bars. Where the fiery core should be, he is scratching his stomach.

You're trying to figure why you still tell Jonah he's your blessing, a thing you do out of habit. Or duty. His dithering is no longer endearing: the hesitation at green lights, the backwards and forwards between pot and plate, the way he slows in the passage, preparing an apology for an imagined infraction, some wrong he hasn't done. Once he said, 'I do,' but now it's always, 'I'm sorry. I'm sorry. I'm sorry.'

You used to listen to everything he said, when you still hoped there was a chance that a brain scan would explain things that pills could fix. You'd try to reassure him, but you can no longer endure his half-sentences, the invisible torment. When he speaks in a too low stutter you can't fill in the gaps; you don't try to make sense of it. There was a time you thought he'd get better, but now you snap at him. 'Jonah! Why are you sorry? What have you done?' You can't forgive a non-slight. 'There's nothing to repent for.'

The texture of the beaten metal of the burglar bars takes you back to the blacksmith you interviewed in Hartebeesfontein; back when you worked for a trade magazine. You've forgotten his name now but you remember the heat the day your shutter clicked to capture the smooth welds by his furnace. Such deserted roads you drove to find his small-holding. So far away, you could have been in Australia. All bluegums and dust. No passing cars. Just his dogs. And a hired hand whose name you didn't catch.

Once you were gentle with Jonah, hoping you could help him if you stayed calm and talked nicely. You'd say, 'Ease up, Bean, your brain is just playing tricks.' But you've stopped bothering to soothe; you can't calm him. You've quit saying, 'It's okay,' and, 'Don't worry.' You don't withhold your own affectionate caresses because your body has its own compulsions and your hand seeks out his skin with the inevitability of a compass spin-ning north. You wish your strokes were reciprocated, but they aren't, and you fear that soon you will slip into tenderness with another.

A puppy with a quivering snout slept under the blacksmith's work-bench, unperturbed by the ringing hammers, the hiss of the white-hot metal thrust into cold water. Its huge paws twitched as the bellows of the smith pitched and gasped.

You wanted it all that different day: the humble cottage, the dogs, the wind in the papery leaves that soughed in the heat. You ached for the blacksmith's body, even though he was a stranger. Because he was. You watched the moon, full and lonely in the afternoon sky, wishing you could reach out and pluck it from the emptiness and hold it to your cheek. You took no photo of the moon because your camera would reduce it to a sorry speck, devoid of magic. When it was time to go, you shook hands with the blacksmith, clutching your desire, your yearning kept private.

Later you stared at the photos of his hands, wishing you'd felt the copper bracelet around his wrist. You had photographed the tattoo that ran like a hoof track down the back of his legs, disappearing into the leather sandals that contained his big feet that kept the earth solidly beneath them. Behind his goggles he hadn't noticed where you aimed your lens.

That night you'd said to Jonah, 'Come, Bean, come to bed.' But the sweetness was gone from your voice. You bristled as Jonah slurped his water and gulped his pills. You flinched when he slammed the glass down on the wood. You tethered your mouth while a watermark pooled on the bedside table. If you'd pointed it out, he'd have rubbed at it a hundred times, saying, 'I'm sorry. I'm sorry. I'm sorry.' When he retreated to the bathroom you replaced the glass on the coaster and dried the wood with a tissue.

There's a dress behind the bars of the boutique, a wedding dress, oyster voile with an ivory satin sash, low on the waist. Amber beads circle the neck of the headless dummy, armless and unarmed in the boutique window. In front of the bridal gown, a flapping motion catches your eye, like a trapped bird beating against the cheek of the man on the other side of the street. He holds the paper up to his eyes, reading slowly, mouthing the words.

It's your favourite place, this restaurant with the gold wooden window frames surrounded by wisteria leaves, fresh and green. A through-breeze cools the morning, and the fronds of the winding vines yield, fluttering in the sunlight. It's one place you'll never show Jonah. Its antique gramophones, bay windows and red concrete floor are yours alone. Under the high, pressed ceilings flits a secret you can't share because he will spoil it with apologies.

Last night again you suppressed a sigh even as a scream's pressure rose when Jonah ambled from the bathroom, pinging the floss between his teeth. Your prince has turned froggy and the rising pond-stink permeates your sheets. The once crisp linen is soggy, the air muggy with discontent. Your princess curls have turned into wild witch's locks, and a curse, like a scorpion, blossoms on your tongue.

The man's jeans are crossed at the ankles. His feet twitch as if he is flicking away flies. Ghost flies, because he surely can't feel anything through all his clothing. His hand arcs up his side, under his ribs, down to his hips, scratching, scratching. He inspects his fingernails, scraping each with the opposite nail, one by one. He undoes his buckle. You stare, fascinated, rude. He redoes his belt, tighter, without exposing himself.

The waiter brings a latte, velvet froth curling over the rim. On the red bench the man rolls up his clothing, examining the insides, searching for something. Will he find a brittle label on the seam or a leaf shard stuck in the weave of his vest? A sharp twig?

Although the pavement is shimmering hot, he is wearing several layers. He peels them back, all the clothes he owns: a pale jacket showing the dirt, overshirts, shirts, undershirts. The wrinkled creases on his stomach are visible from across the road. You think about Jonah, who sleeps turned away from you, curled up like a dog. If you leave him, will he come to this?

From his pocket, the man takes the flapping-bird paper and writes on it. He forms each letter with painstaking slowness, as if pricking out sparse syllables of a haiku with a seed husk. If you had a telephoto lens you could capture the poetry of the lines in his face. If you had a telescope, you'd see the nits in his belly hair hatching into nymphs, tan-coloured body lice, smaller than sesame seeds.

The waiter asks what you'll have to eat. You are hungry, but the menu is costly, and you can afford only one latte. You say you're fine; you want water now, no ice. You finger your chipped crown, which is rough to the touch. You wonder how you will pay the dentist.

The waiter crosses the street, hands the old man a hunk of bread, a carton of mageu. You watch as he tears the soft whiteness, with both hands, filling his mouth, open and moist. When he drinks, hungrily and unashamed, you imagine he smells like dry grass and crushed leaves. You guess he tastes bitter like bluegums, sour as the veld. The ground will be even and unyielding beneath your knees when you lie with him in a nest of his vests, under a new moon.

Light years from home, when you start to itch, you'll remember every-thing you've forgotten you still love in your Jonah. You'll thank the old man. You'll tell him he's your blessing.

lauren
beukes

Easy Touch

Dearly beloved

is a good way to start.
     So is:

Hello my friend

Or:

Greetings to you and your family

Or even an exotic:

Salut

In the end, it doesn't matter how you address them. You don't even need a name. They will give you everything. Roll over to show you their bellies like dogs, their tails still wagging. Money talks, you see. It roars like a stadium of soccer fans, drowning out that little voice of doubt.

     Laryea has never had any doubt: people are greedy and stupid; they get what's coming to them. People like Hilda Varone, whose name is printed in big block capitals on his cardboard sign, so she can't miss him in the clog of people waiting in the arrivals hall of OR Tambo International. Not that she could miss him anyway. He is a big man, more fat than muscle these days, if he is honest, but still good-looking, in a button-up shirt and chinos and a flattop you could stand a glass on.

He knows from experience that Hilda will be feeling anxious, that all those hours and hours on a plane from Mexico City via New York will have given her too much time to think. And it's her first time without Oscar. In these kinds of circumstances, it's important to stick to routine. People like routine. It makes the world seem safe and predictable.

The glass doors to baggage claim glide open and spit out a flurry of people armed with suitcases and backpacks and wheelie carry-ons. Hilda looks rumpled and tired, dragging her big grey suitcase with the dodgy wheel that veers out capriciously. He has chosen a spot right in front of the doors, but her eyes skid over him and his neatly lettered sign, searching the crowd as if she is expecting someone else.

He's always thought of her as roly-poly but she's lost weight since he last saw her. Now, she's just poly, a short, compact package of a woman with over-plucked brows and a frizz of dark hair that doesn't like being told what to do. Much like Hilda herself.

Laryea has always found Oscar easier to deal with. For an ambulance driver, Oscar is a meek man, as if all the shout has been drained out of him by the yawl of the sirens as he navigates the sprawl of Mexico City with his arthritic hands clamped on the wheel, wishing for power steering. He should retire, but how can he, considering the circumstances?

The couple has been to Johannesburg three times since they first made contact eighteen months ago. But Oscar opted to stay home in sunny Me-hi-co this time round. It gets expensive, all these flights, all these meetings, all the administration. Supposedly, this is the last trip. A mere formality and it will all be done.

Laryea knows better.

'Ms Varone!' he calls out to Hilda. 'Over here.'

'Laryea,' she says, noticing him at last, but she sounds less than thrilled.

Jet lag is a bitch. He moves forward to welcome her with a kiss on both cheeks.

'You still dragging this old thing around?' he says, taking the suitcase from her. 'Don't worry, soon you'll be able to afford Louis Vuitton. A matching set for you and Oscar!'

'I think we have *más importante* things to spend the money on, no?' she says, sharply.

'Of course. Forgive me, *señora*. How *is* Gael?'

'The same,' she says, bleakly.

Life can change in an instant. One moment your six-year-old son is stepping out of a bodega, the next he is on his back under a car, with the axle pressing down on his stomach, crushing his spine, his spleen, his pelvis, so the doctors say he will probably never walk again. A burst tyre. A freak accident.

It's not that Laryea doesn't feel sorry for Hilda and Oscar. But the world is full of tragedy.

PLEASE HELP TSUNAMI VICTIMS!

THE RED CROSS INTERNATIONAL AMSTERDAM, THE NETHERLANDS ZONE (B) HEREBY APPEALLING TO YOU FRIENDS,PUBLIC,FAMILIES AND COMPANIES, TO HELP US WITH ONLINE FUND RAISING TO ENABLE US TREAT OVER 1.5 MILLION CHILDREN AFFECTED WITH QUAKE/TSUNAMI DESASTER ACROSS ASIA.VISIT WWW.CNN.COM/ TSUNAMI TO SEE WHY YOUR HELP/MONEY IS HIGHLY NEEDED.

HELP THE NEEDY,POOR AND SICK,NO AMOUNT IS SMALL FOR GOD LOVES A CHEERFULL GIVER.

Hilda is quiet on the drive to the restaurant. But the question still lurks in the tension of her shoulders, the clench of her jaw. *When?*

'You have to be patient,' Laryea soothes her. 'These things take time.'

'These things take time. These things take time,' she parrots angrily. 'This is what you always say, Laryea.'

He imagines her telling off her water-cooler clients in the same tone, more fluently perhaps in her native Spanish, but no less bolshy. He imagines entire office complexes living in fear of Hilda Varone, employees willing to risk drinking Mexico City tap water rather than face her wrath.

'This is the way Third World governments work,' he says. 'This is what makes it all possible. You know that. Your mother—'

'Leave my *mamá* alone.' She glares out the windscreen at the hawkers selling superglue at the traffic lights.

'You know what I'm saying, Hilda, if Pinochet hadn't—'

'I said to leave it. It was different in Chile. There was none of this … *lawyers.*' She spits the word out.

'Of course not. She didn't have time to set anything up when she fled the country.'

'She leaves everything. Just pack up and go.'

'Imagine if she had managed to hide her money away before she left; how hard it would be to get it out of the country? This is par for the course. You shouldn't expect it to be easy. Have patience, *señora*. This is the last time, I promise.'

He suspects it will have to be. They have taken her for $47 453 so far and he can't see how they will squeeze any more juice from her.

The secret is in not using round numbers. Round numbers are too much like a bribe, a ransom. All those gaping zeros like holes in a story. To short-circuit suspicion you need the kind of numbers beloved by bureaucrats and auditors. Numbers that suggest 14 per cent tax or built-in administration charges or adjustments for the exchange rate. Official numbers. Numbers that can keep clicking up, because there is always another cost, another agency fee, another unforeseen surcharge.

'I can't do this again,' she says, staring out the window as if the sweep of trees lining Jan Smuts Avenue requires her fullest concentration. '*No puedo más.*' Laryea pretends not to notice her dabbing angrily at her eyes.

'The last time. I promise. Mr Shaik is waiting for us at the restaurant. In half an hour, less, the last of the paperwork will be signed and sealed. If you want, we don't even have to check in to the hotel. You can get straight back on the plane and go home to Oscar and Gael. *Si?*'

'Yes, okay,' she sniffles. 'But this Mr Shaik is corrupt. I read the news-papers.'

'Do you know a lawyer who isn't? And his corruption, *señora*, is what we are counting on.'

It is a fact that names in the news have more credibility.

I know that this mail might come to you as a surprise as we have not met before, My name is Mrs. Grace Mugabe, the wife of Mr. Robert Mugabe the president of Zimbabwe. Our country is currently facing international saction all over the world and my effort to so speak peace into my husband prove abortive because he already have a wrong notion towards the western nations.

As the first lady of our country i have been able to use my position to raise some money from contracts which i deposited with a European diplomatic security company the sum of US$35M(Thirty Five Million US Dollars) knowing fully that our government will soon be brought down by international communities because of the manner at which things are degenerating in Zimbabwe.

I contacting you because I want you to go to the security company and claim the money on my behalf. I ask you to also pray for me to survive the internal threat i am experincing from my husband President Robert Mugabe because as i am sending you this urgent proposal tears flow from my eyes as i am living with a human monster.

Laryea is *not* a monster. He is a student of human behaviour. He admires Oscar and Hilda's fortitude. They are not without their resources. They borrowed that money from family and friends. They could have used it to fly Gael to a private hospital in America. It would have paid for the specialist spinal surgery at least. Instead they've given it to Laryea's syndicate. Is it the syndicate's fault that the couple is so naive and greedy as to believe a fairy tale about $12.5 million?

It helps that the fairy tales are set in countries too far away to be able to check up on the details. It helps more that Laryea's format, his bait, is grammatical, with none of the gross spelling mistakes or lazy typos endemic to the genre.

> First my Father was a king in our village before he died and left
> behind some Gold as the King of our town that God bless with Gold,
> he was enntitle to some quantity every end of the Month this was
> the way he acquired the quantities of Gold the family is having
> today. the only thing i want from you is either you buy the Gold from
> me or you help me for shipment of the gold to your destination and
> sell it on my behalf and get your own percentage.

No, Laryea's English is excellent. He has a talent for languages, a way with words. It's why he was bumped up from catcher to guyman. Now, instead of fielding emails, he does fieldwork. He deals with actual clients, in person, face to face. This is not why his mother worked sixteen hours a day as a post-office administrator to pay for his university education. Still, he has been able to put his political science degree to some practical use. Current affairs make for topical lures. So do Hollywood movies.

> My name is Captain Andrew McAllister; I am an American Soldier
> and serving in the US Military in the 3rd Armored Cavalry Regiments,
> Patrols Tail Afar, in Iraq. I am desperately in need of assistance and
> I have summoned up courage to contact you. I am presently in
> Iraq and I found your contact particulars in an address journal. I
> am seeking your assistance to evacuate the sum of $1,570,000
> (One million Five Hundred and Seventy Thousand US dollars) to the
> States or any safe country of your choice, as far as I can be assured
> that it will be safe in your care until I complete my service here. This
> is no stolen money and there are no dangers involved.

Better that he had become a journalist. Like the photographer he had assisted in Ghana in 2005. Since then, he has seen his name around a lot, that photographer. He keeps an eye out for it, in the newspapers, sometimes on the cover of fancy art magazines. While he was waiting for a client in the lobby of the Sandton Sun once, Laryea picked up a flyer for the photographer's new exhibition. His photographs were selling for R20 000 each. Easy money. Fame. And for what? Pointing and clicking? Now *that's* a scam.

The Zoo Lake Restaurant is a tourist destination, which means, Laryea supposes, that tourists don't have to *destine* any further north. It's just enough, a taste of the real Africa, diluted, exaggerated. A glamorous movie-land of ornate masks and hanging lamps of dyed leather and food tamed for feeble western palates.

'Did I ever tell you about the bees?' he asks, as he pulls out Hilda's chair for her. It's a signature story in his repertoire. He uses patter to set clients at ease, to make them feel like they're bonding. You aren't supposed to use real stories, in case you reveal yourself in the details. But Laryea would take a bet, any amount you like, that the famous photographer doesn't remember his name, let alone know how to find him.

'The bees? No. I do not think so. Is Mr Shaik coming *pronto*?' Hilda looks anxiously around the restaurant.

'He'll be here any minute, just relax. Have a glass of wine. The food here is excellent. Really authentic.'

'You know I have trusted you all this while, Laryea.'

'I know, Hilda.'

He has arranged a happy ending for her. Or the semblance of one. In return for the last outstanding $6 572, which is the absolute limit of her gullibility he reckons, she will receive 108 pages of paperwork from Mr Shaik, filed in triplicate and stamped by the Reserve Bank as evidence of the transfer to her account in Mexico City.

She will have about a week to enjoy the idea of her wealth before she realises that it is all fake, that the money has not been deposited, that it never will be. But by that time she will be 10 000 kilometres away and Laryea will have switched to a new cellphone number, a new email address. It could be worse. Ask the Swedish businessman who was kidnapped last year. Or the Greek who was murdered …

Laryea has always thought of the syndicate like a swarm on the move.

If the queen dies, you make a new queen; if a worker bee dies, you replace it with another drone. Their business is decentralised. Untouchable. The hive will always survive. And honey is one of the best ways to catch *mugus* of course.

> Hi my friend,
> it's nice and lovely for me to mail you and, I thank God that I find you, Am kristinacain female, 24 years of age and i am from USA ... I will like us to be friends because friendship is like a clothes, without clothes one is naked and without friends one is lonely and to avoid loneliness we all need friends, i guess i am right?
> Kristina

Romance scams always seemed too cruel to Laryea – and too much trouble. Like catching a shark; they're easy to hook but a struggle to reel in. Besides, there is too much typing involved with all the instant messages and emails that stand in for passion these days.

Laryea takes a sip of wine – Warwick Trilogy 2006, because he likes to indulge his clients in these final meetings. He likes to think it is an act of grace, although he notes with irritation that Hilda has barely touched hers. She is fiddling with her fork, tapping it nervously on the edge of the table. Rat-tat. Rat-tat. The restaurant is filling up, conversation and the clatter of cutlery relegating the Senegalese gospel album that has been on repeat since they sat down to ambient noise.

'Now, this story,' he says, trying to recapture her attention. 'It's more about honey collectors than bees, really. I was working with a photographer, a famous one, you might have heard of him—'

'Was this before or after you work in Burger King?'

He had forgotten he'd told her about that. Why had he told her about that? About exactly where a political science degree will get a young man with big dreams and no work permit; not to *The Economist*, but the Burger King at Paddington Station, lost like the storybook bear with his red Wellington boots.

'Before,' he says, trying to recover himself. 'The photographer, he did these hyena photographs. You might have seen them?'

'No.' She fishes a battered soft pack of smokes from the bowels of her bag and distractedly taps out a cigarette. Laryea pinches it from her lips before she can light it.

'We're in the non-smoking section,' he says, laying the cigarette on the table perfectly parallel to the woven place mat. Her mouth twists into a stony pout in its absence.

'Anyway, I was translating for him.' This part is a lie. He was carrying the photographer's equipment, all the lights and battery packs and loops of cable. It was only when the real translator, an environmental journalist for the UN, fell ill with gastro-enteritis that Laryea had stepped in to untangle the local dialect.

'It was about an hour and a half from Techiman, where the jungle runs right up to the highway, like it's trying to swallow up the road. The whole town was three houses. *Mashambas*, you know, like mud huts? Maybe forty or fifty people living there, women pounding cassava or sitting with blankets spread out on the ground selling soft drinks, fruit, loose cigarettes, warm beer and gin. They call it gin, but it's actually liquor they make themselves in Coca-Cola bottles.'

'We have towns like this in Mexico.'

'Maybe not quite like this, but close enough I'm sure. So the women sell basic stuff and pound cassava and the men collect honey.'

'Mmf,' Hilda says.

'No, but it's terrible, just listen. The way they do it. These are African bees. And African bees are crazy. *Loco*.'

'I know what crazy is.'

'They're incredibly aggressive. They'll attack at the slightest provocation. So what these guys do is they smoke them out. They spend hours going through the jungle, sometimes days, trying to find the hives and, when they do, they tie cassava leaves and plastic bags around their heads and hands, because insects don't like the smell, and then they set fire to the bush around the tree.'

'And then the bees fly away and they get the honey.' Hilda is less than impressed.

'The point is that it's a disaster. They burn down half the forest in the process – and they ruin the honey. The smoke gets into everything.'

'You can see this in the honey, *acaso*?'

'That golden glow? Poof!' He kisses off his fingertips. 'Gone. It still tastes sweet, but it's dusty with soot. So, they can only sell it on the local markets. It's an economic tragedy. If they had hives, if they learnt how to cultivate the honey, they could sell it internationally. Organic, fair trade, all that stuff, they could make real money. But instead they're trapped in this subsistence life, burning down the forest, destroying the trees where the bees make their hives, so every time they have to travel deeper into the jungle.'

'This is very sad. But it is like this everywhere, no? All over the world there is *tragedia*. Refugees. Economics. Earthquakes. *Genocides*.' Hilda fiddles with the cigarette, puts it down, exchanges it for the fork. Rat-tat. Rat-tat.

'I'm not comparing it,' Laryea says. 'Not with what happened to *our friend*.' But he doesn't like the echoing of his own thoughts so recently. How does he explain that he was moved by the poignancy of the story, this self-defeating cycle, like a microcosm of the futility of humanity?

The reality is that Laryea is as much a *mugu* to false promises as Hilda, carried on his worthless degree and a British Airways flight to London, only to end up washing dishes in a Lebanese restaurant in King's Cross, flipping patties at Burger King, cleaning the public toilets at an outdoor rock festival. He knows disappointment. It is the reek of shit and teenage vomit in a plastic Portaloo on an August afternoon with distorted guitars buzzing like sick bees in the background.

He was made an offer to move to Johannesburg. He took it. And dealing in dreams seemed easier than drugs.

Need extra INCOME! Become our [MYSTERY SHOPPER]: Earn [NO LESS THAN $500.00] Per Venture: It is Very Easy and Very Simple: No Application fees: Mystery shoppers are Needed Throughout

America Great Pay. Fun Work. Flexible Schedules.No experience
required. If you can shop-you are qualified!

    A mystery shopper is like being 007 at the mall. Mystery shoppers
must complete their assignments and go un-detected. You do not
have to use any money from your pockets. So We will provide you
the money for all your assignments.

The waitress comes over to the table to let them know that their friend
has arrived. 'He's just on the phone. He said he'll be with you in a minute.'
She indicates to a tall man in a crisp dark suit with a cellphone clamped
to the side of his head, pacing up and down in the foyer and talking
loudly in Algerian French. Another deal on the go. Another *mugu* biting.

This is a business proposition. I represent an independent
investment consultancy and brokerage. We have recently been
asked to invest funds outside Scotland and have decided to seek
partners outside Scotland to cooperate with us in investing the
available funds.

'He doesn't look like his *foto* in the newspapers,' Hilda says, staring at the
man across the restaurant. 'And I heard he was sick.'

'You must have him confused with someone else,' Laryea reassures her.

Hilda abruptly stops fidgeting with the fork. She drapes her arm over
the back of the chair, and takes a deep swig of her wine, which is no way
to appreciate a good vintage. But it's as if the question mark knotting up
the muscles in her neck and shoulders has dissolved away like Disprin.

'You know, Laryea, I like your story very much. Now, I want to tell
you a story.'

'Don't you want to wait for Mr Shaik?'

'This is personal. Just for you.'

'All right,' he says, intrigued.

'I know you think I am stupid.'

'Hilda! I've never thought that for a moment.'

'Because my English is not so good, you think that means I cannot think so well. But this is not true.'

'Of course not. I'm hurt that you would even say—'

'Will you listen? You know why I have ask you here? To this restaurant?'

'Because of the ostrich. You said you wanted to try the ostrich.'

'I had a phone call. From the police.'

Laryea pushes his chair away from the table.

'Sit down. It is too late.'

In the foyer, two men approach Mr Shaik, who is really Mr Dansua, and politely but firmly remove his phone from his hand and wrest his hands behind his back.

You have won 450,000 GBP from Nokia Promotion. Please contact our agent Mr Mark Cole;
Regards
Nokia Staff
Nokia Online End of Year Lottery Promotion

There are three more men in plain clothes crossing the restaurant towards their table. Laryea saw one of them in the gift shop on the way in, even noted the slovenliness of his clothes, ill-fitting, creased, like the man had more important things to do than ironing.

'The police?' Laryea laughs uncertainly.

'I thought you were trying to help us.'

'I was. I am.'

LET US DO A GOOD WORK AND HELP THE LIVES OF THE SUFFERING, MY NAME IS Dr. Kenneth Dickson FROM NEW ZEALAND. RECENTLY MY DOCTOR GAVE ME VERY BAD NEWS WHICH IS VERY DISTURBING TO MY EARS, HE SAID THAT IN ABOUT THREE MONTHS TIME THAT I WILL SOON DIE OF MY ILLNESS. I HAVE SURRENDERED MY LIFE TO GOD AND I AM NOW A BORN AGAIN, I WANT TO DO A GOOD DEED BEFORE I DEPART. I WILL WANT TO SET UP

ORPHANAGES IN MY NAME AND ALSO DONATE THE REST OF MY
WEALTH TO THE MISSIONARY OR CHARITABLE ORGANIZATIONS.

'Come on, *señora*. I don't know what kind of lies they have been telling
you, but we can sort this out.'

'You are the one with the lies, Laryea. But this is not the story I want
to tell you.'

'Then what?'

'I lied also.'

'You?' He is trying to understand, but it is like struggling through thick
and scratchy jungle to find the road he was walking only a minute ago.

'There is no Gael. No cripple son. No accident.' Hilda grins, revealing
the skew incisor that Laryea has always found somehow endearing. It is
the first time she's smiled since she stepped off the plane.

'Then you knew? From the beginning? This has been a set-up for ...'
– his head reels, like a hit of nicotine – '... for eighteen months?'

'No. The police, they only contact me now, while we are still in
Mexico. It is terrible shock. We are very angry with you. And that's why
I fly out. To make sure you get what you deserve, *cabrón*.'

I must use this opportunity to implore you to exercise the utmost
indulgence to keep this matter extraordinarily confidential whatever
your decision, as you stand as my only family today.

'But I've seen photographs.' Of a boy strapped to a plastic board, his little
face swollen up like a meaty red and purple flower with a stamen of
plastic tubes sprouting from his nose.

'And *I* have seen papers that show you are going to pay us. Tax cer-
tificates. Letters from the bank.' She shrugs. 'My husband has access to the
children's wards. We have a camera.'

I want you to have it in mind that this transaction is 100% hitch free.

'You're saying you invented Gael? The surgery in America? But what
about Dr Edwards? Dr Friedman?'

'I say you are not the only one, Laryea. We make up Gael so you will feel sorry for us. So you will give us *el dinero* – the money – instead of someone else. But I will not tell this to your police or the judge. They will think Gael is real. That you defraud us, the poor parents of a broken little boy. They will not check. Mexico is so far away. And you will suffer for this. You will suffer *mucho*.'

> Write back as soon as possible any delay in your reply will give me room in sourcing another person for this same purpose. God bless you as you listing to the voice of Reasoning.

Laryea has never felt any doubt. Never felt any guilt. But now, as the police cross the restaurant towards their table, guns held low at their sides, an SAPS badge held before them, opening a pathway between the tables like Moses, he can see that he has lost his golden glow. His honey is tainted, has turned, in fact, to shit.

And the forest is burning down around him.

Note: The author would like to thank Pieter Hugo for sharing his honey-collectors anecdote (photographs at www.pieterhugo.com) and especially the 419 scammers who emailed her their contributions. Scammers can contact the publisher directly for a share of the royalties, although please be advised that there may be a small administration fee involved.

michiel heyns

Long Perspectives

'Oh well,
I suppose it's not the place's fault,' I said.
'Nothing, like something, happens anywhere.'
— PHILIP LARKIN, 'I REMEMBER, I REMEMBER'

'If Larkin was right, and nothing, like something, happens anywhere,' I said, 'this is where my nothing happened.' I gestured over the dusty town huddling in its bowl of scrubby hills, its little cathedral asserting its puny prick of a spire against the wide African sky. The bland light of a winter's morning was marked with a thin drift of smoke over Fingo Village.

'Nothing?' asked Adrian sceptically. 'How long did you spend here?'

'Long enough for something to have happened if it was going to. The last five years of school and, after that, university holidays.'

'The last five years of school and nothing happened?' Adrian persisted. 'The transition from childhood to manhood? Sexual awakening?'

'Oh, I was sexually awake all right,' I said. 'It's just that nobody seemed to notice.'

Adrian and I were standing on Gunfire Hill, in front of the Settler's Monu-
ment, a stranded hulk of cultural presumption overlooking Grahamstown.
We had stayed on, after an academic conference on Romanticism and
Memory, for the Grahamstown Festival.

'To an eye not jaundiced by an uneventful puberty, it's actually an
attractive little town,' Adrian remarked.

'I'm sure it is,' I replied. 'I have only my jaundiced eye to inform me.
I think I hate the place.'

'*Something* must have happened here to make you hate it.'

'No, just nothing. I'll take you up to my old school tomorrow.' I
pointed at the school building squatting on a nearby hill, an unignorable
gesture of Afrikaner triumphalism. 'That's where the festival jazz venue
is. That's one change, at least: in my day, jazz or anything else smacking
of subversive multiculturalism wouldn't have been tolerated anywhere near
the school. But let's go and get tickets. I don't want to bore you with my
forgotten boredom.'

'On the contrary, I'm fascinated,' Adrian said, as we strolled past the
buskers and beggars and vendors and food-poisoning outlets and parking
attendants and shrill school groups and bleary-eyed students to the ticket
office inside the monument complex. 'I'm pleased that I'll be there to
witness your return to the laager.'

'It literally is a laager, isn't it?' I replied. 'Up on that hill.'

'Maybe,' Adrian said. 'I'm less interested in what the place is or isn't
than in your response, which strikes me as very unresolved.'

'I'm flattered by your interest,' I said, 'but I'm afraid you're going to
be disappointed. The place just leaves me cold.'

'No man is left cold by his own youth. That's what Wordsworth meant
– you know, the child being father of the man, bound each to each by
natural piety, all that.'

'You forget that I refuted that sentimental notion in my paper,' I said,
as we joined the ticket queue. I had delivered a paper arguing that the
Romantic concept of memory as master-light of all our seeing was no
longer useful in a time of a truth commission. Adrian, on the other hand,
had mounted a spirited case for a reading of Philip Larkin as a disappointed

Romantic; I privately suspected that this was more Adrian's case than Larkin's.

'I'll get back to you on that over supper,' Adrian said. 'Have we decided what to book for?'

'I think so. You happy with *King Lear* tomorrow afternoon and the African Jazz Pioneers in the evening?'

'Sounds like a good balance to me.'

'And the following evening—'

'I won't be here, remember.'

'Yes, I remember. I was planning my own programme. I think I'll go for more jazz. There's Tu Nokwe … you know anything about her?'

'Nothing, except that she's from KwaZulu-Natal and has a huge following. She should be good.'

'I like the idea of Zulus inside the laager,' I said. 'I have to be there.'

'What will it be, sir?' the young man behind the computer enquired brightly, and I reflected again on how unconsciously patronising the politeness of the young could be.

It was a bright, chilly night as we emerged from the charged fug of the Jazz Pioneers. I was pleased I had brought my down-filled jacket, a relic from a conference in midwinter Toronto.

'Wonderful, eh?' asked Adrian. 'I mean the music.'

'Absolutely,' I said. 'And wonderful that the African Jazz Pioneers should perform here, inside the holy of holies.' I pointed with my chin at the Johannes Schoeman Hall, donated and built by and named for a local builder who had made a fortune out of inflicting sixties face-brick designs on the sober nineteenth-century stone and whitewash of Grahamstown. 'This is where we had scripture and prayers and *skoollied* and *volkslied* and harangues on Monday mornings.' I shivered, in spite of my down-filled jacket. It was always a few degrees colder up here than down in the town. 'Shall we go and find a drink?' I asked.

'Not before you've been back inside.' Adrian pointed towards the school building proper, perched against the hill to one side of the hall.

'What's it to you?' I asked, though I was pleased that he should find my past so compelling.

'Nothing,' he said, 'except that I think it's an event if somebody comes back to his school for the first time in twenty years. You're not going to tell me it does nothing for you.'

'You want to watch me having an emotion? What sort of voyeurism is this?'

'We've just sat through three days of papers on memory. I want to see what the real thing looks like.'

'Don't expect anything,' I said. 'A memory of nothing remains a nothing. But I *am* quite curious to see if the place has changed – if we can get in. It's probably locked.'

But I was wrong. The school was being used to house some hardy student groups from upcountry for the festival, and the classrooms were harshly fluorescent to the standards of the Cape Education Department. We wandered through the dark corridors, lit only by the light from the tarmac playground outside and from the skylights of the inhabited classrooms. As far as I could judge in the blue neon glow, nothing had changed. 'It is now as it hath been of yore,' I declaimed, and Adrian grimaced at my misquotation.

In the corridor leading to the matric classroom I paused. 'There used to be some photographs here,' I said. I had forgotten this: it came back to me with the smell of chalk and stale sandwiches which even the long winter holiday had not been able to dispel. 'The light switch is over there next to you.'

Adrian found it and after a couple of flickers the corridor sprang into stark illumination.

'Here they are,' I said, pointing at a row of framed group photographs on the wall, by now considerably more numerous than in my day. 'Afrikaner youth through the ages.'

'Blindingly undiminished,' Adrian said. 'Hey! Here you are: *Matriekklas 1974.*'

I took off my glasses to inspect the photograph. 'There I am indeed. God, wasn't I a weed?'

'You were thin, certainly. But quite soulful-looking.'

'Oh, I had soul enough. Not much body though.'

'At least you were tall. Can't say your female classmates were much to look at. No wonder you switched.'

'Oh, I never switched. I preferred boys all along. I had the hots for Bennie van der Merwe – there he is, sitting on the floor. He was our lodger for a year after his parents moved away.'

'So did you at least have some boyish fumblings with Bennie?'

'No. Stop slavering for sensational confessions. I told you nothing happened to me in Grahamstown. He had a lovely little body, though – look, here he is in the first rugby team, you can see his neat little legs.'

Solemnly swathed in scarves, booted and blazered, the First Rugby Team glowered at us across the years.

'Bennie was Victor Ludorum in matric,' I continued. 'He was so completely straight he didn't even suspect I had the hots for him.'

'You don't now think of it as a neglected chance?'

'No, I mean, just look at him: have you ever seen a straighter-looking person?'

There, in the courtyard outside, twenty years earlier, Bennie had faced the camera in the harsh November light, forcing a crooked smile, his fringe carefully arranged to flop rakishly over his left eye. I remembered teasing him as he prepared for the photograph in the mirror in the boys' dressing room: 'You think it's going to matter to anyone what your fringe looks like?' And he'd said, 'It matters to me.'

'I don't know,' Adrian interrupted my recollections. 'You look quite straight yourself. I mean in the photograph.'

'Thanks for the qualification. It was more than your life was worth not to look straight. God, the one thing this bloody school taught me was to dissemble.'

'And what happened to Bennie?'

'I don't know. He went to the University of Pretoria on a sporting bursary. I had one letter from him in which he enthused about the beauty and availability of the women at university. I didn't reply, and we lost touch.'

A young man appeared out of one of the classrooms and looked at us curiously: two middle-aged men peering at old photographs in the middle of the night.

'He was at school here,' Adrian explained. 'He's in these photos.'

'Izzatso?' said the young man, not interested. He handed us a leaflet advertising a student production of something called *The Electric Meat Puppet Rebellion*. 'Come and see our show.'

'Sure,' said Adrian, 'sounds like just our gig.'

The young man, looking unconvinced, went back into the classroom and said, 'Two old *ballies* looking at the photies.'

'There,' I said, 'we've done our bit for natural piety. We are not suited to the long perspectives, as your man Larkin would say. Let's go and find a drink.' I put on my glasses.

For another second or two I met the still-familiar gazes of twenty years ago, not quite for ever panting and for ever young – the stock of the school's photographic club was too bad for that – but confidently peering into the future, ignorant of their own fading; and then Adrian snapped off the light.

The following morning Adrian duly left for Johannesburg, where he lectured. I had not booked for any festival events in the morning, and allowed myself the luxury of wandering around without any particular destination or plan. I strolled down the main thoroughfare, Beaufort Street. Even the festival crowd couldn't lighten the place's air of fusty respectability, genteel overlay to the dismal poverty of the majority of inhabitants. On the corner of Glanville and Beaufort, though, was a cheerfully painted converted house, a coffee shop-cum-art gallery. It had a high stoep overlooking the street where a young couple was examining the festival programme over coffee and croissants: pale, fashionable, a studied ensemble of black clothes and white skin, so cool they chilled the bright morning sun.

I walked up the steps and sat down at a table next to theirs, hungry for a whiff of confident ego-projection in this defeated little town. The man's hair was very short, but beautifully cut to enhance the elegant shape of his small skull. His sunglasses – Killer Loops – were wrapped smoothly over the sculpted bones of his cheeks, and his black jeans fitted snugly yet sensuously around the trim legs, the bulky Caterpillars emphasising the slenderness of his calves. A tiny silver stud in the lobe of his right ear sparkled prettily in the sunlight. The woman had cropped hair, bleached to within an inch of its life, and her skirt was so short that nothing of her shapely legs was hidden from sight. She, too, was wearing Caterpillars, but her sunglasses were Armani. She had a diamond stud in her left nostril. They were smoking, exchanging the odd comment in Afrikaans: the new generation, arty, sexually liberated, careful experimenters with the unconventional and the illicit. In five years' time they would be married, probably to other partners, and become only as interesting as their latest BMW. But in the meantime, conscious of being more stylish than their surroundings, they were beautiful, they were *now*.

'*Daar's net 'n klomp kak aan,*' the woman pronounced authoritatively, nothing but a load of shit. And the man said, 'Can you *believe* a play about a man who eats his own father?' The woman said, 'Probably the only way to avoid food poisoning in this place.' She added: 'This festival sucks.'

I ordered a coffee, drank it quickly and left, intimidated by the confidence of the dismissals, such clarity of judgement, like razor wire of the mind.

At the counter, waiting to pay, I noticed a display of earrings, beautifully simple hoops of silver with a slight fern-like filigree. I bought one, thankful to have found a present for Peter with so little trouble. The young woman behind the counter looked pleased. 'I made these,' she said. 'Shall I gift-wrap it for you?'

'How do you know it's not for me?' I joked, and she blushed.

Tu Nokwe ended in a blaze of joyful noise, and the organisers anxiously hustled us out of the hall, preparing for the midnight concert to follow. Going out, I paused over the night-time panorama of Grahamstown, its lights brilliant in the cold air, and felt a sudden wish to revisit the photographs, to face on my own the silent tribunal of my past.

I went straight to the corridor with the photographs, but when I got there I heard the unmistakable sounds of a student party from the classroom next door. Suddenly self-conscious – what if the supercilious young man were to find me there again? – and impatient with my own attempt at recovering the irrecoverable, I turned my back on the photographs and, making my way downstairs by another staircase – the boys' staircase, I remembered – found myself in the dark corridor on the ground floor. Opposite me was the door to the boys' toilets and changing rooms. Odd that I should have forgotten about the changing rooms. In their Spartan austerity they represented the closest thing to a centre of erotic activity that the school had to offer: the twice-weekly stripping for Phys Ed, with obligatory showers afterwards in the communal shower stalls.

The door opened to my tentative pressure; the facilities were probably being used by the visiting student groups. It was quite dark now, except for the blue light from the quad outside. The door thudded shut, its automatic mechanism too worn to cushion the impact. I didn't switch on the light; it seemed more appropriate to revisit the place in the unreal half-light. The layout was unchanged: urinal against the far wall, cubicles on the right, to the left some steps leading up to the rows of benches and clothes hooks where we used to undress. And beyond these the shower stalls – a row of four shower heads protruding from the wall over a cemented area.

I pissed in the urinal, trying to create a ceremonial libation out of it, but unsuccessfully: the bladder is too practical an organ to lend its function to the sentiments. I climbed the stairs to the clothes hooks: empty amper-sands of metal on wooden frames. Against the wall was the mirror in which Bennie had arranged his hair for the photograph; peering into it, I could see only the outline of my padded jacket, my face mercifully indistinct in the twilight. I tried to picture again Bennie pulling on his white gym shorts, but the place remained blankly unirradiated by the fantasies of my youth. It was merely empty. I walked towards the showers. Cold water only, of course, for which I used to be grateful as a deterrent to undiplomatic erections. I tried a tap, just to recover the feel of the thing, and it yielded unexpectedly, gushing water on my shoes. I swore and stepped back, and only then noticed somebody leaning against the wall of the shower en-closure. Swallowing an impulse of blind fear, I heard myself say, 'Evening.' I managed to close the tap, uncomfortably aware of my wet feet.

'Naand, oom,' a young voice said in the respectful tones of the well-raised Afrikaner child.

I switched to Afrikaans: 'I was just wondering if the taps still stuck. I was at school here a long time ago.'

'They stick sometimes, but not all the time.'

'I hope I didn't splash you.'

'No, uncle.'

There was a silence. There seemed nothing more to say and yet this strange encounter had created a situation I couldn't just walk out of.

'So you're at school here?' I asked.

He nodded. 'Yes, uncle.'

'Which standard?'

'Grade 12, uncle.' That at least had changed: standards had become grades. The light outside in the quad, softened by the frosted glass of the shower area, gave the boy an ethereal quality which he probably did not have in the light of common day. He was tall and thin, but well proportioned, with large eyes that in the twilight appeared dark blue. His hair was fashionably cut in a style that I was willing to bet he couldn't have worn in term time, very short around the ears, long on top.

The boy was clearly nervous. There was a smell of cigarette smoke about; he was probably afraid that I would confront him about it. So I took out my own cigarettes, and offered him one.

'Smoke?'

'No thank you, uncle. I don't smoke.'

'Come on,' I said, 'I can smell you've been smoking. It doesn't matter. It's not a good habit, but it's not a sin either.' I held out the packet again. This time he took one, uncertainly. I flicked my lighter and held it out. His hand trembled slightly as I reached the light towards him, and I steadied it with my left hand. I don't suppose he'd ever had his cigarette lit for him before.

'Thank you, uncle.'

We smoked in silence. He smoked very badly, but with great aplomb, in imitation of every Marlboro ad he'd ever seen.

'Have you been to the jazz?' I asked.

'Jazz?'

'Yes. Over in the school hall.'

'Oh, the festival. No, uncle. The festival is too expensive, and my father says it attracts foreign influences.'

I nodded. The foreign-influence phobia had been a feature of my youth too. 'Then what—?' I started, but interrupted myself. I couldn't interrogate this strange boy as if I had a right to his secrets. But he had guessed my question.

'I come here,' he said, in a sudden access of confidence, 'because of Mr van der Merwe.'

'Who is Mr van der Merwe?'

'He teaches us Phys Ed. This is his part of the school.'

So that too hadn't changed. I remembered the Mr van der Merwe of my day, except he was called Mr Wiid, tyrannising over us while we were showering. 'And why—?'

'I don't know why,' he said, 'but I like coming here to smoke. It would piss him … make him mad to know that I was smoking in the showers.'

'Do you hate Mr van der Merwe that much?'

'No, uncle. We mustn't hate anybody. But he's … for me he stands for all of them …' – he pointed out towards the quad, the rest of the school – 'this place with all its rules.'

'You don't like rules?' I asked, in mock-sternness.

He didn't pick up the mockery, only the sternness. 'I know rules are necessary,' he said earnestly. 'But you don't know what it's like here. They use rules to …' – he was thinking hard to capture the particular effect of rules on himself – '… to make us turn out just like them.'

'Like them?'

'Like Mr van der Merwe. And Mr Rossouw. He's the principal. And my father.'

'And you don't want to be like them?'

'No,' he said flatly, without vehemence, but with complete conviction.

'Why not?'

'I don't know.' But he did know. 'Because nothing has ever happened to them.'

'Nothing?'

'Nothing,' he repeated firmly.

'Your father has had you,' I said lightly. 'That's something.'

'Tell him that,' he said, suddenly bitter. 'He says I'm a disgrace to the family.'

'Why?' I wondered what delinquency this mild boy could have been guilty of.

'Because I had my ear pierced.' He pointed at his left ear lobe. 'My father said if he laid eyes on me wearing an earring he would cut off my ear, ring and all, with a rusty knife and mount it on the sitting-room wall between the portrait of my grandfather and the kudu head. My father says I must let the hole close up again, but I put a straw in it at night to keep it open.'

We smoked again. The boy was now strangely calm, relaxing into his own misery and the opportunity to tell a stranger about it.

'And you?' he asked.

'Me?'

'Where are you from?'

'Cape Town.'

'Oh,' he said gloomily. 'I could see that.'

'How?' I asked, amused at his morose certainty.

'I don't know. That jacket. It's not Grahamstown.'

'Well, it's Toronto, actually,' I said, and then regretted what must have come across as the swagger of the traveller. But he didn't seem to notice.

'Toronto,' he said wistfully. 'Then what ... why are you here?'

'In Grahamstown?'

'No, here. Now.' And he pointed at the deserted dressing room.

'I told you. I was at school here long ago. I came to look at the old photographs in the corridor. And I wanted to see if the school had changed. So I wandered in here.'

'And has it changed?'

'Not as far as I can see. And not from what you tell me. I also had a Mr van der Merwe and a Mr Rossouw. And a father,' I half-joked, but he remained starkly serious.

'And you ... got away,' he said, after another pause.

'Yes,' I said. 'You will too.'

He shook his head. 'My father wants me to help him in the business. He's a builder. My grandfather built this school,' he said with sudden inconsistent pride.

'Johannes Schoeman?' I asked.

'Did you know him?'

'Yes,' I said. 'Everybody knew Johannes Schoeman. You should be proud of him.'

'That's what my father tells me,' he said. 'But I don't want to live in Grahamstown for the rest of my life and build ugly houses. I tell my father I'll go and study architecture first, not here but anywhere, Cape Town or Pretoria, then we can build better houses, but he says what was good enough for Johannes Schoeman should be good enough for me. He says architects just push up the costs and most of them wouldn't recognise a brick if they shat one.' He remained as solemn as a young priest.

'Your father is clearly a man of strong opinions,' I said, trying to lighten the tone.

'Fuck, yes,' he said.

We had both finished our cigarettes. I stood around with the butt, wondering how to get rid of it. He took it from me.

'Give it to me,' he said. 'I know what to do with it.'

He stubbed out our butts on the cement ledge of the shower enclosure, and walked to a single locker that I hadn't noticed before. He fiddled with the combination lock. A dull click, and the padlock fell open.

'It's Mr van der Merwe's,' he said, a sudden grin transfiguring his solemnity. 'He doesn't know I know the combination.'

'What are you going to do?'

'Leave the stompies in his locker. By the time school starts he'll never get the smell out of his things.'

'Are his things still in there?'

'Some of them.' He produced a towel, gym shorts, a pair of training shoes. He carefully placed a cigarette end in each shoe and put them back into the locker with the other things. I thought he would leave now but he came back to where I was standing and said, 'He'll shit himself when he finds it,' and giggled in sudden joy.

I laughed. His rebellion was touching in its intensity.

He remained standing in front of me, making no show to leave. He passed his tongue over his lips, evidently wanting to say something he didn't quite have the courage to say.

'You know ...' he said, and stopped.

'Yes?' I encouraged him.

'I ... I usually ... after my cigarette ... I like to ... you know?'

'You like to what?'

He passed his hand down his body and clutched his groin. 'You know,' he said, rubbing himself with slow deliberateness. He was looking at me intently. My eyes flicked down to the growing bulge in his jeans, then back to his face.

'Yes, I know,' I said, after a brief hesitation; to acknowledge that I knew what he meant was to become part of what he meant. 'Why do you do it here?' I asked, hoping to shift the focus back to him and his situation. 'Because of Mr van der Merwe?'

He nodded. 'He tells us it uses up the energy we need for sport. But I don't believe him,' he said, with a slight catch in his breath. Then he cut through his own hesitation and my reserve. 'Why don't you ...' he said, 'why don't you ... do it with me?'

Then he undid his fly. There was no doubting his commitment to the moment; I had forgotten the fierce affirmation of the young erection. I fumbled with my own fly; his eyes were fixed on my groin. I hesitated. I had no desire to be found in a compromising position with an under-age boy. But he had taken charge; his respectful manner was subordinated to a desperate recklessness.

'Take it out,' he said. 'I want to see it.'

I obeyed mutely, conscious of a certain abjectness in my response. Why couldn't I just tell this boy that his demands were outrageous and that he should be ashamed of himself? Probably because he had divined from the start my own suppressed excitement. As I revealed my by now full erection, he took in his breath and said, 'I've never seen that before.'

'Don't you think we should go somewhere safer?' I asked. How was I going to explain this to Peter?

'No,' he said. 'I want to do it here.'

He came closer and reached out. As I put my hand on him he shivered, and a tremor rippled over his body. He closed his eyes and started exploring me, inexpertly but very minutely; he was cherishing the event, storing the details in his memory, his passion making up for an evident lack of experience.

I undid his belt carefully, and slid his jeans to his knees. My own desire took charge and, abandoning caution, I undid my belt and dropped my trousers. He leant up against me. I took off my glasses and put them in the soap dish.

'Hold me,' he said, 'hold me tight.'

His pent-up arousal erupted; he seemed to want to touch every part of me. His hands were everywhere, and I found his mouth on mine, blindly imploring, his tongue searching for mine. I closed my eyes and yielded to this unexpected tryst with my past.

It was over for him more quickly than for me, but instead of rushing off in confusion as I might have done at his age, he stood watching me, engrossed in the spectacle of adult arousal. As I finished, he started panting too; his vigorous young lust was already stirring again.

'Phew,' I said, to break his concentration. 'What a mess.' I stooped to look for a handkerchief in my discarded trousers, but he said, 'No, wait,' pulled up his jeans without closing the fly and went over to Mr van der Merwe's locker. I hoped he would be quick: in the desolate aftermath of passion, standing with my pants around my ankles suddenly seemed more dangerous than exciting.

'A nice clean towel,' he said, and grinned again. 'Mr van der Merwe always tells us that a dirty towel is the mark of a slob.' He passed me one end of the towel and started cleaning himself with the other. I hesitated for a moment, and then did likewise.

The boy took his time, wiping himself carefully, apparently reluctant to let go of the moment, or perhaps just mindful of a mother who checked his laundry. The almost companionable little ceremony was interrupted by the violent opening of the changing-room door. The light was switched on, and in the brief flicker before total illumination I saw scandal, prosecution, dismissal, ruin. I closed my fly and gestured at the boy to do the same and to come and stand next to me against the wall. He dropped the towel and did so.

Two bizarre figures invaded the room. They seemed to be naked, but as they stepped into the full light it appeared that they were wearing flesh-coloured body stockings with pink balaclavas, fitted with flashlights, on their heads. One was trailing an electric cord, and both were carrying cans of beer. The Electric Meat Puppets.

They did not see us in the relative obscurity of the shower stall, and they went over to the urinal with single-minded purpose. 'You can see a woman designed these costumes,' said one, his voice muffled by the balaclava. 'How are we supposed to piss?'

'You're lucky,' said the other. 'I've got a double adapter mounted on my prick.'

'I'll swap you any day. You know what it's like to have a mile of flex with a three-pronged plug attached to your bum?'

'At least we're compatible,' the other said, with the earnestness of the inebriated. 'Oh shit, now I've gone and pissed on my adapter. Could cause a nasty short circuit.' Laughing, the Meat Puppets went back to their festivity, leaving the light on. One had left his beer can on the sill above the urinal.

The boy locked the towel in the locker. In the bright light he was very young – how old could he be? Seventeen? It was difficult to believe that I had just, in common phrase, had my way with him – or, even more implausibly, that he'd had his with me: if I was revisiting my unsatisfactory past, he was renegotiating his unsatisfactory present.

'Well,' I said, 'it's been nice meeting you.' I put my hand on his shoulder; it felt patronising, even to me.

He touched my hand briefly, an oddly adult gesture; then, looking at me attentively: 'I recognise you,' he said, 'from the photograph in the corridor.'

'You do?' I asked lightly, my heart sinking. Was I going to be subjected to a clumsy attempt at blackmail?

But all he said was, 'You were in the same class as Mr van der Merwe. He's in the photograph too.'

'You mean your Mr van der Merwe is *Bennie* van der Merwe?'

'Yes, Mr Ben van der Merwe. He's always saying how he was at school here when there was still respect for discipline. Is that true?'

I thought about it. 'I suppose you could say that,' I said. The idea of Bennie with respect for discipline was new and rather depressing. What strange yoke of years had turned Bennie with the crooked smile and neat bum into this boy's Mr Wiid? Not that Bennie would be much impressed with what I had become: the paedophilic polluter of his spotless towel.

I put on my glasses; they were smudged with fingerprints. I took my handkerchief out of my pocket and a small packet fell out onto the cement. I picked it up and on a sudden impulse of tenderness gave it to the boy. 'There,' I said, putting it in his hand. 'That's for you.' I could hear myself saying to Peter: 'Well, I *did* buy you a present, but ...'

'What is it?' the boy asked, distrustfully.

'An earring.'

'An—?'

'Earring. I just happened to have one in my pocket.'

He was clearly still puzzled, but even more intrigued. He opened the little parcel with scant regard for the young woman's gift wrapping, and shook out the silver ring into the palm of his left hand. He looked at me with something of his earlier reckless joy. 'It's nice,' he said. 'Can I try it on?'

'Of course,' I replied, though uncomfortably aware of the possibility of another Meat Puppet invasion. 'It's yours.'

He walked to the mirror in the changing area, Bennie's mirror, and with the extreme concentration of the unpractised, inserted the ring in his ear. He turned his head this way and that, and then faced me. 'How does it look?' he asked shyly.

'Wonderful,' I said, quite truthfully, for, with the self-conscious tilt of his head to display the ring, his abundant hair flung back, shiny in the overhead light, a slight flush on the taut but pliant skin, the listlessness of earlier sloughed off, he was transfigured by a new radiance, confident, consciously desirable, inaccessible. The ring, small as it was, lent a festive glint to the young head.

And with new joy and pride/The little Actor cons another part, I quoted to myself. Aloud I said, smiling, 'Just don't tell your father where you got it.'

'No,' he said. 'Not yet.'

'Not yet?'

'Not while I'm at school. But one day I'll show it to him and I'll tell him where I got it, and then I'll just clear off.' He turned back to the mirror and said, and now the patronage was all on his side, 'I'll remember you.'

'Thank you,' I said. 'I'll remember you.'

He shook his head. 'No,' he replied, 'you don't need memories. You have a life.' He looked at his own bright image in the mirror, touched his ear, and added, with a fierce exclusive entitledness, 'This is my memory now.'

Note: This story contains phrases from and references to Wordsworth's 'Intimations of Immortality from Recollections of Early Childhood' and 'My Heart Leaps Up'; Keats's 'Ode on a Grecian Urn'; and Philip Larkin's 'I Remember, I Remember' and 'Reference Back'.

Whereas actual places are referred to, all characters and events are fictitious.

emma
van der vliet

Threesome

From the moment they touched, she was hooked …

They'd collided at the swing door into the restaurant kitchen, he look-ing for the gents, and she emerging with a platter of oysters bound for a table full of over-rich American tourists. Shells hailed onto the floor. She bent down to examine one, swore when she found the oyster soiled beyond redemption, and threw it angrily to one side. 'Who's going to eat these now?' she demanded.

He cocked his head, gave her the once-over, and smiled. '*We* eat them,' he said, in his smooth, bad English, and he knelt to gather them up.

The Americans never got their oysters. Somehow he managed to persuade her to wrap the shells and their wet, fleshy contents into her waitressing apron, and they fled laughing into the night. They consumed the whole apron-full in greedy haste all over the seats of his sports car. Then, gorged, they sat in oddly comfortable silence for some time, looking at the sea across the sand. He offered to take her home, but they took a scenic detour and ended up fucking on the pier instead. Fran lost her shoes off the edge of the pier wall, so Paolo threw his in too and they walked barefoot back to the car.

He finally drove her home early the next morning and moved into her tiny shared flat straight away. So little did she know of him that she hesitated uncertainly over his name when she introduced him to her flatmate. He smiled encouragingly. 'Paolo,' she said, rolling it around her tongue in satisfaction. Later, as they climbed into her small bed, she told him her full name was Frances, and he spoke it over and over as he kissed her, relishing the sibilance.

Paolo had lively, almond eyes and curly golden-brown hair, like a pre-Raphaelite heroine or a football star. He also had a penchant for cat burglary. He wasn't ashamed to tell Fran about his past, and for some reason, despite the outlandishness of his story, Fran knew it was true. For years he had made his living primarily as a cat burglar in Paris, climbing up the impossible drainpipes in the old apartment blocks, up to seven storeys high, and making off with the jewellery of Paris's most well-adorned women. He would watch them, sometimes for months in advance, and then seduce them. His skill and success as a toy boy was extremely useful in this regard, allowing him access to the most intimate areas of the house, where the treasures often lay. Even the few women who suspected him had no evidence, and he would carry out the deed when the affair was still at its sweetest, so that he could comfort them afterwards. 'Was anything really valuable stolen?' he would ask. 'Yes? That is terrible, too terrible. What exactly was it, *chérie*?' And he'd get a free valuation of the goods into the bargain.

One such woman, an extremely wealthy German, caught him out, and he became attached to her. Or she to him. She caught him burgling her flat, being a shrewd woman who'd put two and two together after hearing her friends' tales and pinpointing him as the common factor. She promised to keep his secret if she could keep him, and for three years he had been her toy boy, her captive, her slave. It wasn't something he found demeaning – she was nice enough and treated him kindly, and it wasn't that much of a chore to be nice back. She had taken him to live with her and fulfilled her promise to provide him with a life of luxury and excess.

He had an opulent apartment, every electronic toy he could wish for, more pocket money than he could spend, and a Mercedes sports car. He picked up bad, expensive habits and soon found that he couldn't leave. In return for all this, he gave her his body on extended loan.

Paolo had come to Cape Town with her on holiday. The season was in full swing and so was he. When he met Fran, he and his keeper had been dining together and, while he realised it was shitty to leave her at the table and to drive off in her hired car, he was not without honour. The next day he parked the sports car in a large multi-storey car park in the middle of town and dropped the keys in the hotel postbox for her. His own belongings he never fetched: he had moved on, and she had always understood that his departure was inevitable, that it had always been just a matter of time.

Fran stunned Paolo. She blew him away. She was an unknown quantity, riddled with contradictions – audacious, wilful, fiercely independent, childishly spontaneous, easily hurt. Uncompromising. She was on her own mission. But Paolo stunned Fran too. In her romantic mind, he stood in stark contradiction to any of the men she'd met before – a one-man assault on all that was drab and ordinary and taken for granted. For Fran, Paolo was a living monument to the unexpected.

They rented the outside room in the garden of Mad Mrs Mitvak. Its derelict, secretive hedges, clotted with builder's rubble and sweet wrappers and rampant Black-Eyed Susans, appealed to them. Their room was a cheaply converted servant's quarters, shaded by a sprawling Lucky Bean Tree, which was alight with coral-coloured flowers when they first arrived. Mrs Mitvak resembled her garden. She was a voluptuous, blowsy lush, much despised by her small-minded neighbours, whose own hedges were clipped into submission. When Mrs Mitvak first showed Fran and Paolo the place, the woman next door craned her neck over the fence and shot her a look of undisguised loathing and scorn, her mouth pinching up into a little dog's arse of disapproval. Their future landlady's spirits drooped visibly, anticipating failure. 'We'll take it,' said Fran with an arch smile at the neighbour, and she and Paolo kissed excessively in celebration.

Mrs M liked to sunbathe on her lounger in the garden wearing a great deal of paste jewellery and very little else, paring her corns with a small kitchen knife and occasionally talking listlessly on her cellphone to salesmen. Fran often wondered whether there was really anyone on the other end of the line. Not that it mattered. The arrangement suited them all, and an odd sort of kinship developed. When Mrs M went through a phase when she was convinced her late husband was trying to communicate with her through her hairdryer, Fran dutifully put her ear to the warm air to listen and even called Paolo to try. Fran knew she herself was not untouched by the loony brush, and she was fond of Mrs M. She'd watched her own mother's mental crumbling and knew what it was to be damaged goods.

Their landlady asked no questions. She remained unfazed by the shrieks and exclamations of their lovemaking, untroubled by their post-coital joints under the Lucky Bean Tree. In the beginning, when they were still supplied by funds from Paolo's keeper, the lovers would venture to one of the local restaurants for a meal, inspiring or distressing the locals with their ardent displays of affection and sensuous delight. They ate voluptuously and threw their chicken bones under the tables. 'Para os cachorros,' Paolo said, leading the game, 'For the dogs.'

As the months wore on, Fran and Paolo barely noticed anything but each other. They began to believe that they were untouchable, invisible. Like a child who puts her hand over her eyes, they believed that since they saw no one, no one could see them. They clung closer and closer, their room a hot, musky den, inaccessible to anyone but them, clogged with junk and books and takeaway cartons which they brought back to feed the double-backed beast they'd created in their lair. Even in their sleep their bodies sought each other out, as if their nerve endings were suddenly exposed and their bodies were putting out fronds like ferns, searching. They talked little. She learnt the essentials in Portuguese – coffee, joint, bed, water – and they developed their own fuck-focused fanagalo. He called her baby. He called her *querida*, and darling, and even once *Schatzi*, though the German endearment smacked of his former keeper and she bit him for that, till it bled.

One day Paolo brought home a visitor – a car guard he had found working nearby on Camps Bay's main road. Paolo had rejoiced in being able to speak to the man in Portuguese, and in his enthusiasm he brought him home to their retreat. He left the man at the door, silhouetted against the bright outside light, and called Fran's name. She was dressed, at least, sitting with her back to them on the bed. She turned to look. The visitor hesitated on the doorstep of their room until his eyes adjusted to the darkness. The air was redolent of sex and McDonald's, and he sniffed it.

The three of them drank tea in the warm, cramped space, the couple seated next to each other on the edge of the bed and the man opposite them on their only chair. Fran and the visitor sized each other up with wary glances. The Portuguese conversation which had brought the visitor to them in the first place had long since dried up. Paolo reached his hand out to Fran, touching her neck to reassure her, and she leant the back of her head into his touch like a cat, softening, stroking his hand with her hair. He cupped his other hand around her head and pulled her to him, kissing her neck, grazing her with his teeth until she let out a small cry and pulled herself astride him. Paolo swivelled around to lie her back on the bed, kissing down her body, a hand on each of her splayed thighs. The visitor got up from his chair and stood silently next to them, aroused by what he saw and uncertain of his role in it all. He touched Fran lightly on her stomach, but she flinched, and Paolo shook his head and gently pushed his hand away. The man dropped his hands to his sides and watched.

When it was over, the visitor left without saying anything. Fran never knew his name, and she never saw him again. She nursed another cup of tea, warming her hands on it, although the day was hot. She blinked in surprise at what had just happened, as though she'd been in the middle of a particularly vivid and intense dream and someone had ripped open the curtain, letting in the glare. She'd lost herself, and was startled to find herself again. At first, Paolo was anxious that he'd taken things too far, that she was traumatised. He watched her drink her tea, her back to him on the other side of the bed. When her shoulders began to heave he ran to her, kneeling at her side, fearful and solicitous. But she was laughing. Then they were both laughing. Lazily, playfully, they started all over again.

Then one day Fran got sad. She found that the only things that could cheer her up were Melrose cheese and lemon-curd sandwiches, or pasta covered in tuna fish and honey. She dispatched Paolo to the local super-market with lists of increasingly unlikely ingredients to buy. At first, he shook his head, smiling indulgently. At some point she began secretly to pick the paint off the wall behind the bedstead and eat it. Eventually Paolo caught her at it. She was scratching frantically and licking her fingers like a rabid rodent, her mouth, when she turned to him, flecked with white specks. He inhaled sharply in shock and, without thinking, took a step back, away from her. As the days went by and the crazes continued, he became frightened. Although she denied it even to herself at first, Fran found she didn't want Paolo near her. When he returned from the shops, she'd send him straight back out so she could pick away at the walls in peace.

Fran soon began to find the smell of Mrs Mitvak's room insufferable. 'Why does it stink in here?' she raged, raking savagely over the contents of their nest to search for the source of the odour. But Paolo couldn't smell anything different. One day, when he was out buying her bananas and condensed milk and bubblegum-flavoured lip balm, she took against the furniture and threw it all out onto the lawn, convinced that something inside the sofa was causing the stench. When he returned, Paolo could barely look at her. 'We have to go to the doctor,' he said.

Of course the doctor only confirmed what they already knew, and in that moment they came unstuck. The scan revealed that it was a boy. Fran put her fingers to the ultrasound screen and moved her face right up to the shifting, flickering image which pulsed and blurred like iron filings drawn by a magnet. Afterwards, they walked home in divided silence. As Fran's belly swelled, Paolo seemed to shrink and recede, his presence waning as the new one waxed. When he went out, which happened more and more, Fran lay still on the bed, her hand on her belly, smiling to feel the kicks and flutters. 'Baby,' she called him. Just Baby.

Paolo was crowded out. Money was getting scarce, and he moved from drinking in the local bars to hanging out in dark dives a taxi ride away. He made new friends without Fran and gave up telling her where he'd been. She never asked anyway. On the rare occasions they were both awake in their tiny room, they moved wordlessly around each other in their own separate orbits.

He finally left, unexpectedly even to him, one Saturday night, with a crowd of Italians bound for a trance party – or so said one of the waitresses from the restaurant where Fran had worked. The baby came the next week, a month early, signalled by a rush of blood. Mrs Mitvak took Fran to the hospital in her ancient Ford Cortina and sat with her until she was hurried into theatre.

Then it was a babel of medical terms, a flurry of masked faces and rustling green clothing and needles and machines and alarming numbness and glimpses of blood over the barrier they erected on her belly. She was a human sleeping bag being rummaged through by numerous urgent and insistent hands. And then the cry, the strange, sharp bleat as he emerged, telling her he was outside her now, alive. They lifted him and held him aloft: a livid, mottled-red astronaut against the circular spaceship lights.

From the moment they touched, she was hooked. And this time she knew it was for keeps.

About the Authors

Lauren Beukes is the author of the critically acclaimed dystopia *Moxyland* and the rollicking non-fiction *Maverick: Extraordinary Women From South Africa's Past*. She is also a TV scriptwriter and a recovering journalist (who occasionally falls off the wagon). She has an MA in Creative Writing from the University of Cape Town under André Brink, but she received her real education in journalism, hanging out with teen vampires, township vigilantes, AIDS activists and homeless sex workers among other interesting folk. Her new novel, a muti noir set in inner-city Johannesburg, is due out in 2010. She lives in Cape Town with her husband and daughter.

Elleke Boehmer has published three widely acclaimed novels, *Screens Against the Sky* (shortlisted for the David Higham Prize, 1990), *An Immaculate Figure* (1993) and *Bloodlines* (shortlisted for the Sanlam Prize, 2000), as well as short stories and memoir sketches, many of which are set in Africa. Known world-wide for her research in international writing and postcolonial theory, she is the author of the bestseller *Colonial and Postcolonial Literature: Migrant Metaphors* (1995, 2005), the monographs *Empire, the National and the Postcolonial, 1890–1920*

(2002) and *Stories of Women* (2005), as well as editor of the acclaimed edition of Robert Baden-Powell's *Scouting for Boys* (2004). Elleke Boehmer is Professor of World Literature in English at the University of Oxford. Her study of Nelson Mandela, published by Oxford University Press, appeared concurrently with her novel *Nile Baby* in 2008.

André Brink's novels have been translated into over thirty languages. They include *An Instant in the Wind, A Dry White Season, A Chain of Voices, Imaginings of Sand, Praying Mantis* and, most recently, *Ander Lewens (Other Lives)*. He has won the CNA Award three times, has twice been shortlisted for the Booker Prize, and was awarded the Martin Luther King Memorial Prize (England), the Premio Mondello (Italy), the Prix Médicis Etranger (France), and the Ordre National de la Légion d'Honneur (Officier). His memoir, *A Fork in the Road ('n Vurk in die pad)*, was published in February 2009.

Willemien Brümmer is a prize-winning journalist from Cape Town who works as a features writer for the Afrikaans newspaper *Die Burger*. She has degrees in drama, journalism and creative writing. Her debut collection of short stories, *Die dag toe ek my hare losgemaak het*, was published in 2008 to major critical acclaim. She has never given her father a cat.

Imraan Coovadia was born in Durban. He was educated at Yale, and has published three novels, *The Wedding* (2001), *Green-eyed Thieves* (2006) and *High, Low, In-between* (2009). His critical monograph, *Authority and Authorship in V.S. Naipaul*, is due to be published in 2009. He is a member of staff in the English Department at the University of Cape Town.

Damon Galgut was born in 1963. He has published six books, including *The Beautiful Screaming of Pigs, The Good Doctor* and *The Impostor*. His work has been shortlisted for the Man Booker Prize, the IMPAC Dublin Award and the Commonwealth Writer's Prize.

Nadine Gordimer's many novels include *The Lying Days, The Conservationist* (joint winner of the Booker Prize), *Burger's Daughter, July's People, My Son's Story, None to Accompany Me, The House Gun, The Pickup* and *Get a Life*. Her collections of short stories include *Something Out There, Jump, Loot* and, most recently, *Beethoven Was One-Sixteenth Black*. She also edited the anthology of stories *Telling Tales*. In 1991 she was awarded the Nobel Prize for Literature, and in 2007 she received the Legion of Honour, France's highest accolade. She lives in South Africa.

Michiel Heyns grew up all over South Africa and went to school in Thaba 'Nchu, Kimberley and Grahamstown. He studied at the Universities of Stellenbosch and Cambridge, and lectured in English at the University of Stellenbosch until 2003, when he retired to write full time. Apart from a book on the nineteenth-century novel and many critical essays, he has published four novels and three translations, among them Marlene van Niekerk's *Agaat*. He is also a regular reviewer for the *Sunday Independent*.

Maureen Isaacson is the literary editor and an assistant editor of the *Sunday Independent*. Her short story collection, *Holding Back Midnight*, appeared in 1992. Her short stories have been published both locally and internationally.

Liesl Jobson is the author of *100 Papers: a collection of prose poems and flash fiction*, and a volume of poetry, *View from an Escalator*, both published in 2008. Her poetry and fiction have appeared in journals and anthologies locally and abroad. She has been awarded a grant from the Centre for the Book (2007), the Ernst van Heerden Creative Writing Award (2006), the POWA Women's Writing Poetry Prize (2005) and a special mention in the Pushcart Prize anthology (2008). She is the deputy editor of Book SA, an online news source and social network celebrating southern African literature that can be viewed at www.book.co.za.

Anne Landsman is the internationally acclaimed author of *The Devil's Chimney* and *The Rowing Lesson*, both nominated for several awards both in South Africa and the US, including the M-Net Book Prize, the PEN/Hemingway Award and, most recently, the Harold U Ribalow Prize. She contributed essays to the anthologies *An Uncertain Inheritance* and *The Honeymoon's Over*, and her work has appeared in many publications, including the *Washington Post*, the *Guardian*, the *Telegraph*, *Real Simple* and *O Magazine*. She lives in New York City with her husband and two children.

Byron Loker has been called by Ben Trovato 'a talented writer who will go far if he can just stop surfing and chasing women'. His debut short story collection, *New Swell*, has been prescribed as a Grade 9 set-work book in English literature in Gauteng and the Western Cape. He presently lives in Kalk Bay, and still surfs.

Julia Smuts Louw is a freelance wordsmith and a graduate of the University of Cape Town's Creative Writing master's programme. Her story 'Paper House' is inspired by her unpublished novel, *The Second Beast*. She currently lives in London.

Susan Mann is the author of *One Tongue Singing* (2004) and *Quarter Tones* (2007). Her first novel was translated into French and Swedish, won a University of Cape Town Merit Award and was shortlisted for the Sunday Times Fiction Prize. Her second novel was shortlisted for the Commonwealth Prize. She lives in Noordhoek, Cape Town.

Alistair Morgan was born in Johannesburg in 1971. His short stories have been published in the *Paris Review* and the *PEN/O. Henry Prize Stories 2009*. He is the first non-American to have won the Plimpton Prize for fiction. His debut novel, *Sleeper's Wake*, will be published in August 2009. He lives in Cape Town.

Henrietta Rose-Innes was born in 1971 in Cape Town. She has written two novels, *Shark's Egg* (2000) and *The Rock Alphabet* (2004). Her short pieces have appeared in anthologies in South Africa and the UK. *Dream Homes*, a collection of short works, appeared in German translation in 2008, and *The Rock Alphabet* has also been published in Romanian. She has compiled an anthology of South African writing, *Nice Times!*, which was published in 2006. She won the 2007 HSBC/SA PEN short story award and the 2008 Caine Prize for African Writing for her story 'Poison', after being shortlisted for the Caine Prize the year before.

Alex Smith's first novel, *Algeria's Way*, was published in 2007 and her first non-fiction novel, *Drinking from the Dragon's Well*, was published in 2008.

She has been shortlisted for the 2009 PEN/Studzinsky Literary Award for 'Soulmates', and was a finalist in the 2009 SA Blog Awards in the category 'Best Post on a South African Blog' for *A Video to Celebrate International Mother Language Day and the Official Close of the International Year of Languages,* a blog post written in twenty-nine languages of Africa.

Jonny Steinberg is the author of several books about everyday life in South Africa in the wake of the country's transition to democracy. Two of them – *Midlands* (2002), about the murder of a white farmer, and *The Number* (2004), about crime and punishment in Cape Town – won South Africa's premier non-fiction literary award, the Sunday Times Alan Paton Award. Steinberg is also the author of *Thin Blue, Three-Letter Plague* and *Notes from a Fractured Country*, a selection of his journalism. He is currently writing a book about African immigrants in New York City.

Emma van der Vliet worked in film production for almost a decade before returning to the University of Cape Town, where she has lectured in film and media studies for eight years. Her first novel, *Past Imperfect,* was published in 2007. She lives in Observatory with her family and other animals.

Ivan Vladislavić is the author of five works of fiction, *Missing Persons, The Folly, Propaganda by Monuments, The Restless Supermarket* and *The Exploded View.* He has also edited volumes on architecture and art. His most recent book, *Portrait with Keys,* is a sequence of documentary texts about Johannesburg. His work has won the Sunday Times Fiction Prize and the Alan Paton Award.

Mary Watson's collection of interlinking stories, *Moss,* was published in 2004. She won the Caine Prize for African Writing in 2006, and has contributed several short stories to various anthologies, including works in translation in Afrikaans, Italian, German and Dutch. She lectured in film studies at the University of Cape Town until 2008 and currently lives in Galway, Ireland.

Zoë Wicomb was born in Namaqualand. She currently works as Professor in English Studies at the University of Strathclyde, Glasgow. Her critical writing focuses on postcolonialism and South African writing and culture. Her fictional works include *You Can't Get Lost in Cape Town, Playing in the Light* and *The One That Got Away*.

Acknowledgements

'Easy Touch' © Lauren Beukes 2009

'The Father Antenna' © Elleke Boehmer 2009

'Surprise Visit' © André Brink 2009

'A Cat of Many Tales' © Willemien Brümmer 2009

'File Under: Touch (Avoidance of, Writers); Love (Avoidance of, Writers).
(1000 Words)' © Imraan Coovadia 2009

'The Crossing' © Damon Galgut 2009

'The Third Sense' © Nadine Gordimer 2007. Previously published
in *Beethoven Was One-Sixteenth Black* (Bloomsbury, 2007). Reproduced
here with kind permission of Nadine Gordimer and Penguin Books
(South Africa)

'Long Perspectives' © Michiel Heyns 2009

'Love in Lalaland' © Maureen Isaacson 2009

'Nymph' © Liesl Jobson 2009

'Imprints' © Anne Landsman 2009

'Your Stop' © Byron Loker 2009

'Paper House' © Julia Smuts Louw 2009

'Salt' © Susan Mann 2009

'Living Arrangements' © Alistair Morgan 2009

'Promenade' © Henrietta Rose-Innes 2009. First published in
German translation (with the same title) in the collection *Dream Homes:
Schnappschüsse und Geschichten aus Kapstadt,* merz&solitude (Stuttgart, 2008)

'Change' © Alex Smith 2009

'Sheila' © Jonny Steinberg 2009

'Threesome' © Emma van der Vliet 2009

'Lullaby' © Ivan Vladislavić 2009

'Trinity' © Mary Watson 2009

'In Search of Tommie' © Zoë Wicomb 2009

Do you have any comments, suggestions or
feedback about this book or any other Zebra Press titles?
Contact us at talkback@zebrapress.co.za